GILBERT MORRIS
AND BOBBY FUNDERBURK

THE COLOR OF THE STAR

WORD PUBLISHING
Dallas · London · Vancouver · Melbourne

Library of Congress Cataloging-in-Publication Data

Morris, Gilbert.
    The color of the star / Gilbert Morris and Bobby Funderburk.
        p.   cm. — (The Price of liberty series : #2)
    ISBN 0–8499–3495–8
    I. Funderburk, Bobby, 1942– . II. Title.   III. Series.
PS3563.08742V3   1993
813'.54—dc20   92–44518
                                                              CIP

Printed in the United States of America

3 4 5 6 7 8 9 LBM 9 8 7 6 5 4 3 2 1

To Amy Elizabeth Funderburk

At your birth
You were so fresh
From Heaven
You showered us
With His radiance

I gathered
Those drops of Glory
And stored them
Like Fireflies
In a jar.

Their shining
Never Fails
To light my way
When the Path
Grows dark

Dad

CONTENTS

PROLOGUE

Butcher Knife Annie turned her face to the sun, her time-washed blue eyes squinting under heavy brows. She seemed drawn to the light as some flowers are, but if she could be compared to a flower, it would be one cast aside after a funeral—parched by the sun, torn and bedraggled by the rain—breathing the sickly sweet smell of decay.

Even as a young woman, Annie had never been pretty—now her thin, drawn lips reflected a soul drawn thin and hard by life. Her face, sharp-featured under the carelessly cropped brown hair, was burned by days spent shambling through the alleys and side streets of the town, pulling her little wooden wagon laden with plunder. A castoff herself, Annie survived from the castoffs of others.

"You git out of that garbage can, you ol' *witch!*" Dewitt Fikes stood in the alley behind Bates's Market, a broom in his hand pointed toward Annie. His pimply face tried to be fierce but only succeeded in being sullen. "Mr. Bates don't want the likes of *you* hangin' around here! Git yourself on home now!"

Hearing the commotion in the back alley, Cooper Bates stepped out the door. Middle-aged and stocky with a round, hard belly, his warm brown eyes took in the situation at once. "Ease off, Dewitt," he said evenly, taking the boy by his arm.

Annie placed the lid carefully back on the garbage can. With the downcast, stoic air of one who had been through this a thousand times, she trudged away down the alley, her little wagon following like an obedient puppy.

"Hold on a minute, Annie!" Bates called out, hurrying over to her. He took out his coin purse and gave Annie a dollar.

Almost smiling, Annie's blue eyes held Bates's for an instant as she took the bill with her rough, heavy-knuckled hands. Then she turned and trudged away again, accompanied by the discordant sounds of rattling bottles, cans, and old pieces of scrap iron.

"Why do you put up with that ol' woman, Mr. Bates?" Fikes whined, slicking down his thin brown hair with a comb Annie wouldn't have picked up.

Ah, the folly of youth, Bates thought. "That might be you one day, Dewitt—or me—hoping somebody would show us a little Christian charity. You know, one time Annie was richer than either of us will ever be."

"Annie?" Fikes exclaimed, watching her as she sorted through a pile of trash behind the next building.

"Yes, Annie," Bates said thoughtfully. "Her family owned a big chunk of Liberty not too many years ago. Now all she's got is the old home place out at the edge of town by the cemetery. That . . . and the girl."

Fikes's dark eyes held the expression of a poleaxed steer. "No kiddin'? What happened?"

"Her daddy blew most of it on bad whiskey and worse women. The rest Annie spent on her younger brother, Taylor—the best schools, clothes—the whole works. But he had his daddy's appetite for whiskey and his taste in women. He left ol' Annie broke, married a tramp, and hit rock bottom. The girl was the only thing he had to show for his marriage . . . and he come back just long enough to dump her on Annie."

"Who'd have thought she ever had money?" Fikes mused.

Bates watched Annie load a short, heavy piece of pipe onto her wagon. "Some people have it tougher than others. That ol' woman and the girl—I reckon they've had it pretty bad—" He broke off as if he'd said too much. Running his fingers over his bald head to push back the vanished hair, he turned and went into the store.

Fikes leaned on his broom, watching Annie and her little wagon down the alley. He could hear faintly the song she was singing in her cracked voice: "Pack up all my cares and woes. Da da dee . . . Da da dee. Bye, bye . . . blackbird . . ."

Part 1

1

RETURN TO LIBERTY

*T*he dark green Model A hummed smoothly along the blacktop road, a bearded man in somber clothes at the wheel. His dark, remote eyes missed nothing on the road and kept a close watch on the man seated next to him. "Much further?"

"What? Oh—no, not much." The man answering was tall and fair with blue eyes and light brown hair that needed barbering. He had thin lips that he chewed on sporadically and a chin that had given up trying to be strong. With his long, aristocratic fingers twisting slowly in his lap, he had the beaten look of a salesman who couldn't make his quota—and knows he never will. His gray tweed coat looked as limp and worn and downtrodden as he did.

Under a leaden sky, the inconstant wind moaned through dry cornfields like a leftover goblin from Halloween. Looking out the window at the bleak November landscape, a third passenger sat in the back seat biting her nails. She was slim and fair like her father— her eyes a darker blue. Her blonde hair hung in stringy waves to her thin shoulders.

The five-year-old child, her large eyes almost luminous in the gathering gloom, shivered more from what the sound did to her, than from the biting cold that the car's heater could not quite keep at bay.

"You doin' all right back there little lady?" the driver asked absently, smiling over his shoulder.

Startled, Jordan quickly nodded her head. "Yes sir," she replied in a subdued voice.

Turning around, leaning over the back of the seat, Taylor Simms took his daughter's hand in his. "I thought you might be asleep, baby. We've got time if you want a nap."

Jordan pulled away, but her father held to her hand. She relented, sitting passively while he spoke.

"Don't be afraid, Jordan. We're going to my sister's house. You remember Aunt Annie. I know she'll remember you."

Sitting quietly, Jordan stared at her small hand, dwarfed by her father's. She noticed the redness on the ends of his long fingers and around the cuticles where he had bitten his nails. *Mine are like that too,* she thought.

"You're going to stay with your Aunt Annie for awhile. It'll be a nice visit—just until I get back."

Jordan remembered that her mother had left her for "nice visits" before, coming back days later to pick her up. She thought of the long nights in strangers' beds or on floors—the noise and loud music and people drinking all the time out of bottles and glasses—how she had to sneak into the kitchen late at night to find something to eat. She didn't want any more "nice visits."

"Will Mommy be there?" Jordan asked, wondering what had happened to her mother, thinking maybe she might be at this new place—this Aunt Annie's. All grownups seemed to be either "Aunt" or "Uncle" somebody.

"N-no. Not for awhile."

"Daddy, please don't leave me again! I don't want aunts and uncles any more. They don't like me."

Simms watched two tears, gleaming in the dim light from the car's dashboard, streak down the dirty cheeks of his little girl. A sharp pain, springing from the guilt he felt, caught at his chest. He thought of all the nights he had come home in a drunken fog, his wife gone or asleep on the couch, Jordan crying in her bed. All the nights he had cradled her in his arms in self-loathing or rage . . .

"Go to sleep, baby," Simms murmured, releasing her hand. "It'll only be for a little while."

Even at five, Jordan knew it was never *for a little while.* All the visits were for a long, long time. With a child's capacity to live in the present, she soon thought only of how very tired she was and fell into a deep sleep on the back seat of the car that carried her farther and farther from the only life she had known.

Jordan awoke to the sound of her father's voice. "We're stopping for gas in a minute. You want something, Jordan?"

Sitting up, Jordan yawned and rubbed her eyes. She looked out the window of the car, seeing houses scattered along the highway. Down one road, in the distance, she could see more houses, some signs, and large buildings. In a few minutes, they turned into a parking lot, pulling up next to a red gas pump in front of a store.

Jordan recognized the Coca-Cola, Nehi, and R.C. Cola signs tacked to the roughcut one-by-twelve planks of the store. She saw a Prince Albert Tobacco sign and thought the man on it looked like the big man driving the car.

As the driver of the car got out from behind the steering wheel, the owner came walking out of the store toward the car. He had dark brown hair going white, parted in the middle and combed straight back. His handlebar mustache was already white and made him look like a gunfighter. His khakis and light blue shirt were neatly pressed.

"Fill her up, Pop," the big man said.

"Name's Clark," the owner corrected the man flatly, turning his cool gray eyes on him. "Morgan Clark."

"No offense," the man offered, holding both hands in front of him, palms out.

Jordan saw the big man brush against the gas pump as he walked toward the store, his coat slipping back, revealing the long black leather holster at his belt. She had seen it when he picked her and her father up, but she had forgotten about it. Guns, she knew, were worn by cowboys, but this man had no horse and no big hat and no boots. For some reason this made her afraid, although she didn't understand why.

"Let's go in and Daddy'll buy you some candy, Jordan," Simms smiled, buttoning his daughter's frayed blue coat.

As Simms got out, Clark glanced at him. "Taylor Simms. I swan! Haven't seen you in a blue moon! Where in the world you been?"

Looking sheepishly at Clark, Simms mumbled evasively, "Oh, here and there. Haven't been back to the old hometown in a long time."

Clark nodded at the store. "Hope you ain't got official business with Coleman."

Simms looked at the ground. "You know him?"

"By reputation," Clark answered, screwing the gas cap back on. "He's a hard man—fair though, from what I've heard."

"I've made a lot of mistakes since I left here, Mr. Clark. Guess it finally caught up with me."

Clark remembered Taylor as a child—always good-natured but never willing to stand up for himself—taking the line of least resistance, the easy way out. He had been popular in school, getting along with classmates as well as teachers, but there was an almost congenital weakness in him—an inability to tackle problems head on. "Hate to see it, Taylor. Watched you grow up." Clark hung the nozzle back on the pump. "That your little girl in there?"

"Yes sir. She's pretty, ain't she?"

Clark nodded sadly, walking across the gravel parking lot and back into the store.

As Taylor opened the door for Jordan, the wind blew long and hard, sighing high in the tops of the two pines on either side of the store. Jordan thought it was the most beautiful sound she had ever heard—never in the city had she heard anything like it.

"What's that pretty music, Daddy?" she asked, taking his hand.

"What music?"

Jordan pointed upward where the trees were swaying in the wind, outlined against the darkening sky.

Taylor smiled. "That's God's music, baby."

"God's music?"

Taylor picked his daughter up and walked toward the store. "That's what your grandmother used to tell me when I was just about your age."

"How does God make it?" Jordan asked excitedly, her eyes bright with wonder.

"He makes it by blowing His breath through the tops of the pine trees. See them swaying when He breathes on them?" Taylor pointed upward.

"Why doesn't He play His music in town, Daddy?" Jordan mused, unable to take her eyes from the swaying trees.

"He does," Taylor laughed, holding tightly to his daughter as he went into the store. "But there aren't as many trees, and there's so much noise we just don't hear it."

Inside, Jordan saw the man known as Coleman standing next to a counter down an aisle at the back of the store. Morgan Clark was cutting him a thick wedge of yellow hoop cheese with a large knife. He tore a length of brown paper from a roll behind the counter, carefully wrapping the cheese and sealing it with tape. They walked back to the front of the store, Coleman taking a long swallow from a chocolate Nehi he was holding.

The two men passed next to a display advertising Palmolive Soap for ten cents a bar. On the ad was a beautiful girl with short brown hair and flawless skin and a slogan advising any interested parties that either she or the soap was "Naturally Lovable." She wore a white blouse and a red sweater hung carelessly over her shoulders. Below her in large black print was the information that she had "That Schoolgirl Complexion."

Jordan's favorite ad hung over the front door—a hobo with a straw in his mouth wearing a battered, black derby slept next to his bundle. He leaned against a sign that pictured a little boy in a night-shirt carrying a tire over one shoulder and a candle in his hand. The ad said, "Time to retire? Buy Fisk."

The stacks of Hersheys, Baby Ruths, and other candy and packs of gum reminded Jordan of the stores in her own town. Here though, there were all kinds of clothes, shoes, pots and pans, tools, and dozens of other items the town grocery stores didn't have. As she looked about the store, shadows wavering slowly from the sixty-watt bulbs hanging from their long cords, she spotted a shiny blue ball high on a shelf behind the front counter—and next to it was a Raggedy Ann doll with pretty red yarn for hair.

"Two packs of Chesterfields, Mr. Clark," Simms said. "And a box of matches."

"Twenty-one cents," Clark said, leaning on the counter with both hands as he smiled down at Jordan.

Taking two dimes and a nickel from his pants pocket, Simms glanced down at his daughter. The expression of wonder on her face caused him to look upward at the doll on the top shelf. He dropped the change on the counter, staring at the cigarettes Clark had placed there—then at his daughter. Simms thought of how cigarettes gave him a kind of security—something to hold on to when the going got rough. He thought of his daughter—alone in that big old house with his sister. *I wonder if they still call her Butcher Knife Annie?*

Simms fidgeted, still looking at the cigarettes on the counter. "How much is that doll, Mr. Clark?"

Clark remembered giving the salesman a dollar and a half for two of them. "Twenty-five cents."

"We'll take it," Simms smiled, feeling a sudden and pleasant rush of emotion.

Jordan couldn't believe what her father had just said. She stared wide-eyed at him and then at Mr. Clark as he climbed a short ladder to retrieve the doll.

"You want to pay him, baby?" Simms asked, handing the nickel and dimes to Jordan.

Jordan took the nickel in one hand and the two dimes in the other, holding both outstretched hands up to Clark.

"Here you are, little lady," Clark said, handing the doll to Jordan. "You be a good mama to this baby, now." Morgan Clark was a good businessman, never giving things away foolishly, but this child had touched his heart with raw emotion. He also saw the wonder, the disbelief on her face when he had handed her the doll. *Poor little thing—maybe she never had one before.*

"Yes sir," Jordan smiled, taking the doll with both hands and hugging it tightly. It was the most wonderful gift Jordan could ever remember. Now she felt she had someone who wouldn't leave her—someone she could love.

"You ready, Simms?" Coleman grunted, finishing the last of his chocolate Nehi.

"I guess so." Simms took his daughter up in his arms and turned to leave the store.

Clark appeared beside him at the door. "Take care of yourself, Taylor," he encouraged, slipping the Chesterfields and matches into his coat pocket.

"Thank you, Mr. Clark. I will."

Clark switched the outside light on and stood in the front door, watching Taylor carry his daughter out to the car. The little girl waved her doll's hand at him through the window as the Model A circled the lot, heading east on the highway. *Poor Taylor. He could've made somethin' of himself—smart, nice looking—just like his daddy. Reckon that's the whole problem. He's too much like his daddy was.*

*   *   *

As Taylor Simms rode through the twilight, the taste of desolation was in him like a mouthful of old copper coins. He forced the journey's end from his mind, thinking of all the lost autumns of his youth—those crisp, windy mornings on the way to school with leaves tumbling red and rust and yellow from the trees—the clear golden light of October and the sharp presence of wood smoke in the air.

Simms thought of the Liberty High band thundering on the afternoon practice field before Friday-night games—of the red-cheeked, fresh-scented football girls that he walked to the stadium and snuggled with high up on the wooden bleachers, holding them close and feeling their warm breath against his cheeks.

Glancing over the seat at his daughter clutching her new doll, combing its hair with her tiny fingers, Simms remembered a passage from his mother's favorite Psalm, "He shall give his angels charge over thee, to keep thee in all thy ways." *God, please do this for my little girl!*

Coleman turned right, off the highway, onto a gravel road. The rocks pinged against the bottom of the Model A as they passed a cemetery bounded by a piked iron fence. Tilting tombstones near the front were worn smooth by a hundred years of wind and rain and cracked by the roots of the giant live oaks.

Just past the cemetery, they turned onto a gravel drive overgrown with frost-burned weeds, except for a narrow, worn path on the right side. Gnarled old cedars lined the drive, leading to a two-story house behind an almost-white picket fence. A brick path ran from the gate to wide wooden steps that led up to an even wider white-columned gallery across the front and around the right side of the house. The front gable had a single window—the light glinting dully off the dust and old cobwebs on the other side of the glass. Two dormer windows jutted out on either side of the slate roof, one facing north, the other south.

The car bounced to a stop, and Jordan saw her new home for the first time. With a turret to the left of the gallery, it rose in front of her like a castle from one of the storybooks her mother used to read to her. But it was a castle in a haunted wood, with an untended rose garden and weeds growing against the brick pillars on which the house rested. A trellis in front of the gallery held the skeleton of a wisteria vine.

"I think I saw her around behind the house," Simms informed Coleman. "I'll be right back."

"Take me, Daddy."

Simms took his daughter by the hand, pausing to look back at Coleman. "Couldn't I stay the night—just to help her get used to the place—and Annie?"

"Can't do it, Simms," Coleman replied, shaking his big head. "I'm taking a big enough risk as it is."

Jordan held firmly to her father's hand as they walked around the lofty turret of the house to the back yard. Toward the back of the yard, she could see a fire burning, its yellow and orange flames flicking at the dark smoke billowing from the still-damp leaves at the bottom of the trash pile. Beyond the flames, a bulky, dark figure stood among a grove of peach trees, pruning them with a curved saw.

"Hey, Annie!" Simms shouted with mock confidence. "It's me—your favorite brother!"

Annie Simms looked slowly over her shoulder, finished sawing a limb off the tree and turned toward them.

Jordan stood next to her father, clutching his hand, holding her doll tightly to her chest. Through the flames, she saw Annie shambling toward them, carrying the heavy, curved saw like a sword in her right hand. She was a big woman, wearing men's overalls, scuffed boots, a heavy denim jacket, and a floppy felt hat with a large brim that cast her face in shadow. *This must be the monster that lives in the haunted castle,* Jordan thought, remembering the story her mother had read to her. *In the book, nobody loved it.*

Annie looked down at Jordan. "She's growed some. Not enough."

"I need to talk to you, Annie," Simms said in a subdued tone.

"Figured you needed somethin'. Come on in." Annie walked up the high back steps onto the porch. "Well, don't just stand there, come on in," she urged.

A look of embarrassment mixed liberally with disgust for himself crossed Simms's face. "I have to go around front first." He trudged along the side of the house toward the front where the Model A idled, a thin white plume rising from its tailpipe into the evening air. A terrible fear chilled him, and he shuddered at what awaited him at the end of his ride with Coleman. *If I could make it to the river—get across somehow—hide out in the woods—catch a westbound freight.*

As Simms caught sight of Coleman's bulk in the front seat, he knew he could never get away from this man. He was almost to the point of believing that a bullet from the man's pistol would be the best thing for everybody involved.

As he approached the car, Simms said evenly, "I'll just be in there long enough to let her kind of get used to the place. Don't worry about me trying anything."

Coleman looked at Jordan, clinging to her father's hand, shivering in the cold. Shaking his head, he made a quick decision, "I'll get a room for the night. Pick you up at six."

"Thanks, Mr. Coleman," Simms beamed, as the car backed sharply and bounced down the drive. He felt like he had gotten a last-minute reprieve from the governor, and his spirits soared briefly. *Who knows what could happen by morning,* he thought with the desperate optimism of a man with little left to lose.

Inside the house, Jordan stared in wonder at the high-ceilinged foyer with its marble floor and crystal chandelier. It was completely devoid of furnishings, except for a single slim vase on the gleaming floor. Hand-painted with delicate yellow and white flowers, it stood as solitary as a single candle burning in a cathedral.

In the long, oak-floored hall, rectangular areas, a shade darker than the rest of the walls, revealed where paintings had once hung. Jordan and her father continued down the hall, past an expansive living room on the right with a massive stone fireplace, and a dining room on the left, to the kitchen at the back of the house.

"Come on in and set down," Annie said, setting a kettle of water for coffee on the wood-burning stove. "Did I hear a car pull off?"

"That's my, uh, ride. He'll be back to get me in the morning," Simms replied, sitting at the long, heart-pine table with its massive scrolled legs and beaded edges.

Jordan pulled one of the heavy chairs out from the table, scrambled up in it, and set her doll on her lap. She noticed a coal-oil lamp hanging from a bracket on the wall next to the stove—another from a long hook suspended from the high ceiling. The huge black stove provided the only source of heat and helped to make her drowsy as she sat and listened to her father talk to this strange woman, her blue eyes glinting like marbles in the soft amber light.

"Where's Sally?" Annie asked, now peeling potatoes with a large butcher knife.

"She left me three months ago," Simms replied, staring now at his daughter, who was trying to keep her eyes open. "I'll have to tell you about it later."

"I can just about figure it out myself," Annie grunted, dumping the potatoes into a pot of boiling water.

"Where's the icebox?" Simms asked, noticing the large empty space at the end of the counter.

Annie dumped cornmeal into a bowl, added water, and stirred it with a wooden spoon. "Sold it."

"How do you keep things from spoiling?"

"Got a small one. Keep it on the back porch in cold weather," she said woodenly, pointing out the back door. "Takes a long time for the ice to melt that way."

After they had talked for a while, Annie rose and placed a crock of boiled potatoes, a plate of cornbread, and a sliced onion on the table. Using a gourd for a dipper, she filled two glasses with water, put them next to her and her brother's places, and went out the back door with another glass. She returned with it half-full of milk and handed it to Jordan.

Adding salt and pepper to the potatoes, Annie said in her husky voice, "Well, it ain't exactly like mama used to make—but it'll serve to keep body and soul together."

"Tastes fine to me, Sis."

Annie frowned at her brother. "A little butter would make it a lot better."

Jordan thought the hot cornbread was so much better than the white bread her mother always bought in the city. She ate two large pieces with three potatoes, washing it all down with the cold milk. With her stomach full, she climbed down from her chair and sat in front of the stove, playing with her doll. Soon she was asleep, curled up on the floor, her arm around the doll.

"How you managing these days, Annie?" Simms asked, remembering her expression when he had called her "Sis."

"Don't take much. Grow some vegetables and peaches out back. Sell a few—can a few."

Simms got up and looked at the nearly bare shelves. "You got any sugar?"

"Nope. May get some next week. Don't suppose you'll be around to enjoy it then." Annie sipped the steaming, black coffee from a china cup, incongruously small and delicate in her rough hands, chapped and red from the cold weather.

Simms returned to the table. He looked at his older sister, at what time and poverty had done to her. He remembered she had always been a little on the tomboy side, but good-natured and witty, making fun of herself as much as anyone else. She never worried about getting an education or training for a job, because she thought her family's wealth would take care of them for the rest of their lives. "I wish I could do something to help you with expenses, Annie."

Annie looked at the little girl lying at her feet. *He should have been the girl in the family.* "You can't even take care of yourself . . . and that child, Taylor. Don't worry about me."

Simms looked at Jordan asleep on the floor.

"What kind of trouble you in?" Annie's blue eyes had a mica glint as she turned them on her brother.

"Took some money from the hardware store where I worked. Planned to put it back, but it didn't work out."

Annie, remembering all the money she had spent on her brother, bore in. "Gambled it away, huh?"

"It was a sure thing, I . . ."

"It always is, Taylor," Annie declared bluntly, her eyes never wavering from his. "It always is. I learned that from Daddy. He bet on nothing *but* sure things. The only thing sure about it was it sent my mama and him to early graves."

"Well, after Sally left I . . ."

"Caught you with another woman?" Annie had stored this up for five years and would not let go of it now.

Simms drank his coffee in silence.

"What're you going to do with the girl?"

"That's why I'm here. Thought I could leave her with you."

Annie scraped her chair loudly on the floor as she got up. "No, Taylor. Nothing doin'. Not this time."

Jordan stirred from her sleep, awakened, and lay still until she knew what was going on about her—a habit she had picked up while staying with her "aunts" and "uncles."

"No place else to leave her, Annie!" she heard her father say. "Please, let her live with you! I don't have any friends left and you're my only family."

Annie began cleaning off the table. "Look around you, Taylor. Is this any place to raise a child?"

Simms looked directly into his sister's eyes. "It's a palace compared to where I'm goin'."

Annie looked at Jordan, curled up on the floor with her doll. "Lord help us!"

As the conversation quieted down, Jordan drifted back to sleep. When she awoke, the kitchen was bathed in the dim light of early morning. She still lay next to the stove, but a blanket had been put under her, and her head rested on a pillow. Rubbing her eyes, she sat up slowly, hugging her doll. "Where's my daddy?"

"He's gone, child. You'll be livin' with me for a while," Annie replied from her chair at the long table.

Jordan looked around the huge barren room and began to cry. "I want my mama!"

"Cry for her, Jordan, and for your daddy, too. But people can't cry forever when they lose something. You'll learn to live here." Annie gazed at the frail child sobbing on the floor, rubbing her dirty face, her hair matted to her head. "Let's get you a bath. You'll feel better then." She filled the copper kettle with water from the bucket and set it on the stove.

"I want my daddy," Jordan sobbed.

Annie picked her up, held her in her lap, and began taking off her shoes. She knew she did not deserve a child—had no right to one. *Reckon I'm better than nobody at all—just barely.* "I'll do the best I can for you, child."

2

J.T. AND WASH

J. T. Dickerson came that first morning while Jordan was playing with her doll on the kitchen floor in front of the stove. Annie had washed the little girl's red corduroy jumper, white blouse, and underwear—they felt soft and clean against her body. Her hair fell in glossy waves to her shoulders. The big bowl of oatmeal she had eaten felt warm and comforting in her stomach, almost like getting a hug from the inside. Now Annie was slicing apples and dumping them into a huge pot that was boiling on the stove.

"Hey, Annie!" came the shout from near the front of the house. "You up yet?"

"'Course I'm up, J.T.," Annie yelled back, walking out on the back porch. "It's ten o'clock, ain't it? Come on 'round the back, that is, if you think you can walk that far."

J. T. Dickerson came sauntering around to the back porch, singing, "I Can't Give You Anything But Love, Baby." The navy pinstripe suit showed the beginnings of wear. The Harvard sweatshirt he wore beneath the jacket was threadbare with washings. His brown eyes were too bright, a touch of redness in the whites. He tossed his head, flicking back a cascade of thick brown hair. A long-necked bottle with a cork, almost full of a clear liquid, was tucked under his left arm.

Annie shook her head slowly. "J.T., can't you wait till afternoon to hit that hooch?"

"That's the only thing I've plenty of, baby," J.T. sang from the bottom of the back steps, his right hand stretched out in supplication to Annie. "Annie, I'm appalled at your lack of faith in my physical prowess. You actually doubt my capacity to walk to the back of your house. Have you forgotten, Anne of the Almost-White Gables, that I quarterbacked the team that made it to the state finals in 1910? Closest Liberty High has ever come to a state championship."

Jordan peered out the screen door at this singing intruder. He acted a little strange, but then she thought most all grownups were a little strange. There was something about his smile, though, that made her not afraid of him—even with his loud singing. She knew that people who sang like that sometimes got mad for no reason and hurt other people.

"How 'bout some coffee?" Annie asked, wiping her hands on her stained apron.

J.T. sat on the bottom step and leaned back against the rail. Popping the cork out of the bottle, he took a long pull, tapped the cork back in, and wiped his mouth with his hand. "I'm celebrating, Annie. Settled a case on the courthouse steps this morning that's been dragging on for two years. That's usually the way it works out. Two lawyers joust at each other with paper lances interminably, then just before it goes to court, the one with the weakest case capitulates. My fee, Anne of the Perpetual Overalls, was substantial and should keep us in the necessities of life," he continued, lifting the bottle toward her, "for quite a while."

"J.T., if you don't lay off the 'necessities' a little, your law practice is gonna fly right out the door along with all your girlfriends." Annie stood on the porch gazing down at the man who had been her closest friend for the past few years. She did indeed remember when he had been the finest high-school quarterback in the state of Georgia and when he had gone on to Harvard Law School, graduating with honors. J.T. returned to Liberty to begin his law practice. Annie also remembered when things had started to go wrong for him.

"Sure glad it warmed up some today." J.T. set his bottle on the step next to him and looked out at a stretch of clouds across the mild blue sky. "I saw Ellie a while ago," he mused, as if that single fact held the answer to all mysteries. "She was going into the courthouse with ol' Hartley. Never could figure that pair out."

Here it comes, Annie thought. *Happens nearly every time he sees her. Thank goodness he don't see her much.*

Glancing over his left shoulder at Annie, J.T. smiled sadly. "We were the perfect couple, you know. The beauty queen and the grid-iron hero. Lord, what times we had back then!" J.T. uncorked the bottle, taking another long pull. "Never can tell what the scent of money will do to a person, Annie. Sometimes it overpowers even the not-quite-eternal, bittersweet fragrance of love."

"You should have studied poetry at Harvard, J.T. You just ain't suited for the real world. Might as well come on in the house," Annie shrugged, clomping back to the kitchen in her heavy boots.

J.T. rose almost painfully, climbed the steps, and entered through the screen door. "Well, hello, sweetheart," he said brightly, seeing Jordan sitting on the floor with her doll. "Where in the world did Annie get a pretty girl like you?"

Jordan smiled briefly at him and then looked down, hugging her doll with both arms.

"She's Taylor's," Annie corrected him quickly. "Her name's Lisa Jordan Simms. We call her Jordan."

"Come see me, sugar," J.T. beamed, sitting at the big kitchen table, his bottle beside him.

Jordan got up and shyly eased over to where J.T. sat. She squealed as he lifted her high into the air, bringing her down in his lap. Although this man's breath smelled like her daddy's, Jordan knew instinctively that he would never harm her. With a child's wisdom, she also knew that he sincerely liked her.

"You want to know something, Jordan?" J.T. asked, his eyes wide with mock wonder at whatever it was he knew.

"Yes sir," Jordan nodded, still smiling from her brief flight above J.T.'s head.

J.T. took a long swallow from his bottle, looking around as if protecting a great secret. "A friend of mine named Ellie, from a long time ago, when I was little like you, grew up and got married to a very rich man. Now she's got a little girl that looks a whole lot like you. Her name's Debbie and she's got pretty blue eyes and blonde hair just like you."

"She does?" Jordan said brightly, hugging her doll. "Maybe she can come here and be my sister."

J.T. chuckled, took a quick hit on his bottle, and announced to Annie, "How 'bout it, Annie? Think you could handle another ready-made daughter? They could pass for sisters."

Annie glanced away from her apple peeling toward J.T. "Maybe you better ease off the hooch a little, J.T."

Ignoring her, J.T. turned to the child. "Tell you what, Jordan. I don't think Debbie could come live with you, but you might be able to go play with her sometime."

"Oh, good!" Jordan said excitedly. "Can I bring my doll? We can play mamas and babies."

"Why, sure you—"

"That's enough now, J.T.," Annie snapped. "You quit building that baby's hopes up. She's got about as much chance of playing with Debbie Lambert as I do being crowned homecoming queen."

"I wanna go see Debbie," Jordan pleaded.

Annie glared at J.T., then spoke to Jordan in a level voice. "J.T.'s just kiddin', baby. Sometimes he gets a little carried away. Don't pay him no mind."

Jordan remembered that some of the best times she had had were when she lived where there were other children and her mother would go with her into the yard or the park to play with them. She felt that she might never again see another little girl in this big old house. "Please take me to see Debbie, Mr. J.T."

"You happy now?" Annie chided over her shoulder.

J.T. took a long swallow. "You're a tad feisty this morning, Annie, ol' girl. What you need is a touch of the grape to settle your nerves," he expounded, forgetting about Jordan as soon as he set her down on the floor. He took his bottle over and opened the cabinet, fumbling around until he found a large water glass.

Annie watched while J.T. poured the glass half full of the bootleg whiskey. "You know I'm tryin' to lay off that stuff, J.T."

"Aw, c'mon. One little drink never hurt nobody," J.T. coaxed. "Think of it as medicinal. You can't afford to come down with a cold, living way out here by yourself."

Annie gazed at Jordan, now playing with her doll on the floor. Hesitating for a moment, she conceded, "Well, maybe just one." She reached for the glass and took a long swallow.

Two hours later, Jordan watched through the screen door as J.T. and Annie sat on the back steps, J.T. drinking from a silver flask and Annie from her delicate china cup. They were singing "I'll Get By." When they finished, J.T. struggled to his feet, leaving the household bottle with about two inches of liquor remaining on the step.

Squinting in the afternoon sun, J.T. began weaving his way toward the front of the house. He stopped suddenly. "Sorry, Annie. I forgot to bid you farewell. Slipping a bit in my old age, I guess. Got some briefs to work on. See you in a day or two."

Annie waved to J.T., eased herself up to the porch, and leaned back against the wall. She heard the soft clattering of J.T.'s Model A pickup in front of the house and hoped he could keep it between the ditches until he got home.

In a day or two, Annie thought. *That might mean tonight or next month.* She slipped the ten-dollar bill he had given her into the pocket of her overalls. In a minute's time she was snoring softly, her lips moving slightly with a soft fluttering as she exhaled.

Standing behind the screen door, Jordan clung tightly to her doll. In a few moments, she placed the doll in a chair at the table. She pulled another chair over to the counter where she picked up some of the apple slices. Returning to her chair, she placed them on the table next to her doll. Then she went out on the screen porch and brought the quart of milk in from the refrigerator.

Sitting alone in the drafty kitchen, she ate the apple slices and drank the milk, feeding her baby and talking to it as she ate. "Eat your apple, Raggedy Ann. You'll grow up to be a big girl." Chewing on an apple slice, Jordan looked thoughtfully at her doll. "You're like Annie. She's kind of raggedy too. I'll just call you Ann."

The westering sun sailed low in the sky, moving further south daily, on the way to its December rendezvous with the winter solstice. Toward the back of this troubled plot of ground, the peach trees stood in rigid formation, stoically awaiting the hard time. A shadow passed through their ranks as a single crow rode the thermals above them, above the two-hundred-yard strip of woods between Annie's house and the river, alighting in the top of a tall pine on the high bank. Its harsh cries rang through the bright air and reached the house where Jordan was putting Ann to sleep and where Annie lay in dreams on the back porch, snoring softly in a swatch of autumn light.

* * *

The high-ceilinged bedroom at the rear of the house, located directly above the kitchen, now belonged to Jordan. She lay in the mahogany four-poster, high off the heart-pine floor, feeling good and clean from her hot bath in the galvanized tub in the front of the stove. She was full of cornbread, potatoes, and milk. Lying on hand-laundered sheets covering the fluffy feather mattress that almost swallowed her as she snuggled down for sleep, she watched Annie pull the quilts over her and tuck them in.

Jordan listened to the night wind moan and whine in the eaves of the old house. "Can I have a light, Annie? Mama used to leave a light on for me."

"Can't afford it, child. Coal oil costs money," Annie stated matter-of-factly. "'Sides, I'll be in the room right down the hall."

"Please, Annie!" Jordan begged, her blue eyes growing bright with tears. "I'm afraid!"

Annie walked to the door, paused, and turned around. "That's foolish, Jordan! How can you see a light when you're asleep? You don't want to grow up to be a foolish child, do you?"

Jordan sat up in the bed. "I don't mind. Please. Just let me have a light."

Annie sighed deeply and closed the door.

Listening to Annie's heavy tread in the hallway, Jordan stared wide-eyed into the darkness. She thought of the man who had come to see them that day. How he had been so nice to her. And funny—until he drank too much from his bottle. Then he acted like he didn't even see her when he gave Annie some from the bottle, and they both got loud, but not funny anymore. She remembered feeling that this man was different from the others and that he would never hurt her. She saw his smile again, felt him lift her high into the air, and, thinking how good it felt when he held her in his lap, she fell into a dreamless sleep.

Next morning, Annie stood over the bed, envying how peacefully Jordan slept. "Wake up, child," she announced. "It's Saturday. The day we go to town."

Thirty minutes later, Annie was pulling Jordan down the narrow path that ran next to the driveway. She sat at the back of the wagon holding a cardboard box of eggs packed with newspaper to keep them from breaking. Two more boxes sat next to her, and in the front of the wagon were six chickens, lying docilely together, their legs tied with heavy twine. The two-slat rails around the side of the wagon made Jordan feel safe.

Bumping along the edge of the road, Jordan could see pools of rainwater collected in the lowest hollows of the gravelly ditch. Startled by their approach, a green frog croaked his surprise and splashed into one of the pools from the bank. Jordan saw his legs kicking underwater as he frantically sought safety. A mild wind sighed in the pines as Jordan looked at their swaying crowns, thinking how beautiful God's music was and wondering if He lived high, high above the puffy clouds and the pale blue sky.

They passed a white church, with a wooden belfry and hand-painted "stained-glass windows," that sat a hundred yards off the road behind a stand of sweet gums. On the right, Jordan saw a neighborhood of clapboard and tarpaper shacks with chickens pecking in the hard-packed dirt yards and pigs squealing in scrap-lumber pens. Children in shades of color ranging from coffee-milk tan to raven black played among the houses, making no less noise than the pigs.

Jordan was lost in the sights of the journey: Cars spun by them with families on the way to town or for a ride in the country. Convertibles sped by, packed with young people; their shouts and laughter carrying a long, long way on the crisp morning air. Some rode horses or in wagons laden with potatoes and onions and children.

A long, black Cadillac Phaeton convertible, its chrome bumper, grill, and headlight covers gleaming in the sunlight, glided past in quiet elegance. A black-haired man of forty-five sat ramrod straight behind the wheel, his fair-haired wife beside him. In the back seat was a boy of five with his father's hair and his mother's dark blue eyes. Sitting next to him, his sister, a year older, favored her father.

From the back seat of the Cadillac, Billy Christmas glanced at the odd twosome at the side of the road. He had seen the old woman before, but the pretty little girl riding in the wagon was new to him. *I wish I could ride in that wagon with her.*

To Jordan, the car and its occupants looked like they had driven out of an ad in one of her mother's magazines. She gazed steadfastly at them until the car disappeared, making a right turn in the distance. "Who was that, Annie?"

Annie grunted. "That was General Logan Christmas and his wife Agnes. He was a hero in World War I. Reminds me of a picture I saw once of Blackjack Pershing."

"Was that their little boy and girl?"

"Yep. Billy and Helen. You might see 'em again. They buy eggs from me."

In a short while, Jordan was riding smoothly down a paved alleyway between two neatly clipped six-foot hedges. They stopped at a wrought-iron gate set on heavy posts in a break in the hedge. Annie rang a brass bell attached to the left post, and in a few minutes a nattily dressed black man in a cutaway coat appeared.

"Mornin', Amos. Ya'll need anything today?" Annie opened one of the boxes, revealing brown eggs lined up in neat rows.

Amos bared his bright teeth to Annie and then beamed at Jordan. "What a beautiful child! Look jes' like Mr. Taylor."

"She's his," Annie mumbled.

Still smiling at Jordan, Amos remarked absently, "Usual dozen eggs," and snapping his fingers, ". . . and two chickens. General said he wants chicken and dumplings tonight."

While Annie collected ninety cents, Jordan stared across the back lawn at Billy and Helen swinging high in the air on a swing set like one she had seen in a park her mother had taken her to. She thought how much fun it would be to swing high in the air like that or run across the lawn among the flower beds and live oaks and around the still, dark pond, surrounded by well-spaced willows. *I wish Annie would bring me to play with them sometime.*

After they had sold all the chickens and the eggs, Annie and Jordan returned home by the same route they had come—past the children, the squealing pigs, and the church. They went past Annie's house, beyond the cemetery, to the highway and turned left. Several minutes later they reached Three Corners Grocery. Jordan looked up at the towering pines, but they were as motionless as the telephone poles along the road.

Annie lifted Jordan out of the wagon. "I need the wagon for the groceries now, baby. We'll fit you in when we start home."

Morgan Clark smiled down at Jordan as she entered the store. "I see you're takin' good care of that baby, Jordan. Looks like to me she's put on a pound or two. You must be feedin' her good."

Jordan nodded her head, smiling back at Clark. "Yes sir. She's a good baby too."

"I'll just bet she is," Clark laughed.

"I thought you was agin' babies, Annie," a sharp-faced man in his mid-twenties sneered. He sat in a ladder back chair, whittling, his feet propped on the side of the black iron stove. His thin, whitish hair was combed straight back from a low forehead, except for the back of his head, where the comb never touched it—its shape depending on which way his head hit the pillow.

A seven-year-old version of the man sat next to him. "'At's what I heared too, Uncle Moon."

Clark turned his flinty gray eyes on them. "Moon, you shut your smart mouth. That goes for you, too, Sonny. And clean up them shavings before you leave."

Moon Mullins opened his mouth just enough to show his yellowish-green teeth. Seeing the cool threat in Clark's eyes, he lowered his head and returned to his whittling.

"Now, Miss Annie, can I get something for you?"

Annie grinned quickly at Morgan Clark. "Some slab bacon, oatmeal, coffee, butter, milk, and I'll pick up a few other things."

Jordan followed Annie to the back of the store, staring at the man and boy next to the stove. She knew they had tried to hurt Annie by the sound of their voices. Tugging at Annie's overalls, she asked softly, "Annie, why don't they like you?"

"Don't fret yourself about them two, child." She turned and moved on toward the back of the store again, the little wagon tagging along behind with a slight rumble of its wheels on the floor.

Following Annie, Jordan spotted a tiny coal-oil lantern on a shelf laden with hardware items. An angel with golden hair and a long white robe was etched on the globe of the lamp. His arms outstretched, he looked down on a small girl crossing a narrow footbridge over a torrent. Mesmerized by the scene, Jordan stood perfectly still, staring at the lantern while Annie collected her grocery items.

"Jordan? Time to go!" Annie beckoned from the front of the store as she counted out her change to Clark.

Fixated on the scene etched on the lantern, Jordan heard nothing but the water rushing under the bridge.

"Jordan!"

Startled, Jordan looked up at Annie standing next to her.

"What in the world's got your attention now?"

Pointing to the lantern, Jordan said softly. "I need the light so I won't be scared in the dark."

"We got no money for such things, Jordan. Let's go."

With a last look at the shining angel, Jordan followed Annie to the front of the store, climbed into the wagon among the groceries, and bumped over the threshold of the front door.

Grinding along through the gravel of the parking lot, Annie stopped abruptly. "Forgot my change on the counter!" She turned on Jordan. "See what happens when you don't mind? From now on, when I call, you better come runnin', young lady."

Annie trudged away through the gravel, returning in a minute or two. As she walked past Jordan, she pushed the tiny lantern into the little girl's arms next to the doll.

Jordan dropped her doll and held the lantern up to the sunlight. It shone with a radiance that seemed to warm her. *My very own angel. Now I don't have to be afraid.* "Oh, thank you, Annie! I'll always take good care of him!"

Annie never looked back at Jordan, never said a word all the way home and despised the weakness she felt in herself for buying such a frivolous thing. *I never should have done it. Just spoil her, that's all it'll do. People don't get what they want in this life, and the sooner this child learns that the better off she'll be.*

As Annie turned into her driveway, she saw Washington Smith coming toward her, clattering along in his ice wagon behind his swaybacked mule. She pulled her wagon loaded with Jordan and the groceries along the drive and down the side of the house to the back porch. As Jordan climbed down out of the groceries, Wash Smith drove the wagon up beside her.

"Afternoon, Miss Annie. Got some leftover ice for you," Smith grinned, springing from the seat of the wagon, agile as a panther in spite of his six-foot, 220-pound frame. He stood there as solid and immovable and as black as his mule. Wash wore overalls, a long-sleeved khaki shirt, and high-topped brown work shoes. "I declare, if that ain't a *fine* looking little girl! She stayin' wid you, Miss Annie?"

"For a while, anyway," Annie affirmed halfheartedly, carrying her groceries up the steps.

Wash walked to the back of his wagon. Laying a piece of heavy canvas over his right shoulder, he grabbed his ice tongs and snatched a hundred-pound block of ice from the wagon with one hand. With the ice block balanced across his shoulder, he navigated the high, weathered steps, placing the dripping block in the little icebox just as Annie stepped onto the porch from the kitchen.

"Ya'll want to go to church wid us in de mornin'?" Smith asked, smiling brightly down at Jordan from the back porch.

Annie's eyes narrowed, her mouth twisting as the jaw muscles tightened, grinding her molars. "Don't need churchin'," she spat. "We've been over this before, Wash."

"Maybe so, but I still ain't figured out what you holdin' against God. Don't stop Him from lovin' you though."

"Where was God when I needed Him?" Annie shot back, bending to put the slab of bacon into the icebox.

Smith smiled directly into her face as she stood up, a light in his eyes that caused Annie to look away. "Same place He always was, Miss Annie. Waitin' for you wid His arms wide open."

Smith knelt beside Jordan on his way back to the wagon, his white teeth gleaming in his dark, dark face. "My, my! You jes' as pretty as a speckled puppy under a red wagon! What's yo' name?"

Jordan glanced back at Annie, disappearing through the screen door into the kitchen. "Lisa Jordan Simms," she whispered, shyly.

"Well, now, Lisa Jordan Simms! I think you and me gonna be real good friends," Smith grinned. "Missy Jordan—that sound like a fine name to call you."

*   *   *

Jordan awakened slowly to the faint warmth of sunshine as it lay in a pale golden bar against her cheek. Opening her eyes slowly, she stared at the bright angel on her lamp, arms eternally outstretched over the child below him. She went to sleep each night to the soft amber glow of the lamp, and each morning when she awakened, the wick would be trimmed and ready for the coming night.

"Mornin', Miss Annie." Jordan heard the rich, booming voice of Washington Smith below her in the side yard. She quickly sprang from the bed and ran downstairs to the back porch where Smith was talking with Annie. The look on her face told Jordan that Annie was not pleased with the conversation.

Smith sat in his ice wagon that had been scrubbed clean—even the spokes and hubs of the wheels were almost spotless. His wife, trim and bright-eyed as a girl, sat next to him. In the back, sitting on wooden chairs that had been placed on the floor of the wagon were two children. The girl, Jordan's age, wore a red wool coat over a white cotton dress, trimmed with lace. A year or two older, the boy wore a black suit and red bow tie. You had only to glance at Wash Smith to see who the boy's father was.

"Now, Miss Annie, you know that chile need to be in church. Why don't you let her go to preachin' wid us?"

Jordan walked up next to Annie, holding her doll to her chest with both hands. Her bare feet poked out from under the flannel nightgown Annie had worn as a child.

Smith beamed at her. "Well, good mornin', Missy Jordan. This is my wife, Pearl, and these are our chillun, Lester and Hydrangea—we calls her Hy for short."

Jordan smiled and nodded at Wash's family.

"Well, Miss Annie?" Smith added.

Annie sighed deeply. "I'm tired of you pesterin' me about it, Wash." She looked down at Jordan. "You want to go to church with these people, child?"

Looking at the children in the back of the wagon, Jordan nodded brightly.

After Annie had dressed her in her only decent dress, a tan, long-sleeved frock with blue trim that matched her eyes, Jordan sat on the seat between Wash and Pearl, bouncing down the narrow lane that led through the stand of sweet gum trees to the little white church. Glancing to her left, she could barely make out Annie's figure at the kitchen window two hundred yards away across a field of dead grass.

Ahead of them the churchyard was crowded with black people in their Sunday best. Horses and mules were tied to trees, and a dozen or so wagons were parked in an uneven row along the left side of the church. As they climbed down from the wagon, several people came over to greet them.

"Mornin', Reverend—Miss Pearl," a large man with a brown vested suit and gold watch chain said jovially. "Beautiful day for a meetin', ain't it?"

Other people greeted them as Jordan walked with Reverend Washington Smith into his church. Jordan sat on the front row between Pearl and Hy, watching Wash step to the pulpit, his starched shirt white as fleece against his dark face.

Wash Smith looked out over his congregation and gave them a smile brighter than the morning light filtering through the windows. "It's a good day to serve the Lord!"

"Amen!" "Hallelujah!" "Tell it, brother!"

"I *said* . . . it's a *good* day . . . to serve our God!"

There were more shouts of praise throughout the congregation. After a few words of exhortation, Wash opened a hymnal, gave the page number, and led the singing in a rich, bass voice. Pearl had slipped from the front seat and now sat at a battered old upright piano with one pedal missing.

> I'm in the way, the bright and shining way,
> I'm in the gloryland way.

Jordan stood with the rest of the congregation, glancing about in wonder as they sang—some with their eyes closed, some praising God with their hands lifted, some singing joyfully with tears in their eyes.

After several more hymns, Wash made some announcements and then opened his big, black Bible. "I'm reading from the ninth chapter of Luke, the sixty-second verse." He waited until the shuffling of pages had stopped. "'No man, having put his hand to the plough, and looking back, is fit for the kingdom of God.'"

Wash closed his Bible and placed it on the pulpit, looking out over the congregation. "Anybody here ever walk behind a plow?"

There was laughter and good-natured kidding among the congregation as most of the men raised their hands.

Jordan listened while Wash preached, but she didn't understand and soon lost interest. The service ended with another song and about half of the people went forward for the altar call. Jordan watched closely as they knelt and prayed and called out to God.

After the Smiths had dropped Jordan off at Annie's, the two of them sat in the big kitchen at the long pine table eating chicken and dumplings with sweet potatoes and iced tea. Jordan had never tasted anything so good as the tender chicken and the chewy dumplings in their rich, white gravy.

"I like to go to meeting, Annie," Jordan offered as she drank the last of her tea.

Annie finished chewing a mouthful of dumplings, washing it down with the tea. "I hope it does you some good, child. From what I've seen though, it usually don't last long."

3

"DON'T LET THEM MAKE YOU CRY!"

*T*he winter that year was not a hard one. Only on the coldest of nights would Annie place a mattress in the kitchen, where she and Jordan could sleep together for warmth on the floor next to the stove. J.T. and Wash continued to visit: Wash every Saturday afternoon, bringing the leftover ice, and on the Sunday mornings when Annie would let Jordan go to church with him and his family.

J.T. came when the mood struck him, whether it was two or three times a week or as long as a month between visits. He always left money on the kitchen table or stuffed in the pockets of Annie's overalls, and he always had a bottle or two with him. It took less and less persuasion for Annie to join him. They would reminisce about the old days when they belonged to the aristocracy of Liberty.

The first hour or two of the drinking was pleasant for Jordan, with J.T. making her laugh with his funny sayings and playing games with her that he would make up as they went along.

Later, he and Annie would sit on the back porch, if it wasn't too cold, and talk about people and times long before Jordan was born. Or they would build a fire in the massive stone fireplace in the living room, with wood J.T. would bring in his pickup, and sit on the huge old sofa, drinking—J.T. out of his silver flask and Annie out of her china cup—while Jordan played with her doll on the floor in front of the fire. It was the only time the living room was used, as Annie had only enough wood for the kitchen stove. The sofa and a long, carved mahogany coffee table were the only furnishings.

The only painting left in the house hung above the mantle—the sole survivor of the dozen or so others that had decorated the living room and now left their dark rectangular markings behind, like the spoors of some extinct breed of cats that had once crouched along the walls. In the remaining portrait, a ten-year-old Carrie Ann Simms stood next to her father, who sat stiffly in a gold brocade Queen Anne chair. Taylor and Mrs. Simms flanked them to the right and left. Annie often felt her father's demanding eyes on her, sometimes hearing the words ringing down through the years as clearly as when he first spoke them. "You oughta been a boy, Carrie Ann."

"Whatever happened to that fellow who shot ol' Harold, Annie?" J.T. asked one dark February afternoon as they sat together on the sofa, a half bottle into their conversation.

Jordan sat on the floor in front of the fireplace. She amused herself by making imaginary pictures in the flames as they popped and crackled on the hickory logs. Outside the room's high windows, their drapes pulled back and tied, a slow rain fell, the silvery drops on the glass gliding in graceful, erratic patterns toward the window sill. A gray light filtered through the windows, the vast room glimmering in the half-darkness like the bottom of the sea.

Annie's face clouded over at the sound of her dead husband's name. "J.T., in our little jaunts down Memory Lane, there's some side trips I'd just as soon skip. You know this is one of them."

J.T. sat deep in the plush sofa, wearing his Harvard sweatshirt, khakis, and a gray, unlaundered pinstripe suit coat. His brown-and-white saddle shoes were propped on the heavy table. "Aw, come on, Annie, what difference does it make? I was just a kid when it happened, but I remember the whole town talked about it for weeks."

"He moved to Atlanta," Annie answered abruptly, gazing into the flames.

"You mean he didn't go to prison? I know they had a change of venue, but most everybody figured the other judge sent him up."

Annie's gaze went from the fire to the rain, cascading now down the tall panes of glass. "Well, he didn't. Said it happened in the 'heat of the blood.' I believe that was the phrase his attorney used to defend the murder—and that's what it was—murder! Judge gave him a year and suspended it on condition he would leave town. Moved to Atlanta—that's what I heard."

J.T. unscrewed the top of his flask, turned it up, and gave out a loud "ahhhh" when he finished. Screwing the top back on, he slipped it into his inside jacket pocket. "Well, Annie, he *was* in another man's bedroom when it happened."

Annie stared at the rain in silence.

"We don't seem to have much luck in affairs of the heart," J.T. continued, deep into the past now where he felt most comfortable. "Do we, Annie?"

Annie sighed deeply and leaned back on the couch and sipped from her cup. "Too late for me now," she admitted, glancing at J.T. "But not for you. You need to forget about Ellie and get on with your life. A good scrubbing with lye soap and an hour at the barber shop would make a new man out of you. Get your clothes cleaned and pressed. The girls would still turn their heads when you walk down the street."

"They do now," J.T. assured her, a sly smile on his face. "The other way!"

Annie chuckled softly and looked back at the fire. *J.T., sometimes I think you're the only thing standing between me and the nut house—or the graveyard.*

J.T. glanced over at Jordan, sitting before the fireplace with her doll. "Come here, sugar," he called softly to her.

Cradling her doll, Jordan walked over and climbed in J.T.'s lap. She looked into his face, frowning slightly. "Why are you and Wash the only people that come to see us?"

J.T. glanced at Annie and then gazed out at the pewter-gray sheets of rain sweeping through the winter trees. "Because, sweetheart, most people don't know quality when they see it."

Jordan lay her head against J.T.'s shoulder, her arm around the doll resting on his chest. "I don't care if anybody else comes. You and Wash are enough." Jordan kissed him on the cheek and snuggled against him. "I love you, J.T."

As J.T. felt the child soft and vulnerable against him, a foreboding as dark and heavy as the day's weather touched him with a cold ache, like a serpent brushing its scaly coils against his soul. He thought of all the people alone in rented rooms or in houses sliding into decay—knew with an absolute certainty that the best part of him was still spiraling a football downfield in a perfect arc to the addictive roar of the crowd, or standing breathless on a summer

41

night by the river, lost in Ellie's fragrance and touch and the shimmering cloud of her hair in the moonlight. Most of all, he feared for Jordan, knowing that she deserved far more in this world than Annie and Wash and J. T. Dickerson.

Annie watched them until they both fell asleep, remembering all the naps she had taken as a small child with her father on this same couch in the warmth and flickering shadows of the fire.

* * *

Jordan squinted into the afternoon sunlight that glinted on the red Texaco pump. "Ben, can I have a swallow of your Nu-Grape?" she asked, sitting on the bench in front of Three Corners' Grocery.

Ben turned his gray eyes, light and strangely out of place beneath his coal black hair, from the Nu-Grape to Jordan's face. "There's only one swallow left." The moisture from the bottle had dampened the legs of his overalls as it sat between his legs.

"OK, then." Jordan looked at the next bench where Ben's four-year-old sister, Dinah, and his brother, Pete, a year younger than Dinah, sat with their R.C.'s. Feeling the cool smoothness of the bottle against her hand, Jordan glanced back.

"Here, you can have it," Ben offered, a slow smile on his tanned face. "I had enough."

"Thanks." Jordan turned the Nu-Grape up and took a big swallow. It was cool and sweet and tasted like nectar to her. There was a little left in the bottle, just enough to cover the bottom. She swirled it around, watching the light dance and sparkle in the purple liquid. "I wish Annie could buy me my own Nu-Grape," she said wistfully. "I want to drink one all by myself sometime. She says they're a waste of money." Jordan tilted the bottle, letting the few remaining drops run into her mouth and savoring the final fruity sweetness.

"I think they're the best thing in the world," Ben proclaimed.

"Want some of mine?" Rachel Shaw asked, sitting on the other side of Ben. Her chubby face, lightly sprinkled with freckles, beamed at Ben with an adoring smile. Her brown hair was in ringlets, and her clear hazel eyes had flecks of green in them. Like Dinah, she wore a loose dress made from flour sacks. She thought Ben Logan was better than Nu-Grape, and he thought Rachel was a pest.

Ben swung his legs back and forth on the bench. "I'm full. Jordan didn't get one."

Rachel handed the bottle past Ben to Jordan.

Jordan took one long swallow and handed it back. "Thanks, Rachel. Wanna hold my doll?"

Rachel nodded her head as Jordan gave her the doll. "What pretty hair," she cooed, smoothing the red yarn with her hand. "I wish my hair was this color."

Ben jumped down from the bench. "C'mon, Pete. Lets go chunk some rocks."

Pete set his R.C. on the bench, and the two of them picked up rocks from the gravel parking lot and threw them at a yellow-and-black metal sign nailed to a pine tree toward the rear of the store. Three soldiers with red jackets and tall black hats marched across the sign beneath large black letters stating, "Quick, Henry, the Flit!"

Jordan watched Ben hit the sign five times in a row, glancing up as Annie pulled her little wagon out of the store. Behind her, Jewel Logan carried three brown paper bags of groceries. She wore a brown print dress that matched the color of her hair. Her gray eyes were intelligent and full of life.

"Why don't you let Jordan come play with the children sometime, Annie?" Jewel asked, balancing the three sacks in her arms.

Annie gazed down at Jordan. "She's kinda shy. Rather stay home and help me, wouldn't you, baby?"

Jordan glanced at the other children. Staring at her scuffed, brown high-tops, she said softly, "Yes ma'am."

"Well, she's welcome any time," Jewel added with a smile, pointing to Rachel. "This one here's like my own child. Another one won't make no difference. Ben, come get one of these sacks. Here, Dinah, you take this little one."

"Hop in the wagon, child," Annie nodded.

Jewel's eyes caught Jordan's for a moment as the child settled herself among the groceries. Behind their dark, blue beauty she could see a well of loneliness. "Remember, Annie, Jordan's welcome to come home with us any Saturday afternoon. I'll bring her home after church on Sunday."

"Maybe," Annie remarked offhandedly, leading the rattling little wagon across the parking lot.

Jewel watched the two of them as they crossed the highway, Jordan clutching her doll to her chest and smoothing its hair with her hand. *God bless that child—and Annie, too. Give your angels charge over them to protect them in all their ways.*

* * *

Spring drifted lazily into the bright, hot days of summer as the sun moved steadily northward in its diurnal crossings of the sky. Jordan never got to visit with the Logan children, but she played with them briefly almost every Saturday afternoon when Annie bought groceries at Three Corners—and Jewel Logan always bought her a Nu-Grape soda. Sometimes the children would go into the woods behind the store and play hide-and-seek or listen to the songbirds and watch the squirrels' acrobatics in the hickories, beeches, and oaks.

Three times during the course of the summer, Ben, Dinah, and Rachel came to play with Jordan while Jewel and Annie sat on the back porch in wicker chairs drinking tea. It was after their last visit that Jordan heard J.T. singing "Side by Side" in his off-key, but pleasant baritone. Throwing corn to the chickens on a mild September afternoon, she and Annie were admiring the new biddies trying out their new legs among the pecking hens.

"J.T.'s here, Annie!" Jordan shouted. "J.T.'s here!" She went running toward the house through the chickens, their loud clucking drowning out the shrill peeping of the biddies. Her overalls, a smaller version of Annie's, flapped in the wind as she ran. She caught him just as he reached the back steps.

"Maybe we're ragged and fun—uh!" J.T. grunted as Jordan leaped into his arms. He held her at arm's length above his head, spinning around and around while she squealed with laughter.

As J.T. held her, Jordan began digging into his coat pockets. "What did you bring me, J.T.?"

"And what makes you think I brought you something, young lady?" J.T. asked, setting his bottle on the porch at eye level.

Jordan put her arms around his neck, kissing him hard on the cheek. "You always do. That's why."

"Irrefutable logic," J.T. grinned slyly. "Maybe we ought to take a look in the pickup."

Annie strolled up at that moment, hands in the pockets of her overalls. She went into the kitchen and then returned, placing her china cup next to J.T.'s bottle. She wore a red, long-sleeved flannel shirt and her heavy boots in spite of the mild weather. "You gonna spoil that girl, J.T. She thinks you're a whiskey-drinking Santa Claus now."

"It's my calling, Annie," J.T. beamed, holding Jordan with both arms, "to spoil this child. I've been ordained to bring some semblance of joy into her life."

"Let's go to the truck," Jordan begged, climbing down and pulling on J.T.'s hand.

"Right you are," J.T. nodded and began a slow loping run along the side of the house, Jordan close on his heels.

When they reached the truck, Jordan clambered onto the seat through the open door. She grabbed a big black-and-white Hightower's bag, digging into it with both hands. "Oh, look!" she cried. "It's beautiful!" She held up a pink-and-white satin dress with tiny roses embroidered on the bodice and around the hem.

"Glad you like it, m'lady," J.T. grinned.

Jordan slid down from the seat, holding the dress in one hand and the bag under her arm. Running to the back, she shouted, "Annie, look what J.T. brought."

When J.T. reached the porch, Annie was holding the dress, while Jordan brought out a pair of white patent leather shoes and a white ruffled petticoat from the bag.

"For her first day of school," J.T. smiled at Annie.

Annie glanced at Jordan, who was oblivious of them, unlacing her brown high-tops. "Kinda fancy for school, ain't they, J.T.?"

J.T. held up a forefinger, walked to the bag on the ground and pulled out a blue-and-gray plaid cotton dress with a sash that tied in back. He held it out to Annie. "A bit more practical?"

Later, the three of them sat at supper at the long kitchen table, the coal-oil lantern casting its moving shadows along the walls. Jordan had her new clothes piled on the chair beside her, glancing down at them occasionally during the meal.

"Best meal I've had in a long time, Annie," J.T. said expansively, pushing his plate back.

Annie sipped from her cup. "Wouldn't 'a been nothin' but cornbread and snap beans if you hadn't brought that roast."

"Ready for your first day of school, sweetheart?" J.T. asked, leaning toward Jordan.

Jordan looked at Annie with a puzzled expression.

"I hadn't told her yet," Annie explained to J.T. "Didn't want to worry her."

Jordan looked at Annie, an expression of terror on her face. "I don't want to go! Ben said he was goin', but not me. Don't make me go there, Annie!"

"Everybody goes to school, Jordan."

"Not me!" Jordan wailed. "I never go anywhere!"

"Hush, child," Annie insisted. "You have to go to school. Don't you want to be smart like J.T.?"

Tears ran down Jordan's face. Clutching tightly to her doll, she begged, "Just let me stay home till Mama and Daddy come to get me! Please, Annie!"

"Don't think of that, child."

Jordan scrambled down from her chair, climbing into J.T.'s lap. Burying herself in his arms, she clung to her doll and sobbed until Annie picked her up to get her ready for bed.

*   *   *

Jordan rattled through the streets of Liberty in Annie's wagon, the early sun breaking in green-gold salients of light as it struck the high limbs of the elms and oaks that lined the sidewalks. As they neared the school ground, she saw the boys and girls walking singly and in twos and threes toward the two-story red brick building. Some of them had stopped and were looking at her and Annie as they approached along the sidewalk.

"Look at the funny lady!" one of them giggled.

"She's the one that's crazy," Jordan heard another say.

"Why's the little girl in that wagon? Can't she walk?"

Annie stopped at the front walk that led up to the school. "I'll pick you up here after school." Even after all the years of ridicule, the remarks of the children still hurt.

Jordan climbed out of the wagon. "All right." She trudged up the walk, looking back once as Annie pulled her wagon along the sidewalk toward home.

Just inside the door, Jordan saw Ben Logan walking down the hall. "Ben! Wait for me, Ben!"

Ben stopped and waited for Jordan to catch up.

"You know where first grade is?"

"Sure. Mama brought me up here last year so I'd know how to find it. C'mon, I'll show you."

As they entered the room, Ben glanced at the far corner, waving to a tall, skinny boy with straw-colored hair. "There's Tom Shaw. You OK now?"

"I—I guess so," Jordan stammered.

Ben left Jordan standing by the American flag, hanging limply on its upright piked staff.

"Hi, Debbie." Jordan heard a burly, blond boy say to another child near her. He was dressed in pleated navy slacks and a burgundy sport shirt with two flap pockets. His black dress oxfords were shiny and expensive.

Jordan remembered the little girl named Debbie that J.T. had told her about. With her long blonde hair and blue eyes she looked like the one he had described.

"Hi, Keith. That's a pretty shirt," the girl named Debbie replied, smoothing the skirt of her starched blue-and-white dress.

"Do you know J.T.?" Jordan blurted out to the girl.

Debbie Lambert looked at Jordan, then at the dress J.T. had bought for her. "That's a party dress. It's not for school!"

Keith Demerie stepped close to Debbie. "She's the one the funny lady brought in her wagon."

"Oh, yes," Debbie giggled as they walked away together.

Jordan wanted to run from the room, tearing the dress with its tiny roses from her body. She wished that she had listened to Annie earlier that morning and worn her other new dress. *I want to wear my overalls and stay home. Nobody here likes me or Annie! Why don't they just leave us alone?*

A short woman in her mid thirties entered the room and walked briskly to the desk. Carrying a hard-backed gray attendance book under one arm and a *McGuffey's Reader* under the other, she surveyed her charges with eyes so dark they appeared, through the gold-rimmed glasses resting on her short nose, not to have pupils. Her hair, the color of weak coffee, was pulled back tightly from her round face. "Please be seated, class," she stated in a husky voice that sounded like she had a sore throat.

As the children scraped and shuffled into seats near their friends, Jordan found herself alone by the flag. Glancing around, she saw an empty desk on the last row along the windows next to the radiator. With her head down, she slowly walked to it and sat down. Like an open wooden diary, the scarred and scratched surface of the desk carried memories of the students who had used it down through years. Carved deeply into the wood in the upper right hand corner of the desk top, was the name, A. Ditweiler.

"My name is Miss Barron, class, and I'll be your teacher this year," the teacher said, printing her name firmly on the blackboard to the squeaking scrape of the chalk.

The first two hours went quickly with the introduction of classmates, passing out of books and supplies, and a brief look at each subject to be studied. While each child stood and gave his name in turn, Jordan surveyed her classmates. Most of them seemed excited to be in school, happy to be with their friends. She wondered if she were the only who felt so out of place.

Billy Christmas stood at his desk at the end of the row on the opposite side of the room. He wore tan slacks and a dark blue shirt that was a shade darker than his eyes. His black hair was neatly combed, and he sat almost too stiffly erect in his desk. But his smile, when he introduced himself, was easy and relaxed. *I bet we'd have fun if I could go play at his house,* Jordan thought.

"Now class," Miss Barron said brightly, "every morning we're going to have a cleanliness inspection, and we might as well start right now. Each of you will hold your hands out palms up and turn them over when asked to do so."

A muffled groan moved through the room among the boys.

Smiling, Miss Barron took a small tablet with a brown cover from her desk drawer. "Debbie Lambert, would you like to be the first inspector?" She held the tablet toward Debbie, who was seated directly in front of her desk.

"Yes ma'am!" Debbie chirped, jumping from her seat and standing next to her teacher.

Miss Barron handed her the book. "The names of each of our twenty-seven students are on each page. Each page represents one week. You will check the proper boxes as I tell you. Later in the year, you'll be able to read the names yourselves."

Debbie followed Miss Barron around the room, checking the boxes as instructed. When they got to Jordan, she held her hands out, palms up. Debbie made a face. Some of the children giggled until Miss Barron held up her hand. "That'll be quite enough, children!"

Jordan looked at the rusty dirt ground into her palms from the old pipes and pieces of scrap metal she had helped Annie unload over the past months. A reddish-brown stain under her nails was still visible, even after Annie's scrubbing.

"Ugh!" Debbie grunted. "How awful!"

The giggling began again.

"I'll not warn you again, class! The next one who laughs will go to Principal Ditweiler's office."

The laughter subsided abruptly.

"Debbie Lambert! You keep your remarks to yourself!"

"Yes ma'am."

"Jordan," Miss Barron said softly, kneeling beside her desk. "You'll have to ask your mother to show you how to wash your hands a little better. OK?"

"She ain't got no mama!" a husky boy with short black hair and rough good looks shouted quickly.

"Who said that?" Miss Barron demanded, standing up suddenly. "I will personally see that Mr. Ditweiler paddles the next person I catch talking!"

Encouraged by the giggles from his classmates, the boy couldn't resist another try. "Daddy neither!"

Miss Barron was ready this time. "Marcell Duke, you get yourself on down to the principal's office right now! Tell the secretary I'll be there shortly."

With a sullen look at the teacher, the boy rose from his desk. He clomped out of the room in his too-long khakis, frayed at the bottoms from the heels of his scuffed brogans.

Miss Barron and Debbie continued their rounds. Jordan opened her *McGuffey's Reader* and looked at the pictures. She thought of her father she hadn't seen in almost a year . . . and of her mother who had been gone longer than that. *If they would only come and get me! Please come and get me, Daddy! These boys and girls don't like me. I don't know why! I don't know why!*

When the bell rang for recess, the children were up and rushing for the door before Jordan could put her books under her desk. They laughed and squealed in the hall, pairing off or in small groups, acting as if they played together all the time. Jordan edged down the stone steps to the playground, walking across toward the swing sets.

A skinny boy with a sallow complexion, wearing threadbare khakis, walked along next to Jordan. "I seen a mule pullin' a wagon one time—looked better than that woman that pulled you to school this morning," he jeered.

Ben Logan appeared out of nowhere. "Jack Clampett, you leave her alone!"

"Aw, Ben. I was just funnin' her. C'mon. Let's go play on the swings."

Ben looked at Jordan with a forced smile. "Jack didn't mean nothin'. He just ain't very smart."

"Let's go, Ben," Jack called out. "You don't want to hang around with no girl, do you?"

Glancing at Jordan, Ben hesitated for a moment, then called back. "I'm comin'!"

Jordan walked over to a stone bench under a live oak and sat down. She watched the children playing on the swings and see-saws and merry-go-round. After Debbie had made fun of her dress when she spoke to her, Jordan was afraid to talk to anyone else.

Looking at her grimy hands, lying on the new pink dress, Jordan felt a hurting in her chest that would not go away. Two glistening tears dropped from her blue eyes, one splashing softly on the tip of her left thumbnail as if in a vain attempt to wash away the ground-in dirt and rust, the other making a small, round spot on the pink cloth of her dress. She felt a stirring somewhere in her being as though a hand moved inexorably, laying the first stones in a painfully constructed, immovable wall.

A few minutes before the final bell rang, Jordan glanced out the window, watching Annie pull her little wagon across the school ground toward the cafeteria. It was loaded with jars of canned fruits and vegetables Jordan recognized from the pantry at home. She continued on around to the back of the cafeteria, reappearing in a few minutes, heading for the front walk to wait for Jordan.

When the bell rang, Jordan let the bustle of the classroom die down and gathered her books and walked out alone.

"Did you enjoy your first day of school, Jordan?" Miss Barron asked, putting her folders into the file drawer of her desk.

Jordan stopped, giving her teacher a quick look. "Yes ma'am. I guess so."

Miss Barron noticed the stack of books Jordan was carrying. "There's no homework."

"I like to look at them," Jordan said shyly.

"You're a very pretty little girl, Jordan," Miss Barron smiled, gathering up her purse and notebooks. "You should straighten up a little. Hold your head up more."

Jordan lifted her head slightly, a half-smile on her face.

"There—that's better."

As Jordan walked down the front walk of the school between the columns of ancient cedars, she saw some of the children taunting Annie as they passed her. Annie acted as if she heard nothing, standing immobile, with the tongue of the wagon in her work-hardened hand. When Annie spotted her, Jordan noticed something pass across the weathered face like the forgotten remnants of a smile she could no longer remember how to fit together.

Jordan remained silent along all the shady streets, with September sunlight filtering through the leaves in a golden haze around her. The wagon jarred her where the roots of the giant oaks had cracked the curbs and pushed the sidewalk up in peaks. She sat alone with her terrible fear of school, watching Annie trudge along in front of her like some ancient beast of burden that had taken human form.

When they reached the back porch, Annie started up the steps, turned, and looked back where Jordan still sat in the wagon, staring at her shiny new shoes.

"Come on in, baby. We'll have some cookies," Annie said as gently as she could.

Jordan looked at her shoes, her body beginning to shake uncontrollably.

Annie came down the steps to her, standing next to the wagon. "What's the matter, baby?"

Jordan continued to shake as she tried to talk. "Annie . . . they wouldn't play with me! They . . . made fun of me . . . and you!" she gasped, as the tears started to roll down her cheeks. "They said I don't have a daddy. Please don't make me go back!"

Annie knelt beside the wagon, placing her calloused hand gently on Jordan's shoulder.

Jordan fell against her, holding tightly to her. "Why were they so mean to me, Annie?"

Annie put her left arm around Jordan, brushing the tears away with her right hand. "People are just mean, baby. I don't know why."

Annie knelt beside the wagon and held Jordan for a long time. When she finally stopped crying, Annie lifted her face with a grimy forefinger beneath her chin. Looking directly into Jordan's eyes, red and swollen now, she said evenly, "Don't let them make you cry, Jordan. No matter what they do—don't let them make you cry!"

Annie lifted Jordan from the wagon. Exhausted now from the weeping that had torn the deepest part of her, the child still clung weakly to her. Annie made it to the top step, sitting down heavily, cradling Jordan in her arms. From the tall pine on the riverbank, the cawing of the same solitary crow rang through the darkening air.

What's wrong with our family? Maybe it's a curse that passes from generation to generation. Daddy—a womanizer and a drunk. Mama—grieving herself to death over him. Taylor—failing in everything he ever tried, except self-destruction. And me—the worst of all! This poor child—stuck here with me, who can only bring her misery and shame. What did she ever do to deserve this?

Annie sat on the steps holding Jordan, who had drifted into a deep sleep, not realizing that she was rocking gently back and forth, singing an old, old hymn she hadn't thought of since she was a child.

> Rock of Ages, cleft for me,
> Let me hide myself in Thee . . .

4

ANGEL OF THE LAMP

*J*erusalem has only one Wailing Wall—in Wall Street every wall is wet with tears." Thus did one observer describe Black Tuesday, October 29, 1929—the day the stock market took its greatest plunge. Black Tuesday did not cause the Great Depression, but it was the country's most visible harbinger of the wolf-lean decade to come.

Men would leave their houses in the morning to hunt for work, trying to preserve a threadbare gentility in a threadbare suit and polished shoes whose soles were thin as tissue paper. Soon, they would be spending most of the day in the public library or some other hideout to avoid friends who had somehow held on to their jobs.

Next would come the sneaking like a burglar into pawn shops to hock a watch, a wedding ring, or the family radio. Or perhaps they would face that most dreaded of all humiliations, a registered letter with the eviction notice from the landlord.

Especially in the cities, the jobless were the most striking symbol of the American dream slipping into nightmare. They gathered in pool halls and taverns and shared a common misery and frustration. They sat in the parks if the weather was good or stood in empty doorways to shelter them from the wind and the rain. Some panhandled for nickels and dimes on the streets, or lingered for an hour over a nickel cup of coffee in a dingy cafe, staring out at the bleak, endless days.

As the times became more desperate, a migration of jobless workers began across the land, like the great African herds seeking new feeding grounds in a drought. With little hope for tomorrow, they looked for a day's work anywhere—pushing a wheelbarrow, harvesting crops, or washing dishes. If that failed, they turned to robbery or hijacking.

Some traveled the highways, but most took the faster and more certain route of the rails. They threw their battered suitcases or bundles into boxcars, sitting in the open doors and watching the countryside flash by on their way to the same desolation in a different state. The "Hoovervilles" along the roadsides and the "Hobo Jungles" of the railroads became familiar landmarks in the America of the thirties.

* * *

"Wish it wouldn't have closed up," Dinah Logan sighed, standing in front of Penny's Bakery.

Across from the elementary school, the group of children was gathered in front of the little building. A brown bag was taped to the inside of the glass on the front door, next to the brass bell they had all rung on their way in and out of the bakery. Scrawled with a grease pencil on the coarse paper were two words that had meaning for everybody in the country: "Went Broke."

Through the plate glass windows, they could see that the inside of the building was empty. Even the glass display cases were gone. White paper bags, rolls of tape, and a few pieces of chalk were scattered across the floor. DOUGHNUTS/THREE FOR TEN CENTS was neatly printed on the blackboard.

"What difference does it make?" Ben shrugged. "We never get nickels to spend anymore."

"Sure did smell good on the way to school every morning though," Tom Shaw added.

"Nothing ever lasts," Jordan remarked with a stony fatalism. "Let's forget about it."

Ben and Tom walked ahead of Jordan and the two first graders, Dinah and Rachel. The trees had taken on the bright, relentless green of late April in the South. Leaving the tall, white peaked and gabled houses of the town, the children came out into the flame-bright fields of the countryside. Across the barbed wire fences, where sleek cattle grazed, honey bees were settling on and lifting off the white clover blossoms like tiny helicopters.

"Them cows don't know there's a depression," Tom observed. "Look at 'em. Fat as pigs."

Ben gazed at the Jerseys and Guernseys scattered across the rolling pasture land. "They got kinda bony-lookin' back in the winter when nobody could afford to buy feed."

"Can't figure out why times got so hard," Tom shrugged. "Don't make no sense to me."

"Daddy said it all started up in New York City," Ben offered. "Happened at a stock . . . something or other. Market! That's it! Stock market."

Tom frowned in bewilderment. "I didn't know they kept stock in New York City. What kind you reckon? Cows or pigs?"

Ben shook his head slowly as he walked along kicking the gravel. "Ain't nothin' them Yankees do surprises me. I think it's all that cold weather makes 'em crazy."

"That's a pretty dress, Dinah," Rachel observed, touching the ruffles on the sleeves.

"Got it from my cousin," Dinah beamed. "She's two years older than me—same as you, Jordan—and they got money. I get all her old clothes. Mama says we can't afford dresses like this."

Jordan looked at the dress that J.T. had given her at the first of the school year—the last one he had bought her—worn thin from Annie's scrubbings in the black iron wash pot. *Poor J.T., he can hardly afford his own clothes now.* "I'll see ya'll in the mornin'," she confirmed when they reached the two huge live oaks that guarded the entrance to Annie's house.

The other children said their good-byes, continuing on down the gravel road. Jordan stood at the beginning of the overgrown drive and watched them. Dinah was talking to Rachel, who kept her eyes on Ben. In a few seconds, Ben and Tom were racing toward the distant highway. She wondered why Tom bothered trying to beat him anymore.

Jordan walked toward the house along the little path Annie kept clear with her wagon. The weeds were already three feet tall—blue and gold wildflowers in glorious disarray all the way to the woods. The paint on the house was beginning to peel badly, especially on the front, which faced west, and on the east side, along the back porch. Some of the fence posts were sagging, and in places the wire was down where limbs had fallen on it. The weathered gray barn in back, close to the woods, was beginning to lean a little off balance, like its owner.

Jordan dropped her books on the back steps and grabbed a basket on the way to the henhouse. The hens clucked their disapproval as she gathered their potential progeny while the Rhode Island Red Rooster strutted about, lord and master of a forlorn kingdom. With little money for feed, the scrawny chickens had become adept bug and worm hunters. Jordan had propped the henhouse up numerous times with scrap lumber from Annie's foragings, but it still slouched toward the earth.

Returning to the house, Jordan picked up four pieces of stove wood from the back porch and started a fire for supper. She cracked two eggs into a large white bowl, added cornmeal, and mixed up cold-water corn pone. Waiting for the stove to get hot, she clicked on the radio and caught part of a song by Mildred Bailey: ". . . just an old sweet song keeps Georgia on my mind."

"Wonder if she's ever been to Georgia?" Jordan said aloud as she smeared bacon grease around the inside of an iron skillet. "And if she has, why's she singing about it?" After pouring batter into the skillet, she tested the stove with a quick splash of water from the bucket and set the skillet on the hot surface. Collecting her books from the back porch, she sat at the table doing her homework while the bread cooked, sometimes singing along with the radio.

As Jordan got up to turn the bread over in the skillet, Bing Crosby's unmistakable mellow voice came on the radio. "Where the blue of the night meets the gold of the day," he crooned, with Jordan joining in on, "someone waits for me."

Wouldn't that be nice? To have someone waiting for me every day when I get home. Mama standing out by the road wearing a big smile and a pretty apron. She never did wear aprons. We could make supper together and have it ready when Daddy got in from work. And we could all eat together in a pretty dining room with real china and silver. Afterwards, we'd sit in the parlor while I did my homework and Daddy read his paper. Mama would be sewing me a pretty dress for school—one like Debbie Lambert wears.

When the corn pone was cooked, Jordan climbed the stairs to the second floor, leaving the radio on. At the end of the hall she opened a narrow door leading to an even narrower staircase and climbed up into the attic. Walking through a derelict history of the Simms family—old trunks and suitcases, cartons of musty books and papers, toys, hanging clothes and those piled at random on the floor, boxes of loose pictures and albums—Jordan went to her favorite spot in the house, the window seat at the front gable.

Sitting on the green velvet cushion she had left airing outside in the sunshine for two days, Jordan picked up the copy of *Tarzan and the Ant Men* she had found in one of the cartons. The light filtering in through the dust and old cobwebs on the window was hazy bright. Jordan thought it just right for reading. Gazing out the window, she saw a cloud of dust on the road and in front of it a gleaming black Cadillac convertible. She watched Billy Christmas ride by, sitting stiff as a tin soldier in the front seat next to his iron-soldier father.

Poor Billy, all that money and he looks like he just lost his last friend. A mother, father, and sister—what in the world does it take to make some people happy? I'd sure like to trade places with you, Billy, Jordan thought, returning to her book about a race of African warriors only six inches tall.

Lost in the book, Jordan didn't see Annie until she had almost reached the house. Marking her place, she ran for the stairs, taking both sets two steps at a time and rushed onto the back porch just as Annie reached the side yard with her wagon.

Annie took off her sweat-stained, crumpled felt hat, running her hand over the coarse, matted hair that looked like it would rip the teeth out of a comb. "How 'bout unloadin' for me, will you, Jordan? I'm give plumb out today."

Jordan bounced down the steps. "Annie, you don't look good. Why don't you lie down for a while?"

Annie bent over the wagon, lifted a folded throw rug, and pulled out a brown bottle. She picked up her cup, which rested against a column on the porch, and slouched down on the back steps. Pouring the cup half full of the amber liquid, she gulped it down and gave a long sigh. "That'll pep me up."

Jordan began unloading the wagon, tossing the junk up on the far end of the porch where Annie could sort through it and stack it in the storage room that formed the end of the porch. The wagon contained, in addition to the throw rug: a bicycle wheel with the tire still on it, several bricks, two pieces of iron pipe, a short piece of two-by-four, a few magazines and books, a woman's coat with the lining ripped almost out, and two sweat-stained men's felt hats.

"How'd you get the groceries?" Jordan picked up the sack, struggling up the steep steps with it.

"Traded Cooper Bates some copper tubin' for 'em." Annie picked up her bottle, following Jordan into the house.

Setting the bag on the big pine table, Jordan took out a bag of vanilla wafers. "Oh, Annie, thank you so much! We haven't had cookies for such a long time!"

"Bates give 'em to me free. Said they was goin' stale anyway," Annie mumbled, pouring her cup full from the brown bottle.

Jordan put a five-pound bag of flour, a two-pound bag of sugar, two brown bags—one of dried beans, the other of rice—and a pound of hamburger wrapped in white freezer paper on the table. "I made cornbread," Jordan offered. "What else you want?"

Annie sipped from her cup, her cloudy blue eyes glazing over from age, alcohol, and exhaustion. "Whatever you say, baby. I'm not all that hungry anyway."

"You're not eatin' enough," Jordan admonished gently, filling a pot with water and dumping two cups of beans into it. "We got to put some meat on them bones."

Annie smiled wearily. "You're a good child. I'm lucky to have you here for company."

Jordan smiled contentedly at Annie's words. Chopping up an onion, she added it to the beans, along with a spoonful of bacon grease for flavor. Next she made four patties of the hamburger, putting them into a skillet with a little more bacon grease. She listened to the "Little Orphan Annie Show" while she finished preparing their supper.

Serving their plates, Jordan announced proudly, "I made a B+ on my arithmetic test today."

Annie sipped from her cup. "Good," she grunted. Her face had turned a blotchy red color, the veins prominent and her eyes becoming no more than slits.

Seeing that Annie was in no mood to talk, Jordan changed stations on the radio. As the theme song started, she said, "You might like this program, Annie. I heard about it at school today. It's called 'One Man's Family,' and this is the very first time it's been on the radio."

The announcer began: "'One Man's Family' is dedicated to the mothers and fathers of the younger generation and to their bewildering offspring. Tonight we present chapter one of book one. . . ."

The two of them ate in silence as the program continued. Once Jordan remarked, "I'd sure like to see San Francisco where this Barbour family lives. Wouldn't you, Annie?"

Annie only grunted, her head down as she shoveled in the beans, meat, and cornbread.

"Guess I'll get these dishes washed," Jordan said to no one in particular as she got up from the table.

"Let 'em be, child," Annie declared bluntly. "You've done enough. I'll do 'em tomorrow. Set a spell."

Jordan sat back down, wondering what was on Annie's mind, as she usually sat on the porch for a while, or went directly off to bed after supper was finished. She noticed that the meal seemed to revive Annie somewhat.

"I wish you had a nice family like that one on the radio, Jordan," Annie observed, pouring the last of the whiskey into her cup. "I know it's hard on you livin' with a crazy ol' woman like me."

"Oh no, Annie! I don't think that at all. You've been a mama and a daddy to me." *I would love so much to have a family like that, but there's no use in telling Annie. I could never hurt her. She took me when no one else wanted me.*

"Well, I ain't much. Wish I at least had enough money to buy you some nice things. Spent it all on yore daddy though. What a waste!" Annie swallowed the last of the whiskey. "Guess I'd do it all over again though. I loved yore daddy, baby. Still do. Maybe if he'd married somebody else . . ."

Jordan frowned. "You don't like my mama?"

Annie leaned back in her chair, her head resting on its back. "Don't pay no attention to me. I'm just a foolish old woman. Wasn't her fault. Maybe they just weren't right for each other."

Noticing Annie nodding off, Jordan walked around the table to her. "Annie, you think Daddy's ever comin' back?"

"Some day . . . maybe," Annie replied, opening her eyes slightly. "But don't build on him, baby. Don't build on anybody. In this ol' world you got to make it on your own."

Jordan helped Annie to her feet. She knew they'd never make the stairs, so she guided Annie into the cavernous living room and helped her stretch out on the couch. Fetching a quilt from the hall closet, Jordan covered her, bending over to kiss her on the forehead. "Good night, Annie," she whispered.

Upstairs, Jordan touched a match to the wick of her lantern and watched the scene etched on the globe come to life. Crawling under the covers, her head resting on the soft, fluffy pillow, she gazed at her bright angel. She called him Michael, after an angel she had heard Wash preach about once, imagining as she drifted off to sleep that he would rescue her from any danger that might come in the night. "Good night, Michael," Jordan whispered, as she slipped away from the world into a land where she wasn't any different from other children.

* * *

In 1935 Jordan Simms had become a coltish, awkward twelve year old—a late bloomer with the promise of beauty in the delicate planes of her face. It was a fine year for peaches, and the trees in Annie's little orchard struggled to stand upright with their fuzzy, luscious burden. The peaches were bursting with juicy goodness— all the sweetness of the long Southern summer trapped inside their rosy skins.

Jordan was out in time to see the colors in the light-rimmed eastern sky try to outshine the pastel shades of the peaches. Through the glistening dew, she walked to the orchard, selected a particularly appealing peach and sat on a rung of the stepladder while she bit into it. It exploded with flavor, the juice running down onto her chin as she ate ravenously. *These are better than Nu-Grape!* she thought as she flicked the peach pit back into the grove.

Walking toward the sunrise, Jordan found the path that started at the back of the peach orchard and led through the woods to the river. Once inside the woods, her eyes had to adjust to the false twilight. Startled at his breakfast, a rabbit bounded across the path into the underbrush. Ahead of her, a fox squirrel skittered up the trunk of a huge white oak, its fuzzy tail flicking a warning from behind the first high limb to any of his cousins nearby.

Jordan heard the river before she saw it, a deep murmuring sound beyond the underbrush, almost like a gathering of old men on the grassy bank, sharing their years of arboreal wisdom. At the water's edge, she turned north along another path she imagined the Indians had made, a hundred, maybe two hundred years ago. It was old enough to be worn three or four inches below the level of the ground on both sides of it.

The path hugged the riverbank, rising or falling with the lay of the land. It would climb gradually up a twenty-foot bluff over the river with stands of beech, poplar, and pine, or coast along through a hardwood bottom and down to a white-sand beach. Jordan walked under the highway bridge and listened to the dopplered roar of a truck overhead, followed by the cloppety-clattering of a horse-drawn wagon.

North of the bridge the cool, green water splashed over rocks and fallen tree trunks, playing background for the songbirds. Just above this miniature rapids, the river moved almost imperceptibly between a sandy beach and a twenty-five-foot rocky bluff on the far shore. At the upper end of the beach, a huge boulder curved around a spreading live oak, flattening around the trunk and forming natural benches with the tree and parts of the boulder as backrests.

Jordan would come here very early or very late, sit and enjoy the silence or the sounds of the woods and the animals and the beauty of the river. She climbed the boulder just as the sun rose above the heaviest foliage of the trees, angling across the water in yellow paths of light. Sitting in a depression of the rock at the edge of its sheer six-foot drop to the surface of the river, Jordan leaned back to enjoy the beauty of the early morning. Suddenly, she heard shouts as someone approached the river from the main path.

"C'mon, you bunch of slow pokes!"

Jordan recognized the gruff voice of Marcell Duke, who seemed to have taken a particular pleasure in tormenting her ever since that first day of school.

Marcell burst from the trees onto the leaf-covered ground that led to the beach, followed closely by Billy Christmas and Lyle Oliver. Marcell's shaggy, rough appearance was in stark contrast to the well-groomed neatness of Billy Christmas. Both had black hair, but that was the only similarity. Marcell was stocky with bulky muscles, while Billy was a whippet—slim and gifted with a seemingly effortless and controlled balance. Lyle had the round-eyed, owlish look of one enamored of books and indoor activities. He was of average build with the smoothly rounded muscles of the sedentary.

All three boys wore black, high-topped tennis shoes, denim trousers, and white t-shirts and began shucking their clothes before they reached the water.

As he dropped his socks onto the sand, Marcell noticed Jordan sitting motionless on the boulder above the water. "Hey, fellers! We've got company!" he shouted gleefully.

Jordan felt a cold fear rising in her chest.

Billy and Lyle watched as Marcell swaggered toward Jordan. Jordan scampered down from the boulder, trying to outflank Marcell and reach the path by the river.

"Come on Jordan, go swimmin' with us," Marcell teased, darting after her. "Git them clothes off now!"

"Aw, leave her alone, Marcell!" Billy ordered.

Marcell glanced at Billy disdainfully as he grabbed Jordan by the back of her overalls. "C'mon now, you can't swim in this getup," he growled.

"Don't touch me!" Jordan screamed, kicking him in the shins and breaking free.

"You dirty little . . . !" Marcell bellowed in pain. He drew back his fist just as Billy wrapped his arms around him from behind and pinned Marcell's arms to his sides.

"Leave her alone, Marcell!" Billy grunted, holding on tight as Marcell jumped and bucked like a small Brahma. "Can't you see she's scared to death?"

Jordan reached her path and glanced behind her just in time to see Marcell fling Billy to the ground with a vicious whirl of his body. Then she fled along the riverbank.

"You better not do that again—ever!" Marcell growled, glaring down at Billy with his fists doubled up.

Billy stood up carefully, never taking his blue eyes from Marcell's dark, pupil-less ones. They stood that way for a few seconds, neither looking away.

"C'mon now, ya'll, we came here to have some fun," Lyle offered in way of reconciliation.

Marcell gave Billy a sinister grin. "Yeah, he's right. Can't let no crazy girl ruin our fun."

"She ain't crazy as ol' Annie," Lyle remarked, sitting down on the sand to remove his shoes.

"Who is?" Marcell agreed, sitting beside him.

"Jimmy Delaney tried to steal some of her peaches one day last week, and she let him have it with a load of bird shot," Lyle declared, as if this were the accepted medical validation for insanity.

Billy sat on the sand in his white boxer shorts, arms resting loosely on his bent knees. "I'm not afraid of her. I'll steal peaches anytime I want to," he boasted.

"Oh, yeah?" Marcell taunted. "Well, let's just go see right now if there's more to you than yore mouth."

Billy regretted his rash statement, but there was no backing down. He stared directly into Marcell's dark eyes. "Let's go!"

Thirty minutes later, Billy, Marcell, and Lyle knelt together in a pine thicket at the edge of the woods near Annie's peach orchard. The place looked deserted, shadows lying down across the long, dew-wet grass. Billy saw the little wagon parked next to the back porch, but he didn't notice Annie's china cup sitting on a post next to the henhouse.

"Well . . . what're you waitin' for?" Marcell taunted. "Losin' yore nerve, I bet."

Billy glanced stonily at Marcell. "You just watch."

Parting the broom straw that grew at the edge of the thicket, Billy stepped into the open. He stood for a few seconds, peering slowly around like an animal approaching a water hole. Walking deliberately into the shady orchard, he selected a rosy ripe peach and bit into it. As he ate, he picked another, glancing with a big smile toward the thicket where his friends lay hidden.

At that moment, Annie appeared at the other end of the row of trees where Billy stood. She began lurching clumsily down the leafy archway toward him like some huge scowling predator. "You git away from my peaches!" she shouted, waving a shovel at him.

Billy stood wide-eyed, mindless with guilt and fear, the whole and half-eaten stolen fruit dropping from his limp hands. He could hear the heavy thudding of Annie's boots on the ground and felt the deer-quick hammering of his heart against his chest.

Seizing a plum-sized stone at his feet, he heaved it at the fearful crone twenty feet from him—seeing it strike her close to the heart.

Annie stopped in her tracks. A sudden choked cry pierced the morning air. Clutching her chest with both hands, she stood woodenly among her leafy brood, their branches bowing with the fullness of her labor. The shovel bore mute witness on the soft ground.

In the wink of an eye, the world closed in on Billy Christmas. He stood alone on its brink with Annie. He remembered her shambling on a wet December afternoon down some forgotten alleyway, her little wagon creaking along behind. He thought of a hundred other times she had crossed his path, but he knew he had never truly seen her until now.

Billy felt the pain that he saw in Annie's eyes. It sprang not from the stone, but from the endless, awful nights of being alone and *all* the eyes that never saw her. Then for the first time in his life, Billy wept for someone other than himself.

Jordan had watched from the back porch and had run up to Annie as Billy disappeared into the woods. "Why did he hit you, Annie?"

Annie picked up her shovel and trudged slowly down the lane between the trees. "There are some that like to hurt other folks, Jordan."

* * *

For three days Billy Christmas lived with remorseful. And three nights brought dreams of what he saw in Annie's eyes. On the late afternoon of the third day he knew what he had to do. He found Jordan alone, trying to split some stove wood with a heavy double-bit axe she could barely lift with both hands.

"Hi, Jordan," Billy said awkwardly. "That axe is a little big for you, ain't it?"

Jordan dropped the axe on the woodpile, mopping her brow with a white handkerchief she pulled from her overalls. "Only one we got. Never saw one in a girl's size."

"Guess you're right about that," Billy laughed. "Want me to give it a try?"

Jordan sat down on the woodpile, squinting in the afternoon sunshine. "You didn't come here to chop stove wood, Billy."

"You're right." Billy looked at the ground, biting his lower lip. "I'm sorry for hittin' Annie."

"Maybe you ought to tell *her*," Jordan suggested flatly. "She's the one who got hurt."

Billy looked up at Jordan, his dark blue eyes bright with resolve. "I'll just do that!" *Shoot! Why did I say that? I'll have to tell her quick before she shoots me!*

Jordan looked at Billy's hair, glistening with sweat from his long walk in the afternoon heat. "You want some water or something?"

"No thanks," Billy answered abruptly, hefting the axe. "I'll keep busy 'til she gets here."

Jordan sat on a weathered gray nail keg next to the woodpile, watching Billy swing the axe. He had taken his shirt off and his muscles flexed smoothly under his tanned skin. *He looks like that statue of David I saw in one of those old books in the attic. Well, maybe not now, but he will when he gets older.*

As Billy stacked the last piece of wood on the pile, Annie turned onto the little path that led alongside the drive. He spotted her, hurriedly putting his white t-shirt back on. Annie wore her overalls and heavy boots, but she had made one concession to the heat by rolling up the sleeves of her khaki work shirt.

Jordan smiled at Billy and then at Annie as she parked the wagon next to the porch.

"What's this all about, Jordan?" Annie asked, eying Billy suspiciously.

"Billy split all the stove wood," Jordan beamed. "Didn't he do a good job?"

Annie surveyed the newly split pile of wood, neatly stacked, the axe leaning against it. Nodding her head slowly, she gazed at Billy, waiting for an answer to this riddle.

"Ann—Miss Annie," Billy stammered. "I'm sorry I hit you with that rock. Don't know what got into me. Well, anyway, there's no excuse for it, and I'm really sorry."

Confused by the unexpected, as well as by the daylong sipping from her china cup that bulged in her left front overall pocket, Annie tilted her head slightly to the side, as a dog might at the sound of a dull noise outside the house.

"'Bye, Jordan," Billy nodded, hurrying toward the road. "'Bye, Miss Annie."

Annie watched him go, a softness coming gradually into her weathered face. "Funny. I've known that boy's daddy for fifty years. He never apologized to a livin' soul. Wonder what he'd do if he found out his boy apologized to ol' Annie?"

That night the shining angel of the lamp, his arms eternally reaching outward, gazed placidly down on the little child crossing the bridge and on Lisa Jordan Simms as she lay on her bed writing in a Big Chief tablet with her yellow pencil. She had been writing things for a long time now, never telling anyone about it. She wrote of a boy who hurt an old woman and was unable to live with what he had done. Writing quickly, with pauses only to sharpen her pencil, she finished the story.

Jordan took her rose-colored diary out of the Hershey candy bar carton she had picked up at Three Corners one Saturday, placing her tablet back inside it. Glancing at her lamp, she began to write:

> It was strange the way Billy Christmas came. He hated it, I could see. Nobody likes to come here, of course. But he came anyway. Maybe people are afraid of Annie because she's not like they are—or like they think she oughta be. Maybe I'm not either. Sometimes people can't help how they turn out. Sure would be a better world if people were nice to each other— even the different ones. Seems like it would be just as easy as being mean to them.
>
> When I'm a famous writer I'll have enough money to take care of Annie. I'll fix up this old house just like it was when she was a little girl. And I'll hire a cook and buy her a car and lots of pretty clothes. Then maybe she'll be happy and won't have to drink whiskey anymore to feel good.
>
> Then I'll go find my mama and daddy and bring them back here, and we'll all live together. I bet the people in this old town will really stare at us when we drive down the street in a car like Billy's daddy drives. And we can have parties with lots of food and pretty decorations and invite a lot of people over. They won't make fun of Annie and me then, and they can't say I don't have a daddy and mama anymore either. I'll just have to work real hard.

Sometime after midnight, Jordan put her things away in the Hershey carton and shoved it back under her bed. Kneeling by the side of the bed, she prayed that God would let her be a writer . . . and that He would give her family back to her.

As she lay on her pillow, Jordan heard the limbs of the gnarled old cedar outside her window scraping against the glass as the night wind touched them. She gazed at her angel, at his gleaming brightness, but a cold fear slithered along on its raspy belly beyond the edge of the light where the darkness gathered.

5

"THEM THAT ARE BRUISED"

*T*he *Wizard of Oz* is playing up in Atlanta, Annie," Jordan remarked, spreading butter on one of the hot biscuits. "Everybody says it's the cutest movie ever. Judy Garland sings 'Over the Rainbow.' She's got such a beautiful voice! Sure would like to see that movie."

Annie lifted the coffee pot off the stove and poured her china cup half full. Her cheeks and nose were red, webbed with purple veins. Her right eye was cloudy as blue-white milk glass from when she had stumbled drunkenly into the woodpile one night, gouging it on a broken limb from an untrimmed log. "Might as well be in London, England, for all the chance you got of seeing it." She took a bottle of clear moonshine out of the cabinet, popped the cork off, and poured until her cup was full.

"Do you have to drink first thing in the morning?" Jordan asked in a concerned tone.

Annie turned the cup up, swallowed half the mixture, and blew through her lips like a horse, shaking her head from side to side. "Ever hear of an 'eye opener'? I ain't got but one eye, so I got to make real sure it's wide open."

Jordan smiled sadly. "You been hanging around J.T. too much. That sounds like something he'd say."

"Reckon you're right there," Annie smiled forlornly. "Nobody else interested in me though—'cept Wash maybe, and I think he's 'bout had a belly full of me."

"That's not so, Annie," Jordan assured her. "You never had a better friend than Wash. He just won't drink with you."

Annie was biting into her first biscuit, the train of conversation lost in the food. "You know, child," she mumbled through a mouthful of biscuit, butter running down her chin, "you make better biscuits than I could on my best day."

Jordan smiled, seeing Annie devote her full attention to breakfast, knowing the dialogue was over for now. She clicked the radio on and returned to the table. "Oh, this is a good one, Annie," she remarked, listening to the last few bars of the song. "'In the Mood,' by Glenn Miller. All the kids love to dance to it."

"Uh huh," Annie grunted into her biscuit.

As the song ended, the precise and distinctive voice of one of the European correspondents began with a recording of one of his broadcasts from London. *Warsaw is surrounded by German troops trained in this formidable new military tactic, "Blitzkrieg" or "Lightning War." Hitler has announced to his generals that the city is to be regarded as a fortress and destroyed by the use of artillery and bombers. Ironically, there were two General Rommels involved in the fighting. One is the commanding Polish general, and the other is the commanding German general. On September 27th, twelve days after the siege began, Warsaw was forced to surrender.*

Jordan listened intently. "Is that Edward R. Murrow or H. V. Kaltenborn?"

"Beats me," Annie declared offhandedly. "All them radio people sound just alike."

Another journalist spoke from the other side of the Atlantic:

In the early morning hours of October 14, the German submarine U-47, commanded by Lieutenant Günther Prien, sank the British battleship *Royal Oak*. Penetrating the submerged barrier of block ships at the strongly defended naval base of Scapa Flow in the Orkney Islands, north of Scotland, the U-boat launched a salvo of torpedoes. Only one struck its target, hitting the bow of the battleship.

So incredible was this feat that both the admiral and the captain on board looked for an internal cause of the explosion. Twenty minutes passed before the U-boat reloaded and fired a second salvo. Three of these four torpedoes struck the ship, ripping her bottom out. She sank in ten minutes with the loss of 786 men.

Ironically, Scapa Flow is the site where the German fleet was scuttled after the Great War of 1914. The sinking of the *Royal Oak* is a serious blow to the prestige of the Royal Navy, especially since the German U-boat escaped unscathed.

As the news continued, Jordan asked solemnly, "Annie, do you think our country will get involved in that war? "

Annie slowed her eating down a little. "President Roosevelt says we won't. We got enough problems pulling out of the Depression without spending money to fight that crazy Hitler."

"I hope you're right," Jordan declared, her brow wrinkling slightly. "By the way, I may have to work a little late at Dr. Simmons's after school today. His regular nurse is sick."

Annie peered at Jordan over a final biscuit as she paved it with butter. "You ain't a nurse. I thought all you did was answer the phone and clean up."

"Dr. Simmons says that I've got a real knack for nursing," Jordan smiled proudly. "He showed me how to take blood pressure and pulse rates and a few other things to get the patients ready for him to examine. I just might take it up some day."

"Well, I'm 'bout ready if you are," Annie burped. "You sure you don't mind me tagging along with you into town? Won't bother me none if you'd rather walk to school with the Logan or Shaw kids. Maybe people won't look down on you as much."

Jordan gathered up her books and smiled directly into Annie's wasted face, into her good blue eye. "I'd rather walk with you than anybody I know, Annie. What's that J.T. told me years ago? People don't know quality when they see it."

Annie's mouth twisted slightly in an attempt to smile. She took her tattered brown man's suit coat from the back of her chair and struggled into it as a single tear slipped unnoticed down her wind-burned cheek. "You're a good girl, Jordan Simms."

* * *

"Edwin Arlington Robinson," Leslie Gifford began. "Who wants to tell me something about this man—one of the best-known American poets of this century?" Gifford sat on the edge of his desk, his polio-crippled right leg hanging at an odd angle. His strange sad eyes, the color of old pecan shells, dominated his face. He looked at his class with a mixture of humor and fatalism.

"He's dead!" Marcell Duke announced proudly, looking around the class for approval.

There were a few muffled giggles in the classroom.

Gifford lifted his stiletto-slim frame awkwardly from the desk, his right foot softly slapping the wooden floor as he walked over to the bank of windows. Slipping his left hand into the pocket of his brown tweed coat to support the bad left arm, he turned to the class. "Excellent Mr. Duke—and quite true. He died on April 6, 1935. Now would anyone like to create a metaphor using the poet's biological state and Mr. Duke's brain?"

Duke beamed at being the center of attention, brushing his thick black hair back from his face, proud of his dark good looks.

Jordan laughed first, using her hand to suppress it. Duke glanced at her with a puzzled expression as some of the other class members caught on and began giggling. Ben Logan leaned over and whispered something in Duke's ear. His face reddened, and he glared around the room, silencing most of his classmates—all but Billy Christmas, who found Gifford's remark exceedingly funny to the point of having to be told by his teacher to quit laughing or leave the room.

Gifford, his unfashionably long brown hair touching his ears and shirt collar and illuminated from behind by the golden sunlight of late October streaming through the windows, spoke softly. "Anyone else care to comment?"

"President Theodore Roosevelt gave him a job as a clerk in the New York Custom House when he was about to starve," Jordan offered cautiously, then, encouraged by a nod from Gifford, continued more confidently. "He didn't become a success until his late fifties, and he won the Pulitzer Prize three times. He spent most of his time alone. Some people say he was in love with death."

"He must be one of your favorites, Jordan," Gifford smiled. "What do you particularly like about him?"

Jordan narrowed her dark blue eyes in thought, the autumn light turning her hair the color of spring honey. "I think his best writing is about misfits and outcasts."

Gifford rubbed his softly rounded chin with a slim thumb and forefinger. "I agree. Ruben Bright, Miniver Cheevy, Richard Cory—an American gallery of those who, as Thoreau said, lived lives of 'quiet desperation.'"

"Richard Cory wasn't an outcast," Ben Logan chimed in. "He was a rich man."

Gifford looked about the room, a wry smile on his face, enjoying the growing interest of his students. "Comments?"

"You don't have to be poor to be an outcast," Billy Christmas protested. "Richard Cory blew his brains out. His money didn't do him much good."

"Maybe 'misfit' is a better word for him," Jordan offered softly. "People envied him—thought he 'glittered when he walked,' but inside he hurt too much to want to go on living."

Gifford smiled at the bright eyes of his students as others added to the discussion.

"I had an uncle once," Marcell Duke remarked earnestly. "He was mean as that feller Aaron Stark that Robinson wrote the poem about. One time he . . ."

As the bell rang Gifford called for silence. "I want to remind y'all that the tickets for the winter play, *Our Town,* go on sale next week. I'd advise you to get yours early. We expect a sellout. Two of our stars, Debbie Lambert and Ben Logan, will answer any questions you might have about the quality of the production. We don't want anyone throwing hard-earned money away on something amateurish."

Gifford observed Jordan talking with Ben, knowing that her work with Dr. Simmons had prevented her trying out for one of the parts. *Well, Ben can stand in for all the outcasts, I suppose.*

Five hours later, Jordan was sweeping the waiting room, which had been the parlor of the rambling, white frame house Dr. Phinehas Simmons used as his medical office. As she was emptying the dust pan, she thought of how fortunate she was to have her job. It not only gave her and Annie some much-needed money, but it made her feel good about herself as well as affording her the opportunity to learn something that could lead to a lifelong profession.

"I've told you the housekeeper could do that, Jordan," Simmons snorted from the door that led to the two examining rooms in the back of the house. The doctor had a decided resemblance to Humpty

73

Dumpty—everything on him was rounded. He was short with a round belly, a pale round face, chubby hands, and he chewed on a big round evil-smelling cigar.

"I don't mind. Just takes a minute or two. I like to leave the waiting room clean." Jordan emptied the dust pan into the trash and walked toward the kitchen with it.

"Put that thing away and sit down a minute," Simmons growled impatiently, slouching into a metal chair with brown leather cushions. "Something I want to tell you."

Jordan went down the hall to the kitchen, set the can outside the back door and returned to sit opposite Simmons. He was trying to light his cigar with a kitchen match but never could seem to keep it burning. Whenever he tried this, he usually ended up mangling the cigar with his teeth.

"You've got a knack for medicine," Simmons began without preliminaries. "More than that, you have a way of making patients feel comfortable. That's a rare quality. Something they can't teach you in nursing school."

Jordan sat up in her chair, leaning forward, elbows on knees, hands clasped together. "You really think I could be a nurse? I mean, am I smart enough?"

"I made it through medical school, Jordan, and I ain't that smart," Simmons laughed. "What it takes is gumption. They lay so much on you at one time that you have to study every spare minute. Overwhelms you at first, but that's the design—to weed out the ones who can't take the pressure. I think you can handle it."

"Well, I still have a year and a half left in high school," Jordan sighed wistfully.

Simmons gave up on his ragged cigar and tossed it deftly into the small trash can on the far side of the room. "I checked with the school. Your grades are good enough to take the state board and get your GED at the end of this year if you want to. You'll only need three more credits to graduate."

Jordan took a deep breath, made a decision, and looked at Simmons with a shy smile. "It may sound silly, Doctor, but what I'd really like to be is a writer."

"That's not silly. It's admirable! But there aren't many overnight successes among writers," Simmons said, rocking up from the low chair and coming to his feet. "You have to earn a living while you try to get published and nursing would do that for you. I wish you all the success in the world in your writing, but it's a tough business. Somebody said a person should do something with more stability—like play the horses."

Jordan laughed as she got up and collected her books from the hall closet. "See you tomorrow, Dr. Simmons," she waved, pausing at the front door.

"I'm gonna grab a bite to eat and then make a couple of house calls," Simmons coughed, trying to light another cigar. "Be glad to drop you off if you want."

"No thanks," Jordan replied, opening the door. "It's a nice night. I'll enjoy the walk."

Simmons placed both hands in the pockets of his white lab coat. "One more thing, Jordan. Your posture's awful. You look like you're carrying a millstone around your neck. Stand up straight."

Jordan flushed slightly, but straightened up, pulling her shoulders back.

"Much better," Simmons smiled. "One more thing . . . that hairdo's fine if you're eighty-five and live in a nursing home, but pulled straight back and tied with a rubber band ain't exactly gonna drive the boys crazy. Use some curlers, fluff it up . . . something! You're a pretty girl, Jordan. Why don't you act like it?"

Jordan smiled again. "I'll try to do better, Doctor. Thanks for the advice."

* * *

Jezebel, the marquee glared brightly, starring Bette Davis and Henry Fonda. "What a crummy movie," Marcell Duke scowled, walking away from the bright lights of the Liberty Theatre with Lyle Oliver and Billy Christmas. "Next week *Robin Hood*'s playing. Errol Flynn's in that. It'll have some action!"

"Yeah," Lyle agreed. "What say *we* look for some action."

"Action? In Liberty, Georgia, on a weeknight?" Billy mused. "You wanna go smell the bread baking, Lyle, or put some pennies on the railroad track?"

Lyle smiled sheepishly. "Let's just take a ride. We got a math test tomorrow anyway."

Marcell hopped over the closed door into his Model T jalopy, throwing the crank out to Billy. "Give it a turn and let's get on our way in 'Thrill-a-Minute City.'"

Billy inserted the crank into the front of the car, turned it nine times, and the engine fired up, backfiring and sputtering into life. Jumping into the rumble seat, he added jubilantly. "Oh, boy! High adventure in good ol' Liberty."

As they clattered down the street, Marcell spied Jordan strolling along the sidewalk. "Hubba hubba!" he shouted, bearing down on his oooga horn.

Jordan glanced at the car and kept walking, holding her books tightly against her chest.

Marcell pulled alongside of her, driving on the wrong side of the street. "Hey, baby," he growled lasciviously, brushing his thick black hair back from his face. "Wanna go make some whoopee?"

"Leave her alone," Billy interrupted. "Can't you see she ain't interested?"

"Mind your own business," Marcell glared back over his shoulder. "Hey, Jordan, we just saw *Jezebel*, with Bette Davis. You look a little like her. Don't I remind you of some movie star?"

Jordan stopped and stared directly into Marcell's obsidian eyes. "You do at that, Marcell."

"Yeah," Marcell gloated, combing his hair back with his left hand. "Who?"

"Rin Tin Tin. Except he smells better, and he's a whole lot smarter than you are." Jordan turned away sharply, swinging hurriedly down the sidewalk.

Billy and Lyle were hooting and hollering as Marcell gunned the sputtering motor and drove away, making more noise than speed. "She'll be sorry she did that!" he muttered under his breath.

* * *

"The Spirit of the Lord is upon me, because he hath anointed me to preach the gospel to the poor; he hath sent me to heal the brokenhearted, to preach deliverance to the captives, and recovering of sight to the blind, to set at liberty them that are bruised." Washington Smith closed his black Bible, laid it carefully on the podium and clasped his big, work-hardened hands together in front of him. After preaching for an hour and fifteen minutes, his face glistened with sweat, even though the building was damp and chilly.

Jordan sat between Pearl, who hung on her husband's every word, and Lester. He was sixteen now and almost as tall as his daddy, but with the slim suppleness of youth. Jordan, with her honey-blonde hair spilling onto her shoulders, her fair skin and deep blue eyes, looked out of place among the dark-skinned congregation. But she had felt comfortable in this church since the first time Wash had brought her in the ice wagon when she was five. She had gone to several of the white churches downtown, but the people treated her—or she imagined they treated her—differently. That was the only way she could explain it. She just felt different from everybody else.

"To set at liberty them that are bruised . . . ," Smith repeated, his dark eyes bright with emotion. "That may be the hardest part for us to understand. You'd think somebody that was bruised would need healing, wouldn't you?"

There was a chorus of "Amens" and "That's rights" throughout the small crowd.

"What Jesus was talking about is the bruises that nobody can see. The pain that other people have caused us. And we can only find 'liberty' from these kind of bruises through Jesus Christ. When we accept him as Savior and Lord, He forgives us our sins. Then we can forgive the people who have hurt us."

The November wind made a low moaning sound outside the little church building. Inside, there was complete silence, except for a lone man on the back row, coughing into a white handkerchief. Pearl eased from her pew and went to the scarred piano bench at the old upright to the left of the pulpit.

Washington Smith took three steps from behind the pulpit, towering before the congregation. "'If thou shalt confess with thy mouth the Lord Jesus, and shalt believe in thine heart that God hath raised him from the dead, thou shalt be saved.' That's how simple it is, brothers and sisters. It all takes place in the heart."

Holding his arms out, Smith spoke in a rich baritone that needed no amplification. "Jesus said, 'All those that come, I will in no wise cast out.' He'll heal your broken hearts, and He'll set you at liberty from the hate and anger you have against the people who have bruised you."

Pearl began playing "Pass Me Not, O Gentle Savior," singing in a clear contralto. As she sang the last line of the chorus, the man from the back row walked down the aisle, his white handkerchief still in his hand. He knelt at the little wooden rail in front of the pulpit, with Wash kneeling beside him. Laying his big arm across the man's shoulders, Wash prayed for him, lifting his other hand toward the heavens.

Jordan felt a gentle movement inside, saw herself rise from her seat and kneel at the altar next to the man with the white handkerchief. But her hands gripped the bench. She felt trapped inside a swirling darkness and fought against it. Beads of sweat popped out on her forehead. Taking a deep breath, she relaxed, looking again toward the altar, hearing Pearl sing for the last time, "Do not pass me by."

After the service, Jordan saw Wash wrap his big arms around the man at the altar, giving him a hug that almost lifted him off the floor. The man smiled broadly and, as Wash walked away, began talking animatedly with a woman in a bright yellow hat.

"You stayin' for dinner, Missy Jordan?" Wash asked. "Supposed to be out on the grounds, but it turnt off a little cool for that. Gonna have it right here in the church house."

Jordan slipped into her threadbare, gray wool coat Annie brought home on her wagon the past summer. "I'd like to, Wash, but Annie's feeling poorly. Better go check on her."

"Pearl makes the best sweet tater pie in Georgia," Smith laughed. "Make a bulldog break his chain. Better stay and eat some. If you don't, Lester here will sure enough eat yore piece." He clapped his tall son on the back.

"Maybe next time," Jordan smiled. On her way out, she lingered at the church door. Watching the people laughing and talking with each other—fellowshiping, they called it, preparing to eat together—she suddenly, for the first time, felt different from all of them. *Oh God! Am I ever going to fit in anywhere? What's wrong with me?*

* * *

"Oh! It's such a lovely dress, Annie!" Jordan beamed, holding the blue velvet dress up to her and turning around and around with it. "And the pearl buttons. I've never seen anything like it! Oh, thank you so much!"

Annie sat down at the table, basking in Jordan's happiness. "It ain't every day a girl gets asked to the Christmas play *and* a party at the Lambert mansion. That old thing you had just wouldn't do."

Jordan lay the dress carefully across the back of a chair. She hugged Annie and kissed her on both cheeks. "But it looks so expensive! How did you ever afford it?"

Annie took a dirty red handkerchief from the back pocket of her overalls, dabbing at the edge of her cloudy, blue-white eye. "Had a talk with ol' man Hightower at his house. His boy runs the store now, but he remembers me from when our family had money. I was one of his best customers. Let me have the dress for old times' sake. Had one of the salesgirls bring it down from the store."

"This makes the night just perfect," Jordan smiled. "I couldn't have picked a prettier dress myself."

"You run get ready, child. We don't want Lyle Oliver waitin' on you. I know that's the stylish thing to do nowadays, but a real lady is more considerate than that." Annie's face was drawn, a sickly pallor showing beneath the sun-baked skin, but an almost forgotten light gleamed in her one good eye.

Six hours later Jordan stood with Lyle Oliver at the front of the school auditorium near the stage after the performance of *Our Town*. In the clamor and press of the crowd rushing off to their Christmas celebrations, Jordan felt an anticipation at being part of the group—a sense of belonging for the first time. She had heard for years about the Lambert home in the exclusive Pine Hills area and couldn't wait to see it.

"Why aren't we leaving, Lyle?" Jordan asked, flushed with excitement.

Lyle glanced about the crowded auditorium impatiently. "Uh . . . in a few minutes."

Across the rows of seats on the other side of the building, Jordan noticed Ben Logan and Debbie Lambert standing near the doors where the crowd surged through. Ben wore a new pearl gray suit and Debbie was radiant in a blue silk gown that matched the color of her eyes perfectly. *They certainly make a handsome couple. Well, that makes two of us outcasts in with the right crowd tonight.*

Debbie caressed the lapels of Ben's suit, looking lovingly into his gray eyes. Suddenly, Ben slapped her hands away and stormed out the door in the rush of the crowd. *What in the world could have happened to them,* Jordan thought, just as Keith Demerie appeared and put his arm around Debbie's slim waist.

"Let's go," Lyle said abruptly, taking Jordan by the arm, leading her toward the doors.

As they walked across the school ground, Jordan admired Lyle's family car—a 1937 Buick four-door sedan. She had ridden in few cars since coming to live with Annie, and certainly nothing as elegant as this. Two years old now, it looked brand new with its bold whitewalls and its black paint gleaming under the street lamps.

Jordan settled herself into the plush cushions of the front seat. "Did you see what happened with Ben and Debbie?"

Lyle started the engine and pulled carefully away from the curb into the traffic leaving the school. "Yeah, I saw it."

"I wonder what happened?" Jordan mused, straightening the skirt of her new velvet dress, caressing its softness. "They make such a nice looking couple."

"Ben doesn't fit in with our crowd," Lyle remarked casually. "Debbie just led him on—planned on going to the party with Keith all the time if you ask me. She gets a kick out of things like that."

Having had no practice at deception and manipulation, Jordan was shocked. "I think that's *terrible!* Ben had his heart set on going to this party with Debbie. It's all he talked about for months. Why would she do something so cruel?"

Lyle turned left toward the highway instead of right toward Pine Hills. "Gotta run a quick errand," he murmured, ignoring Jordan's comments.

Jordan settled back in the plush seat, enjoying the ride, but she felt something like tiny needles pricking the back of her neck. *What an awful night for Ben.*

Reaching the highway, Lyle turned right, then left onto an old logging road a quarter mile past the river bridge.

"What are you doing, Lyle?" Jordan felt the needles starting down her spine. "This old road just goes into the woods!"

Tight-lipped, Lyle said nothing. He had driven only a hundred yards when his headlights flashed on Marcell Duke's battered old jalopy.

Jordan recognized the other car immediately. "Oh, God! Lyle, you can't do this!" she wailed.

Lyle hung his head. "Wasn't my idea. He just didn't leave me any choice about it."

The passenger door flew open and Marcell Duke stood grinning wickedly in the darkness, his rented tuxedo matching his hair and eyes and the dark intent burning in his face. "Glad you could make it, Jordan! We're gonna have such fun."

Jordan screamed as she felt Duke's rough hands pulling her from the car. "Lyle, please don't leave me!"

But the Buick was already bumping around in a turn, heading back to the highway.

"No use wastin' your breath! Nobody can hear you way out here." Marcell encircled Jordan with his thick arms, holding her motionless in their viselike grip.

"Why are you doing this?" Jordan struggled to free herself, but it was hopeless.

Duke smiled. "Just wanted to give you a chance to get to know me better. All the girls like me. One little kiss and I think you will too." He released her with his left arm, placing it against her face as he pressed his lips against hers.

Jordan almost gagged at the smell of his rank whiskey breath. "Don't!" she gasped, pulling away, as she slapped him across the face with her free hand.

"You little . . . ," Duke bellowed, throwing her to the ground beneath a huge pine.

Jordan lay on her back, taking ragged breaths, staring up at Duke's shadowy bulk in the night, a pale moon gleaming over his right shoulder. Other nights rushed back to her across the years. Another dark figure towering over her in the darkness. Hot tears filled her eyes as a pain, greater than any physical hurt Duke could inflict, burned inside her soul.

Turning on her side, Jordan pulled her knees up and crossed her arms over her breast. *Oh, God! Please make him leave!* Gradually she realized that Duke no longer stood above her. She heard his jalopy sputter to life, back against some brush and clank into first gear. Lying on the bed of pine needles, she remained motionless, her eyes shut tightly.

"You'll never be a woman," Marcell growled in the darkness. "You ain't worth a minute of a real man's time."

Fifteen minutes later, Duke sprawled on a sofa in the expansive living room of the Lambert home, drinking egg nog from a crystal mug. "You shoulda seen her," he boasted, his cronies gathered about him like a returning war hero. "Laying there on the ground, whimpering like a baby. Last time she'll ever mess with Marcell Duke."

Billy Christmas stood at the edge of the crowd, his eyes narrowed in anger. "You're a coward, Marcell!"

Amazed that someone in the crowd didn't appreciate his unique sense of vengeance, Duke rose from the couch. "Oh, it's you. Always sticking up for that crazy girl, ain't you? You oughta stand more with your own kind."

Billy, at an even six feet, stood eye to eye with the blustering Duke but spotted him forty pounds. "I don't consider cowards to be my own kind, Marcell."

Duke's eyes blazed with anger as he jerked his head toward the back of the house, striding heavily from the living room. Billy glanced about at Duke's smirking admirers and followed, walking down the long hall behind his burly opponent. The other boys followed at a respectable distance, mumbling comments about Billy's fate.

The boys behind Billy had been his friends for years, but their eyes glittered now like wolves at the scent of blood, for that's exactly what they were hoping to see, and it didn't matter whose. There is something in impending violence that ignites the atavistic nature of the human race, something tribal that screams for blood.

As Billy stepped through the back door, he felt the jarring impact of the blow against his left jaw before he saw anything. Bouncing off a heavy white column of the portico, he stumbled into the yard, falling onto the dew-wet grass. He saw swirling flashes of color that had somehow turned into pain and then the high, shining stars as he opened his eyes.

Duke stood above him, fists clenched, a twisted smile on his face. "Who's a coward now, boy?"

Billy struggled to his feet. Duke swung with a roundhouse right, but Billy went in under it, slamming a hard left into Duke's ribcage. Duke grunted loudly, regaining his balance, rubbing his bruised ribs with his thick left hand.

Now Duke stalked Billy, moving in a circle, hunched over in an almost simian fashion. Swinging with a left this time, Duke put all his weight behind it. Billy jerked back and, as the big left fist whizzed by his head, he drove in with a straight right to the jaw and a quick left cross that caught Duke squarely in the mouth, splitting his lip.

Duke, bellowing in pain and rage, charged. Billy, caught against one of the huge live oaks, couldn't sidestep him. Duke hit him with all his two hundred pounds like he did opposing halfbacks from his tackle position, head down, massive legs churning like pistons.

Billy slammed backward into the tree, banging his head on the rough bark. He heard a loud roaring in his head, and then he was on the ground with Duke crushing down on his chest. He saw the big fist pull back, felt it slam into his mouth. He felt dully the last blow that battered his left eye, before they pulled Duke off him.

The next thing Billy knew, Lyle Oliver was helping him up from the back seat of his daddy's black Buick. Lyle steadied Billy as he stood under the portico at the service entrance at the back of his house.

"Didn't think you'd want to go in the front door," Lyle muttered, glancing around him. "Not the way you look."

"Hope I don't look as bad as I feel," Billy mumbled through his split lip.

"Worse!" Lyle said, shaking his head. "I'm ashamed of what I did tonight, Billy. Marcell told me it was just a big joke, but I guess it kinda got out of hand."

Billy ran the fingers of his left hand over his swollen left eye, realizing he couldn't see out of it. "Jordan's a good girl, Lyle. She didn't deserve that."

Lyle hung his head. "Reckon I was afraid Marcell would do to me just what he did to you." Glancing at Billy's face with a grimace, he got into the big car and drove slowly down the drive and around the side of the house.

Quietly closing the back door, Billy went into the small bathroom off the mud room, switched on the light and looked into the mirror. His left eye was a mass of bruises, the left jaw swollen, and his lips were split and caked with dried blood. He cleaned his face in the sink and started down the hall toward his bedroom.

"Step in here a minute," his father called from the study.

Billy entered the oak-paneled room with its mementos of war ("The rattle of musketry," his father called it), the bookcases with their leather-bound volumes, and the massive mahogany desk his father sat behind. He wore a burgundy smoking jacket and a dark scowl. "You're a fine sight!" he growled, taking the pipe from his mouth.

Billy sat down in a brown leather chair against the wall, staring at the German helmet with its piked top resting on the edge of the desk.

"Hartley Lambert phoned and told me what happened at his house. Look at you! Brawling like a commoner in front of our friends! How could you sully our name like that?"

"I could change it if you'd like, sir," Billy said flatly, holding his father's stern gaze.

"And for what?" the general continued, ignoring Billy's jibe. "For that . . . that *girl* who lives with that madwoman! She probably enjoyed it if the truth were known."

Billy rose to leave the room. "I'm sorry to have disappointed you—*again!*" he said bitterly.

General Logan Christmas struggled to control his temper, his nostrils flaring as he breathed heavily. "I'm going to assume a mild concussion precipitated that remark. But it would behoove you greatly to get out of my sight. Now! And you keep away from that *tramp!* Do you understand me?"

* * *

"Billy, you look terrible! Whatever happened to you?" Jordan sat on the back steps as Billy walked along the side of the house toward her.

"I had a debate with our mutual friend, Marcell Duke," Billy smiled. "He was more familiar with the subject matter than I was."

"Marcell always was the cerebral type," Jordan replied, trying to make light of the situation, but her humor was feigned as she fought to control her fear. *God just let me forget about what happened!* "You sure you're all right, Billy?" she breathed deeply.

"My manhood got slightly tarnished. Otherwise I'm OK." Billy sat next to Jordan. "How did you get home?"

Jordan shivered as an errant breeze touched her. Drawing her gray sweater around her, she looked across the tawny landscape. Her heart felt as dry as a winter leaf. "Walked."

"Did he . . . *do* anything to you?"

"No. I'm fine."

"I'm sorry, Jordan. But don't judge everyone by Marcell Duke —or Lyle Oliver for that matter—he was just scared to death."

Jordan smiled sadly at Billy, his close-cropped black hair shining in the morning sunlight, his right eye as blue as the evening sky. She shuddered at the sight of the damaged left eye, swollen shut and discolored with yellowish-purple bruises. "Doesn't matter, Billy. I'm leaving after this year anyway."

"Why? You've got another year of school left. You can't quit before graduation! What'll you do?"

"Dr. Simmons said he can get me into a nursing school in Atlanta. All I have to do is pass the state board at the end of the year. I'll have most of my credits by then anyway."

Billy looked around at the old house, almost completely paintless now—at the barn out back that had collapsed, its weathered gray planks and timbers sticking out at odd angles like the skeleton of some monstrously deformed animal—at the peach orchard where long ago, or so it seemed to him, he had caught his first glimpse of life's other side. "I wish I could have gotten to know you better, Jordan."

Jordan glanced at Billy, then across the sweep of tall, brittle weeds toward the cemetery. "You could have."

"Well . . . maybe this spring," Billy ventured, standing up. "After all, we've still got another whole semester left."

"Maybe," Jordan responded absently, knowing that Billy's world made no allowances for an abandoned girl brought up by a crazy old woman living in a derelict house by the cemetery.

After Billy left, Jordan went to her room. She retrieved her diary from the Hershey's carton and lay across the bed. With a glance at her bright angel, she smiled, then her expression changed and she began to write:

I've got to get away from this town. It's obvious now that I'll never fit in with the people my own age. Growing up out here with Annie, I'll always be an object of ridicule. And the other things—before Annie—may have scarred me for the rest of my life.

Annie, J.T., and Wash are the only things holding me here. Wash has his own family and his church. J.T. stays drunk most of the time now, so I never know when I'll be seeing him. And Annie, well, she'd have more money if she didn't have to feed and clothe me. I won't tell her I'm going though, until things are finalized—until it's actually time to leave for Atlanta.

After I graduate in nursing, I can live anywhere I want to—maybe bring Annie with me to live in another city. She's lived in this old house all her life though. If she doesn't want to leave, I'll just stay here and take care of her as long as she lives.

Well, anyway, maybe it wouldn't be so bad if I had a decent job—maybe at the hospital. Then we'd have enough money to buy some nice things and Annie could retire her little wagon and just take life easy for a change. I owe her that much after all she's done for me, to give her a little happiness in this life be-fore—while there's still time.

But then—I'm through with this town!

6

A NEW FAMILY

*J*ordan pushed her cart through the door into the darkened room, walking quietly over to the window and drawing the curtains back. December light seeped into the room like pale gray smoke, filling it with murky shadows. The inside of the oxygen canopy was streaming with water drawn from Minnie Durham's body by the alcohol exchange in her lungs as the oxygen bubbled through the alcohol bottle before she breathed it. Jordan wondered how a woman as small and as frail as Mrs. Durham could possibly hold so much water.

Walking to the head of the bed, Jordan turned the valve of the oxygen tank off and the bubbling noise stopped. She stared at the face and hands of her patient, getting puffier and puffier, even with all the fluid she was losing.

"Good morning, Mrs. Durham," Jordan whispered, pushing aside the canopy of the oxygen tent. "It's time for your medicine."

Minnie Durham smiled weakly at Jordan, her breathing labored as she struggled to sit up in bed.

"Now, you just lie still. I'll raise you up some more where you'll be comfortable." Jordan walked to the foot of the bed, reached beneath the chart hanging from the rail, and flipped the metal crank out. Turning it, she watched the head of the bed rise slowly until it was in the proper position.

"That's much better," Mrs. Durham murmured, barely audibly. "I can breathe a little easier now."

Jordan glanced at the chart, knowing what it would say before she read it. "Congestive heart failure" was the diagnosis; the prognosis was poor.

"Did you sleep well?" Jordan took the water pitcher from the bedside table, poured two ounces into a glass, and lifted Mrs. Durham's head gently.

"Little hard to breathe," she said, sipping the water slowly. "Oh, that's so delicious."

"Sorry I can't give you any more, but the doctor's got you on fluid restriction."

Minnie Durham's long hair fanned out on the pillow behind her, almost as white as the hospital gown she wore. "You're a pretty little thing, Jordan. I bet you've got a lot of beaus, haven't you?"

Jordan flushed slightly as she slid the oxygen canopy toward the back of the rails so it would be out of the way. She dried the inside of the canopy with a towel. "No, ma'am. I haven't got much free time."

With the oxygen off, the minor exertion of speech was already taxing Minnie Durham's meager resources. "Well, I don't mind telling you, I certainly did when I was your age." She began breathing heavily, wheezing from deep in her lungs.

"Maybe you'd better not talk until I get you bathed and back on the oxygen, Mrs. Durham.

"I believe you're right, child. I declare, age catches up to a body quicker than the wink of an eye. Seems like only last week, I could clean that big old house, wash all the clothes, and have dinner ready for Clyde and the children without half trying. Now it's all I can do to draw a decent breath." Minnie Durham lay back on the pillow, trying to fill her tortured lungs with oxygen from an atmosphere that could no longer sustain her. Fear began to brighten her faded brown eyes.

Jordan changed the bedclothes as quickly as she could. Taking a pan from her cart, she filled it with warm water from the small sink in the corner, bathed her patient, and put a fresh gown on her. All the while, Mrs. Durham gasped and wheezed, but she never complained.

When she had completed her tasks, Jordan drew the oxygen tent around the head of the bed, arranging towels at the base to soak up the expelled water, and started the flow of life-giving oxygen.

Minnie Durham breathed deeply, beginning to relax as some color came back to her face.

Jordan emptied the catheter, recording the intake and output on the chart, and sat in the chair by the side of the bed. "Are you feeling better, now?"

"Oh, much better," Minnie wheezed. "I feel a little light headed though, like I used to when my daddy would give me a hot toddy at Christmastime."

"You're supposed to feel better," Jordan assured her, knowing she was becoming giddy from the alcohol her lungs were assimilating in exchange for the water they were expelling.

"You're a good girl, Jordan," Minnie breathed, a little easier now. "You'll make some man a fine wife. And you'll be a good mother, too. You've got all the qualities."

Jordan turned to leave.

"I'm afraid, Jordan. Would you stay with me until I fall asleep?" Minnie whispered. "I'm so tired. It won't be long."

"Yes ma'am." Jordan sat in the chair next to the bed.

"'My days are swifter than a weaver's shuttle,'" Minnie spoke so softly Jordan had to lean forward to hear her. "That's something my mother used to say. Don't know where it came from. It's so dark. My children are all dead. Jordan, I'm afraid."

Minnie slid her hand along the fresh sheet toward Jordan. Jordan eased hers under the edge of the canopy, taking Minnie's cool hand in her own. A web of veins ran like slender cords just beneath the skin. The skin itself was as dry and brittle as old parchment and only a shade darker than the sheet it lay on. Jordan touched the pulse with her finger—felt it quick and light as a hummingbird's. *Tachycardia,* she thought almost unconsciously. The long hours of training had begun to entrench medical terminology into her thought patterns.

Jordan sat at her bedside as Minnie Durham wheezed less and less, her chest rising and falling in a regular motion—the rich oxygen giving her ease as she breathed out the suffocating fluid from her lungs. Already the sides of the canopy were streaming with water as if it were weeping for the frailty and brevity of life.

Holding the hand that felt like a tiny sack of bones, Jordan imagined herself in fifty or sixty years, dying alone in the company of strangers. *Why was I even brought into this world? To go through life alone and end up like this. Who'll be around to sit with me when I'm this old?* She remembered a passage of Scripture from the last sermon she heard Wash preach. "Our days upon earth are a shadow . . . ," and she thought of a poem she had read in one of the old books she had found in the attic of Annie's house:

> The shadows in my room
> Move toward evening,
> To the slow, inexorable cadence of the sun;
> As all mankind moves
> Toward that final failing of the light.

"You goin' to sleep on duty?"

Coming out of her reverie, Jordan felt she had been sitting with Minnie Durham for hours, but, glancing at her watch, she saw it had only been ten minutes. "No," she smiled. "Just thinking too much."

Ronnie Meadow stood next to her, his horn-rimmed glasses glinting in the dim light. "You usually do," he grinned. "Don't think—act. That's my motto."

Action was the last thing you thought of as you looked at Ronnie Meadow. At five-feet-six, he was a shade taller than Jordan, but outweighed her by a good fifty pounds. Twenty-five years old, his light brown hair already thinning in front, above his round, rosy face, he had the appearance of an aging cherub.

"You'd better do a little more thinking," Jordan replied softly, rising from her chair, "or you'll never make it through your first year of residency."

"Got time for coffee?" Meadow asked, waving a folded sheet of white paper in his right hand.

Jordan smiled suspiciously at him as they walked down the corridor toward the nurses' station, her heavy cotton dress rustling against her legs. "I know that look, Ronnie. What're you up to now?"

"Thought you might be interested in your final grades from last semester," he remarked slyly, tapping the folded paper on his left hand. "Maybe we can make a deal."

Jordan grabbed for the paper and missed. "You let me see that right now, Ronnie Meadow!"

Meadow held the grades behind his back with his left hand keeping Jordan at bay. "Oh, I will . . . as soon as you agree to go with me to the hospital Christmas party tonight."

Jordan stormed past him and turned into the break room just off the nurses' station. She poured a cup of strong coffee into a heavy white mug and placed the pot back on the hot plate as Meadow seated himself at the scarred wooden table. Jordan hesitated, then poured another cup, placing it in front of Ronnie and sitting down on the other side of the table. Besides the table and six chairs, the only other furniture in the stuffy little room was a row of metal lockers for the nurses' belongings. A narrow window looked out onto the rear parking lot.

Meadow took a sip of coffee. "Just teasing you about the party," he mumbled. "You do know, of course, that you couldn't get your grades until after the holidays without my, uh, connections." He unfolded the sheet of paper, laying it in front of Jordan.

Jordan unpinned her starched white nurse's cap, fluffing up her honey-colored hair that fell in soft waves to her shoulders. Picking up the sheet of paper, she studied it carefully:

Anatomy	A
Physiology	B
Pharmacology	C
Microbiology	C
Nutrition	C
Surgical Nursing	A

The corners of Jordan's mouth turned up slightly and then became a full-fledged smile. "Oh, Ronnie, thank you so much! I'd have just worried myself sick waiting through the holidays to find out." She stood up, leaned across the table and kissed him on the cheek.

"Glad to help, ma'am," Meadow beamed. "Now what about the Christmas party?"

Jordan looked up from her grades. "Oh, all right. If you promise to bring me home early. Tomorrow's a workday."

"Sure thing," Meadow agreed quickly. Then with a sober expression, he asked, "Jordan, I know you've gone out with a few of the guys, but never more than a time or two. Do you think it could be any different with me? After all we've had *three* dates. That's a record for you if my figures are right."

"You keeping tabs on me, Ronnie?"

"No, no, nothing like that. Just forget it. I'll pick you up about seven. OK?"

"Fine," Jordan replied, sipping her coffee. "Thanks again for the grades."

Meadow stood up. "My pleasure," he smiled and hurried from the room to make his rounds.

Jordan observed him as he left. *A little too narrow in the shoulders, but wide in the heart.*

*   *   *

A soft, fine snow was falling through the darkness as Ronnie opened the door of his Ford coupe for Jordan. She got in, shivering and plunging her hands deep into the pockets of her wool coat. Sleet had begun to mix with the snow, its irregular ticking against the windshield reminding Jordan of the arrythmia she had listened to through a stethoscope that morning.

Meadow got in, started the engine, and revved it up. "I love that sound. It's a 1933 V-8. Seven years old and runs like a sewing machine. Used to belong to the Atlanta Police Department. Ain't many on the road I can't just walk away from."

Jordan noticed the excitement on Meadow's face. *Never pictured him as somebody who'd like fast cars.*

"Now for a little toddy? Gotta keep the ol' bones warm on a night like this," Meadow muttered to himself, pulling a silver flask from the inside of his overcoat pocket. He unscrewed the cap, the whiskey gurgling into his mouth as he turned it up. He held the flask toward Jordan. "Want a snort?"

"You know I don't drink. And I think maybe you had enough at the party."

"Just to ward off the chill," Meadow insisted, the flask in his outstretched hand.

"No thanks."

Meadow took another swallow, screwed the top back on, and stuffed the flask back into his pocket. Pulling out into the almost deserted late-night streets, he glanced over at Jordan. "Wanna make a stop or two. After all, it *is* the holiday season."

"Holiday season," Jordan echoed. "Maybe for some. Not for

me. I've got to get that overtime pay at the hospital just to make ends meet. Dr. Simmons's loan pays tuition, but not food and rent."

"You mean you're not going home for Christmas?"

Jordan was staring through the windshield at the shining streets where the snow and sleet was melting as fast as it hit them. "There's only two or three people I care about seeing anyway."

Meadow took his flask out and took a quick hit. "Your mama and daddy?"

"No," Jordan replied in a leaden tone. "Mama got killed in a car wreck years ago. I haven't seen Daddy since I was a little girl. Don't even know where he is."

"Why don't you come on down to Waycross with me?" Meadow smiled. "You'd like my family. Mama always cooks enough for an army anyway. There's three boys and four girls in our family, and *big* is the only way she knows how to cook."

Jordan felt the warmth in his invitation and was tempted. *Wonder what it's like having Christmas with a family like that. Bet they have a big tree with a lot of presents under it.* "I'd really like to, Ronnie, but they're counting on me to work."

Meadow pulled over to the curb in front of Jordan's apartment building. "This place's a rundown-looking mess, Jordan. Looks like it hasn't been painted since Teddy Roosevelt was in the White House."

"Well, I can walk to the hospital from here, and the price is right," Jordan remarked, thinking that it looked a whole lot like Annie's house.

"Wish you'd come home with me. I'm leaving first thing in the mornin'." Meadow sipped from his flask and put it away. Taking a deep breath, he slipped his arm across the back of the seat and around Jordan's shoulder."

Jordan trembled involuntarily.

Meadow pulled her to him, his left hand brushing the soft waves of her hair, shimmering in the light from the street lamp. "I can't get you off my mind, Jordan."

"Please . . . don't," Jordan protested softly.

"Aw, come on. Just a good night kiss," Meadow murmured, cupping her face lightly in his hand.

Jordan felt her body going tense. She knew that Ronnie Meadow was a kind and gentle man, that he would never hurt her, but a cold fear and an ever greater revulsion rose inside her like a dark heavy cloud, blotting out all reason. "No!" she cried sharply.

Meadow quickly released her, almost jumping back across the seat of the car.

Jordan saw the shock on his face, the bright pain in his light brown eyes. "I'm sorry, Ronnie," she said in a sincere tone.

Meadow looked out the driver's window, his back to her. "It's all right," he mumbled.

"No, it's not all right," Jordan insisted. "You're a fine man. You don't deserve to be treated like that by someone like me."

"What do you mean, 'someone like you?'" Meadow asked with a puzzled frown, turning toward her.

Jordan took his soft round hand in both of hers, looking into his boyish face. "I'm . . . I'm just not . . . ready for this now. It's not your fault. Any girl would be lucky to have you."

"I don't want just *any* girl," Meadow said earnestly. "I'm in love with you, Jordan."

Oh, Lord, not again! Why can't they just be friends? Why does it always come to this? "Ronnie, you've only know me four months."

"Doesn't matter. I know how I feel." Meadow's face was flushed from emotion and alcohol as he poured out his feelings.

Jordan felt trapped—suffocated. She knew she had to get out of the car. "I have to go now, Ronnie. I'll see you after the holidays. Be careful on your trip home."

Meadow sat gloomily behind the wheel as Jordan hurried across the sidewalk to the apartment building. At the door, she turned and waved cheerily to him. After glancing at her, he sat behind the wheel of his shiny Ford V-8, staring down the street. Listening to the erratic clicking of the sleet on the roof of the car, he thought of Christmas at home with his brothers and sisters, their wives and husbands and children, and wondered what was wrong with him.

Jordan watched him career away from the curb, the back end of the car swaying back and forth as he gunned the engine. She choked back a sob and ran up the three flights of stairs. *He's such a nice man. What's wrong with me?*

Entering her room, Jordan switched on the light, lit her tiny lamp by the bedside, and switched the light off. She dressed in some flannel pajamas, thick white socks, and a heavy cotton robe. Taking her Raggedy Ann doll from the bed, she sat on the window sill, her feet propped up, left cheek resting on her knees as she looked down on the almost deserted street below. Her fingers moved through faded red yarn, combing the doll's hair in a motion that had become almost as unconscious and familiar and necessary as the beating of her heart.

Jordan sat for a long, long time staring out at the empty night and the protean shapes that appeared in the shadows of the buildings. A stray cat, yellow and scrawny, glided through a circle of light beneath a street lamp, disappearing like a wraith into a dark alley.

Jordan felt something drawing her toward the street, saw an image of herself diving from the window sill into the amber pool of light, drifting beneath its wavering surface in an eternal warmth. As her hands moved to the sash, she heard a voice softly call her name. Startled, she looked about the empty room and rubbed her eyes, surprised by the warm wetness she felt.

That night she slept, as she always did, under the outstretched arms of her bright angel.

* * *

September 1941 saw Jordan register in nursing school with one full year and two summer sessions behind her. She had fought hard through that black depression of the first winter, finding a tempered strength inside herself she didn't know was there. Her grades were holding steady, even with the long work week at the hospital, and things were looking up for the quiet, lovely blonde from Liberty. Except for school social functions, she seldom went out, giving her long hours as an excuse.

All this changed on the first morning of the first day of the semester. A secretary brought word that she was to come to the main office immediately. When she returned forty-five minutes later, her face clouded with concern, she gathered her belongings and left without a word to anyone but the instructor. The next morning she was on a bus to Liberty.

* * *

Dr. Simmons sat nodding on one of the two concrete and wood benches beneath the blue-and-white sign picturing a greyhound in full stride. Startled from his nap by the sound of the bus's air brakes, he threw his mangled cigar into the trash bin and stood up wearily to greet Jordan.

Jordan found it easy to smile when she saw the Humpty Dumpty form of Dr. Simmons, his wrinkled gray suit draped carelessly about his squat body. "Hello, Dr. Simmons. It's awfully nice of you to come and meet me."

"You know me . . . nothing but free time," he snorted back.

"How's Annie?" Jordan kissed the doctor on his pale round cheek and smelled the acrid cigar smoke about him like an invisible wreath.

"*Hardheaded*—that's how she *is!*" Simmons walked over to the bus, taking the twine-wrapped cardboard box Jordan used for a suitcase from the driver.

Jordan caught up with him as he waddled to his black Chevrolet coupe parked on the corner. "You don't have to tell *me* that. What's wrong with her medically?"

Simmons dropped the box into the trunk of his car, closed the lid and fumbled for his keys. "Too much bootleg whiskey and not enough food for too many years."

Climbing into the car, Jordan heard the school bell ring. She saw herself that first morning twelve years ago, riding along in Annie's little wagon, dreading what lay before her. "Cirrhosis?" Jordan asked cryptically, sure of the answer already.

"What else?" Simmons mumbled, shucking another of his tree-trunk cigars.

"I shouldn't have left her," Jordan mused, gazing at the shady old streets and houses of the town. "Annie can't take care of herself anymore. She didn't look good the last time I was home."

"You did just what you should have done. Annie wouldn't have wanted it any other way." Simmons glanced at her. "You got two days to get things squared away out at the house, then you start to work at the hospital."

Jordan stared at him blankly. "I don't understand."

"Got you a job on the surgical ward. Won't be as exciting as Atlanta, but it'll pay the bills."

Jordan felt a great burden lift from her shoulders. "Oh, Doctor Simmons. I had no idea how we were going to make it. Thank you so much. You're wonderful!"

"Ain't I though," Simmons grinned around his cigar. "Too bad most people don't have your discernment."

When they reached the house, Jordan found Annie in the kitchen propped up on an old army cot that had been in the attic. It stood next to the bank of windows that looked out across the open field toward the graveyard. Annie smiled weakly as soon as she saw Jordan.

"Annie, how did you get yourself into such a mess?" Jordan chided with mock anger. "You're yellow as a Chinaman."

Annie's dull eyes regained a trace of the vanished brightness of her youth. "Ain't never used much sense, I reckon."

"Well, we'll just have to get you fixed up," Jordan beamed, hugging her neck and kissing her on the cheek. "Plenty of healthy food and no more of J.T.'s 'liquid dreams,' as he calls that nasty stuff."

Annie looked out at the ancient tombstones, cracked and tilting beneath the live oaks. "Doc said you quit yore job in Atlanta. Gonna come back here and work at the hospital. I don't mean to be a bother to you, child."

Jordan knelt beside the cot, hugging Annie tightly. "That's the last thing you are to me, Annie. I'm tired of that big city life. This is my home." *The closest thing I have to one anyway.*

For Jordan, the days settled into a monotonous routine of work at the hospital, household chores, and taking care of Annie. With plenty of rest and wholesome food, Annie's health began to improve. She helped around the house, but Jordan insisted that her little wagon be given an extended vacation. Most of all, Annie's spirits lifted so that she was happier than Jordan had ever seen her.

In addition to visits from Wash and J.T., Dr. Simmons now came once a week to check on Annie and usually ate supper with them. J.T., in deference to Annie's condition, slipped out onto the back porch when he wanted an occasional pick-me-up from his flask.

Jordan felt this time coming to an end as Annie regained her health. A restlessness, bordering on panic, filled her, and she felt driven to see something of the world outside Liberty, Georgia. She worked hard and read incessantly, but always in the quiet times, as she looked at her bright angel in the stale hours past midnight or stared at the flames in the great stone fireplace on a dreary afternoon, that haunted, shadowy feeling would come to her like a recurrent nightmare.

Wash continued to insist that Jordan and Annie needed to be in church. "It ain't fittin' for folks to sit home on Sunday mornin'," became his by-word. Annie, as always, steadfastly and bitterly refused. Jordan hadn't been back since the day the man with the white handkerchief had gone to the altar, but in the wake of Wash's unflagging devotion to his faith, she eventually succumbed.

It was a bright December Sunday that Jordan chose to return to the little white frame church across the field from her house. She took her usual place on the front row next to Pearl and joined in with the singing, feeling out of place as the people raised their hands toward the heavens, praising God. Jordan sang with the congregation, "I once was lost, but now am found, was blind but now I see."

Washington Smith stepped behind the podium and opened his big Bible. "In him was life; and the life was the light of men. And the light shineth in darkness; and the darkness comprehended it not."

Suddenly, Jordan saw her tiny lamp, shining as it had at her bedside for thirteen years, but somehow it was as though she were seeing it for the first time. She saw herself as the child on the bridge, and she saw who had watched over her through the long nights.

Wash's voice sounded as if from a great distance, but with power and clarity: "But as many as received him, to them gave he power to become the sons of God, even to them that believe on his name."

The small congregation listened as Washington Smith preached. Jordan heard again the words from the last sermon she had heard him preach. "'To set at liberty them that are bruised . . . If thou shalt confess with thy mouth the Lord Jesus, and shalt believe in thine heart that God hath raised him from the dead, thou shalt be saved.' It all takes place in the heart."

Jordan bowed her head, not seeing the puzzled stares of those around her. *Lord Jesus, I believe that you're the Son of God and that He raised you from the dead. I receive you now into my heart as my Savior. From now on, Jesus, I'll live for you.* There came no blinding light to Jordan Simms, no great rush of emotion, but she knew that what had taken place in her heart was eternal.

Jordan lifted her head. Pearl, her eyes bright with tears, smiled warmly at her and gave her a big hug. Holding her tightly, Pearl whispered, "Welcome to the family of God, Lisa Jordan Simms."

When Wash gave the altar call, Jordan went forward and confessed before the entire congregation that she had accepted Jesus Christ as her Lord and Savior. Her new family welcomed her with praise and great joy. As soon as the last hug was over, she raced across the field through the dry winter weeds, briars scratching her legs and pulling at her dress. Taking the back steps two at a time, she burst through the kitchen door. "Annie! I've got good news!"

After sharing her heart with Annie and witnessing to her for an hour, Jordan took a red pencil and circled the date on the Purina Feed calender that hung on the kitchen wall—December 7, 1941.

Part 2

7

LIBERTY AT WAR

*B*ombs were still falling on Pearl Harbor when most Americans first heard the news of the Japanese attack. Millions of them heard about it on CBS that afternoon when John Daly's familiar voice broke in on the New York Philharmonic a few minutes after 3:00 P.M.: "We interrupt this program to bring you a special news bulletin. The Japanese have attacked Pearl Harbor . . ." Americans would always remember the day they heard about Pearl Harbor. It was as though the shutter of a camera had clicked in their minds, printing a memory of exactly where they were and what they were doing at that precise moment.

In their hour of fear and uncertainty, the American people turned their hopes toward the White House. Large crowds formed on the sidewalk near the Pennsylvania Avenue entrance. They milled about for the most part in silence, hoping for a glimpse of their president, some sign that everything was going to be all right. That night a misty three-quarter moon hung over the darkened White House. As Cabinet officers and congressmen began arriving, the people, gathered on the sidewalk and in Lafayette Park across the street, broke into choruses of "The Star Spangled Banner" and "God Bless America."

Americans had put their confidence in the right man. Franklin D. Roosevelt was no stranger to adversity—a condition that seemed to bring out the best in him. After surviving polio at the age of thirty-nine, he once remarked, "If you have spent two years in bed trying to wiggle your big toe, everything else seems easy." Edward R. Murrow, who spent time with him that first evening after Pearl Harbor later wrote, "I have seen certain statesmen of the world in time of crisis. Never have I seen one so calm and steady."

* * *

Taking the backspin from the sliced approached shot, the ball skidded low as it hit two feet from the sideline in the far corner of the court. Billy took his first step before the ball crossed the net, sprinting to his left. He cradled the throat of the racquet in his left hand as his right turned counterclockwise on the leather grip, preparing for an Eastern backhand. Moving parallel to the baseline, he took the racquet back until its head was pointing in the opposite direction from which he was running, keeping his right elbow close to his body.

As the ball bounced, Billy planted his right foot, kept his head down, and whipped the racquet around and through the ball, meeting it dead center on the cat gut two feet in front of his right hip. The white ball zipped down the sideline two feet above the net, kicking up a tiny cloud of chalk dust as it skipped off the baseline.

"Game, set, and match!" Billy cheered, jumping into the air, his arms outstretched above his head. At that precise moment the cannon thundered on the parade ground, shattering the peaceful Sunday afternoon. "Why in the world would they shoot that thing off today?"

"Beats me," said Todd Greer. Todd was Billy's lanky, redheaded roommate who now stood at the net where he had positioned himself to return Billy's volley. "I know one thing though. If you can make shots like that, you're a shoo-in for the varsity squad. Nobody else would have even gotten to the ball."

Several boys suddenly came running by, heading for the parade ground.

"Hey! What's the hurry?" Billy yelled.

"The Japs bombed Pearl Harbor! We just heard it on the radio!"

Billy stood just inside the baseline where he had won the final shot of the match, the toe of his right tennis shoe coated with chalk dust as he had stepped into the perfect backhand. Sweat ran down his brow from his exertions in the unseasonably warm weather; his black hair glistening with health and sweat. The cannon thundered again and he thought of his father's favorite phrase—"The rattle of musketry."

Three hours later, Billy was zooming along a stretch of highway at eighty-five miles an hour in his 1937 Cord Westchester convertible. As he flashed by a billboard with a red-cheeked Santa Claus drinking an icy bottle of Coca-Cola, he heard the sound of a siren rise quickly and then fade behind him. Looking into his rearview mirror, he saw a black Ford sedan with white decals on its doors screech out onto the highway after him.

Billy kept glancing at the mirror as the Ford gradually pulled closer. Soon they would be able to read his license plate. When he made his decision, the Lycoming V-8 roared and lurched ahead as he floored the accelerator. When the speedometer began rocking on 110 miles an hour, Billy saw that the Ford was now no more than a dark speck in the mirror.

Later that night, Billy glided around the back drive and parked under the portico at the rear entrance of his home. Lifting his two tan leather suitcases from the car, he walked up the stone steps, entered the back hall, and turned into the kitchen. His mother stood at the counter drinking tea.

Agnes Christmas was a handsome woman for her fifty-six years, in spite of having a weight problem that she constantly battled. Billy got his blue eyes and easygoing nature from her, but he rebelled against her wanting to choose 'acceptable' friends and female companions for him. Her perfectly shaped eyebrows rose at the sight of him. "Billy! Whatever are you doing home?" She set her cup down, hurried over, and kissed him on the cheek. Holding him by both shoulders, she stepped back. "Surely you aren't finished with finals already?"

"No ma'am," Billy said solemnly. "I'm joining the Army."

Agnes Christmas blanched, her arms dropping limply to her sides. Taking a deep breath, she turned away. By the time she reached the counter and retrieved her cup, she had regained control. "Your father won't hear of it."

"I'll talk to him right now," Billy declared bluntly, dropping his suitcases in the corner. He walked briskly down the hall and knocked once on the door of his father's study.

"Come in," the voice barked from inside.

Billy entered and sat, as always, in the brown leather chair against the wall. His father held the black telephone to his ear, his right hand toward Billy, palm outward. "Yes, General, I understand." His hand dropped to the desk and fumbled with a brass shell casing. "Yes, General. Two days at the most." He leaned back in his chair, laughing. "No sir, I don't doubt that at all. See you soon, General."

Billy noticed the slack skin under his father's chin where there was a hint of gray stubble. "Who was that . . . the general?" he smiled, hoping to put him in a good mood.

Logan Christmas glared at his son, a mica glint in his dark eyes. "That was General George C. Marshall, the Army chief of staff. Tomorrow the president will declare war on Japan."

"That's why I'm home," Billy said flatly. "I'm going to join the army. A lot of the guys are doing it."

Logan Christmas gave his son a steely grin. "You're not like a lot of the guys. You'll finish college and go into the officer corps, maybe before you graduate if things get as rough as I think they will."

"But, sir! I . . ."

"You heard me!" Christmas snapped. "No son of mine will ever be an *enlisted* man." He used the word *enlisted* as one might use the word *degenerate*.

Billy glared back at his father. "Thank you, sir. I knew I could count on you to hear me out." He rose quickly to leave the room.

"Don't slam the door on your way out," Logan Christmas demanded, dialing the phone as he gazed at his directory.

Returning to the kitchen, Billy snatched up his suitcases and turned to leave.

"Sit with me a while, Billy," his mother pleaded softly, pouring him a cup of coffee.

Billy glanced at her, sat down at the heavy oak table, and spooned sugar into the steaming coffee. "Should have gone straight to the recruiting office with Todd. After all, I *am* eighteen."

"Your father and I only want the best for you, son. Finish your education, then go into the army if you want to." She reached over and patted him on the hand.

"The war may be over by then," Billy shrugged.

Agnes smiled. "I was an army wife for twenty-five years, son. If it gets rough enough, you'll go in all right, but as an officer."

Billy gulped the last of his coffee. "Guess I'll get on back to school."

"You can't leave now. It'd take you the rest of the night. Tomorrow's soon enough. We'll have a little supper, and you can get a good night's rest."

"Might as well, I guess," Billy agreed sullenly.

"You might want to spend some time with your father, Billy," Agnes encouraged. "He's being called to Washington in some sort of advisory capacity. It's not supposed to be permanent duty, but in wartime one never knows for sure."

"He's too busy," Billy replied cryptically. "He'll be on the phone all night—winning the war."

Agnes let it drop. "Have you written Gloria Prentiss yet? She tells me you never answer her letters."

Billy shook his head. "Mama, Gloria's a nice girl, but I'm just not interested in her."

"Well at least give her a chance," Agnes insisted. "After all, she comes from a good family. Her father was a captain in the navy."

"Mama, will you just fix me some supper?" Billy sighed. "I'm starved."

* * *

Billy sat next to Lyle Oliver at the last booth near the jukebox in Ollie's Drugstore. Leslie Gifford sat across from them, his copy of the *Atlanta Constitution* spread on the table before him. He had dropped a nickel into the jukebox and punched in his favorite song: "And these few precious days I'll spend with you . . ." The lyrics told of the swift, bittersweet passing of the years, sounding as though Gifford could have written them himself.

"So you've gone and joined the Marines, have you, Lyle?" Gifford asked pleasantly, folding his newspaper.

Lyle grinned at Gifford, then at Billy. "Yes sir, I sure did. Billy here went with me."

"Fastest way I can think of to see some action," Gifford responded in a solemn tone. "If that's what you want."

"It is, sir. We've got to keep the Japanese out of this country," Lyle smiled confidently.

Gifford glanced at Billy, whose face spoke of frustration bordering on despair. "I don't think Japan's likely to invade us, Lyle. They'd have done it right after Pearl. The Germans are another story. Their U-boats are sinking our freighters and tankers every day up and down the Atlantic coast. Friend of mine from Florida saw a tanker blown out of the water right off the coast of Miami. Once he saw the bodies of three crewmen that had washed ashore. Says you can see ships burning at night before they go down."

"I hadn't heard about that," Billy remarked in a surprised tone.

"They try to keep the news coverage down," Gifford continued. "To prevent a panic, I suppose. From what I'm told, the U-boats are even sinking supply ships coming out of the mouth of the Mississippi River."

"Do you think we can whip Germany *and* Japan?" Lyle asked anxiously.

Gifford smiled sadly. "Oh, we'll win the war, Lyle. It'll be long and bloody, but we'll win. This country's never had such unity in its entire history. Arthur Krock wrote in the *New York Times*, 'You could almost hear it click into place.'" Gifford continued, opening the newspaper again. "Listen to what John W. Flannagan, a congressman from Virginia, said, 'It is a war of purification in which the forces of Christian peace and freedom and justice and decency and morality are arrayed against the evil pagan forces of strife, injustice, treachery, immorality, and slavery.'"

Billy and Lyle stared wide-eyed at Gifford.

"A little overstated, even for a politician," he said evenly, "but it does, to some degree, reflect the mood of the country."

Hearing a racket outside, Billy and Lyle glanced at the plate glass window at the front of the store. Passing in front of it was a ragtag group of very young and very old men carrying shotguns and squirrel rifles. Two or three even had black-powder weapons. "What's that bunch doin'?" Billy asked.

Gifford didn't bother to look around the corner of the booth when he heard the shouted orders. "Oh, you boys wouldn't know about that, being away at college. It's the Liberty Militia. They're sworn to protect us from the dreaded Hun. Makes you feel all warm inside just to look at them, doesn't it?"

"Makes me feel like I better learn to speak German," Billy laughed, "if that's the best we can do."

"Well, I gotta go tell the folks I'm an official 'jarhead.'" Lyle stood up to leave. "Got a few days before I take off for Parris Island, Billy. Probably see you before then."

Billy's face was stony as Lyle left. "Hope he gets along all right. He never was very tough."

"That's why he joined." Gifford's strange eyes met Billy's. "To prove to himself—and to the town—that he can make it in the toughest branch, the Marines. Why do you want to go, Billy?"

"What makes you think I want to join up?"

"It's all over your face." Gifford stood up awkwardly, lifting his bad leg with his left arm. "People go to war for a lot of reasons. Patriotism is only one of them. Be sure you know what you're doing when your time comes. Sometimes decisions can be more deadly than combat."

Billy walked to the door with Gifford. "Thanks, Mr. Gifford. You're a good friend."

Standing in the door of Ollie's, Billy watched Leslie Gifford limp down the street, his right foot slapping loosely against the sidewalk with each step. *There's a man that oughta know about fightin' battles.*

"Hi, Billy. I thought you had gone back to college." Gloria Prentiss had come up behind Billy, smiling brightly at him, her eyes as dark as his father's. Her narrow face was pale, but her long hair was as straight and black as an Indian's. A pink sweater hung from her shoulders, and her gray wool skirt showed too much of her slim, shapely legs. "Your mother told me I might find you over here."

Billy felt trapped. "Uh, I decided to stay a little longer. Probably leave tomorrow. Spring semester starts Monday."

"You know you really should answer my letters," she pouted. "Talking to your mother is the only way I can find out anything about you."

"I'm sorry, Gloria," Billy mumbled, glancing at Gifford as he made his unsteady, awkward way down the sidewalk. "There's just so much studyin' to do, and I'm tryin' to make the tennis team and all . . ."

Gloria took him by the arm. "Well, why don't we just go on into Ollie's and have a soda or something? We can have a nice visit."

"Ah, I don't think so, Gloria. Got to get back home, get everything packed," Billy lied. "Lot to do."

"I want to thank you again for the lovely time at the Christmas party at your house. Seems like our families get along so beautifully," she smiled, straightening his collar, her soft fingers rubbing lightly on his throat.

"Yeah, Mama's good at arranging things like that. Well, I've gotta run," he said, kissing her on the cheek. "See you next time."

* * *

"Did you plumb drop out of college, Billy?"

Billy was threading his way through the crowd that had gathered around the depot. "Oh, hi, Coach," he yelled above the clamor, spotting Bonner Ridgeway standing near the front door of the depot with Alvin Ditweiler, the principal of Liberty High. "No, I didn't—not yet anyway. Just had to see the homecoming of Liberty's only Medal-of-Honor winner."

"We got us a real hero, don't we?" Ridgeway boasted, drawing his bulky frame up as he glanced out over a sea of people, their welcoming signs held aloft.

"We sure do," Billy agreed. "Picture on the cover of *Life* magazine and everything."

"What do you mean, 'not yet,'" Ditweiler asked, a plug of tobacco bulging from his cheek, his chunky Babe Ruth face beaming at being out in the open air away from his office.

Billy gave him a puzzled frown. "Oh, you mean about leaving college. I wanna join the army," Billy answered flatly.

"I bet that made the General happy," Ditweiler grinned. "Can you see that, Coach? General Logan Christmas's boy as a buck private."

Ridgeway laughed, shaking his big blond head. His gravelly voice assumed the tone of a locker room pep talk. "Billy, you just keep yore mind on the books and forget about this war. Maybe you'll catch the next one, cause we're gonna whip Tojo and Hitler in about three months."

"Maybe so," Billy laughed, walking toward the platform. "See y'all later."

Signs, streamers, and banners were everywhere bearing slogans of WELCOME HOME BEN or BEN LOGAN FOR STATE SENATOR—HE'S ONE OF US. People were still streaming into the area around the train station, trying to find places near the speakers' platform, or milling up and down the tracks. Near the lectern, Mayor Calvin Sinclair, who looked like a pudgy Charlie Chaplin in his black suit, argued with burly, blustering Hartley Lambert, owner of the lumber mill.

Billy found an unoccupied three feet of space under a sycamore. Glancing about the crowd, he saw a striking blonde in a nurse's uniform standing gracefully erect at the far edge of the crowd. *Must be new in town. I'll have to go by the hospital and find out who she is.*

Three hours later, Billy watched Ben Logan walk down the steps from the platform, thronged by reporters and hangers-on. Though an inch shorter than Billy's six-one, to him, Ben looked bigger than life in his dress blues—deeply tanned and confident with something about his eyes that reminded Billy of someone else he couldn't quite remember. *Maybe that's what war does to you,* Billy thought. *Makes you bigger than you were before—or smaller.*

After the crowd had dispersed, Billy hung around town talking to a few friends, stopping by Ollie's for a Coke. Restless and dissatisfied, he was drawn to and repelled by the siren call of battle. He drove out to the Logans' house, feeling somehow that Ben had the answers he needed.

"Haven't seen him since he left the platform," Jewel beamed proudly, glad that her son was safe at home. "He might stay in the hotel tonight. There's a lot of people want to talk to him, I reckon."

"Well, thank you, Mrs. Logan," Billy said absently, turning to leave.

"Billy . . . you all right?" Jewel asked in a concerned tone. "You look kinda peaked."

"I'm fine, Mrs. Logan," Billy called over his shoulder as he walked back to his car.

Before he reached Three Corners Grocery, Billy pulled his Cord off the dirt road and parked in a clearing in the midst of a stand of tall pines. In the summertime there were always several jalopies parked here. Now it was empty. He walked along the path leading to the swimming hole and pausing in wonder where it led out of the woods onto the beach. The blonde nurse he had seen at Ben's homecoming sat on the huge boulder under the live oak at the river's edge. Her frosty-white nurse's uniform had been replaced by a pair of faded old overalls and a blue-and-white checkered shirt. Still, she looked elegant.

"Jordan Simms!" Billy walked along the river's edge toward the boulder, his brown-and-white saddle oxfords scrunching in the sand. "I hardly recognized you!"

Jordan stared at Billy's sloppy denim trousers rolled above his white socks and at his torn blue sweater worn over a wrinkled white shirt with its tail hanging out. "Same here, Billy. You used to be such a neat dresser."

"College," Billy shrugged, as if that were to blame for all his shortcomings.

Billy sat on the boulder next to Jordan. "I see you made it through nursing school."

Jordan gave him a puzzled look.

"Saw you at Ben's homecoming," Billy smiled. "You were so . . . far away I didn't know it was you." *You sure don't look like that shy little girl I went to school with.* Billy gazed at Jordan's long lashes, half-veiling her deep blue eyes that held a light he knew had never been there before. The afternoon sun highlighted the honey-colored hair that fell to her shoulders. A secretive smile curved the corners of her lips, which needed no coloring but their own. "You've . . . filled out!"

Jordan blushed under his gaze, looking down on the dark water, which was full of sky and upside-down trees. "Dr. Simmons found a job for me at the hospital." She fidgeted on the boulder. "Ben looked nice in his uniform, didn't he? And his speech was the only one that made any sense to me."

"Uh, yeah," Billy mumbled, forcing his eyes to look at the river. "All those years in school. I never took him for the hero type." He glanced at Jordan. *I wonder what type you are, Jordan Simms? Ben ended up a hero. Maybe you've changed that much, too.*

"How's college?"

Billy glanced again at the swells and curves of her body. "Boring compared to what Ben's doing anyway. I want to join the army, but 'The General' won't hear of it. Says there hasn't been an *enlisted* man in our family for three generations. I just want to see some action before this thing's over."

Jordan propped her feet up on the cold surface of the rock, her arms resting loosely on her knees. "I don't think it's going to be over for a long time, Billy. Maybe you're just restless . . . want to see some of the world outside Liberty, Georgia."

"From the way you said that, it sounds like you're ready to take off yourself," Billy smiled.

"You're right," Jordan declared bluntly, her blue eyes holding his. "This town hasn't exactly been the answer to all my dreams. Maybe I could even help out in the war."

Billy laughed. "Somehow I can't see you storming a beachhead or manning a machine gun."

"I've got a feeling there's more to war than winning medals and getting your picture on magazine covers, Billy. I'm sure there's something I could do."

"Why don't we see how Hollywood handles it?" Billy stood up and took Jordan's hand.

"What are you talking about?" she asked with a slight frown as she climbed off the boulder.

"I'm talking about you and me going to see *Sergeant York* tonight. Gary Cooper's in it," Billy smiled. "How 'bout it?"

"Sorry. I've got to work tomorrow," Jordan protested weakly.

She seems almost afraid of me. I certainly never did anything to make her feel that way. Well, she always was a little strange—she wasn't always this good-looking though. "Six o'clock feature . . . malts at Ollie's . . . home by nine. How can you refuse such a night of raw excitement?"

"How can I indeed?" Jordan laughed.

* * *

"You didn't tell me you were dating Jordan Simms, Billy," Agnes Christmas huffed, making a pot of hot chocolate at the stove.

"First time," Billy replied casually, slouching in a chair at the kitchen table. "How did you find out, anyway?"

Agnes glared at her son. "Gloria saw you coming out of the picture show with her. She called an hour ago, and she's *very* upset. I think you should apologize to her."

"What for?" Billy demanded. "I didn't make any promises to her. I don't even like her. She's too much like her mother."

"I suppose you like Jordan Simms because she's so much like that . . . that creature who raised her," Agnes admonished.

"There's nothing wrong with having to work for a living, Mother," Billy snapped. "We can't all be royalty like . . . I'm sorry. It's just that I enjoyed being with Jordan tonight."

"Well, I'm sorry, too," Agnes replied, pouring the hot chocolate into white mugs. "You'll have to get these things out of your system, I suppose. I know you'll come to appreciate a girl like Gloria—someone with quality."

Billy sipped his hot chocolate. *Quality—money and knowing which fork to use first at a formal dinner,* Billy thought scornfully.

"I'm sure your father will want to speak to you about this," Agnes murmured into her cup. "He'll be home next weekend."

"Think I'll go to bed, Mother. I'm tired and I've got to get up early to get back to school." He bent and kissed her on the cheek, leaving his cup steaming on the table.

Later Billy lay in bed remembering the small red-and-white banner with a single blue star in the center that he had seen hanging in the window of the Oliver home as he drove to Ben's homecoming. *Wonder how ol' Lyle's doing? Better than me I bet.*

8

THE COLOR OF THE STAR

*A*nnie, you look better than you have in years." Jordan walked down the steps from the back porch and began helping Annie unload her wagon. "You should have told me you were going out today. I was worried when I got home from the hospital, until I saw the wagon missing."

Annie took the last of the junk out of the wagon and tossed it to the side of the porch. Then she plopped down on the steps and started unlacing her heavy work boots. "Figured if I told you, you wouldn't let me go."

Jordan helped her with her boots. "Well, there's really no need. I make enough at the hospital to support us."

"You won't be here forever, child. You've got your own life to live," Annie remarked, rubbing her feet through her heavy wool socks. "Besides, what else would I do? Sit around and knit doilies? Have the ladies over for bridge?"

Jordan laughed and sat down beside Annie. "I see what you mean. Well, I think you'll be fine as long as you don't push yourself. Sleep late. Go out in the afternoon when it's warmed up some."

A gust of wind came sweeping across the dry fields. Annie shivered. Glancing at Jordan with her weary, pale eyes, she murmured as if to herself, "You know, baby, I never would have made it if you hadn't come back when you did."

"Sure you would have, Annie." Jordan tried to sound cheerful as she took Annie's calloused hand in her own, soft and white now, reflecting the change in her life. "Why, you're too cantankerous to let anything get you down for long."

Annie looked across the lion-colored winter field where the late sun was laying down long shadows across the graveyard.

"Guess you're right. It's a comfort to have you here though." She stood up painfully, rubbing her back. "Let's get some supper."

"You wash up while I get the food on the table," Jordan suggested, opening the screen door.

"I'm not all that hungry," Annie replied, getting a drink with the gourd dipper that hung from a nail next to the shelf. Then, pouring water from the galvanized bucket into a metal basin, she began to wash up.

"Wait'll you see what I fixed."

Inside, Jordan turned the radio on and served their plates at the stove while Annie seated herself at the big heart pine table.

The Japanese continued to pressure the American positions on the Bataan Peninsula, forcing the Americans to retreat to a second line of defense. Sources indicate that several amphibious landings have also been made at several points along the coast. The president has ordered General Douglas MacArthur to abandon his forces and proceed to Australia. No word from the general as yet. It is expected that General Jonathan Wainwright will assume command.

American naval task forces commanded by Admirals Halsey and Fletcher attacked Japanese air bases in the Marshall and Gilbert Islands. The aircraft carrier USS *Enterprise* was damaged—details are not available at this time.

Elsewhere, British forces under Lieutenant General Arthur Percival surrendered to Japanese forces in Singapore, culminating the greatest disaster in British military history. The entire Malayan campaign was successfully completed by the Japanese in seventy days . . .

"Liver and onions," Jordan announced, setting Annie's plate in front of her. "Good blood builder."

"Good taste too," Annie mumbled, cutting a large hunk and chewing it hungrily.

Jordan sat down and watched with pleasure as Annie devoured the food. "I'm seeing Billy Christmas now."

Annie glanced up from her plate, talking around a mouthful of liver and field peas. "Nice boy. 'Member that time he came back and said he was sorry for hittin' me with that rock?"

"I sure do. He was scared to death to face you. But he did it."

"Well, I hope ya'll have some good times, baby." Annie scraped her plate clean. "But remember, people do crazy things during wartime. Some of us don't even need a war. So be careful and don't rush into anything you'll be sorry for later."

"Oh, it's nothing serious," Jordan mused. "We're just friends. He's taking me to play tennis in the morning. Supposed to be a nice day."

"You don't know anything about tennis," Annie shrugged. "That's for rich people."

"Billy's gonna teach me. He's real good. Everybody at school used to say so. We're going to the country club."

Annie got up, poured herself a cup of coffee and sat back down. "My niece at the Pine Hills Country Club. You reckon the General knows about this?"

"What difference does it make? We're not children anymore."

Annie gazed into Jordan's clear blue eyes, shining with the excitement and promise of youth. "It makes a difference to people who have money. I know. A long time ago I used to be one of 'em."

As Jordan cleaned off the table the newscast ended and Harry James and his orchestra filled the kitchen with the strains of "I'll Get By." "Oh, this is such a beautiful song. I just love the way Dick Haymes sings."

Annie cradled her coffee with both hands, savoring the fragrance and the warmth. "Poverty may come to me it's true, but what care I, say, I'll get by as long as I have you."

* * *

"Oh, my goodness! What is all this?" Jordan stared in wonder at the black-and-white Hightower bags Billy dumped onto the kitchen table.

"You can't play tennis in that getup," Billy laughed. "Besides there's an all-white rule at the club."

Jordan glanced down at her tan slacks and brown loafers. "I didn't even think of that. I thought just the tournament players wore those clothes."

Billy started digging into the bags.

"I can't let you do this," Jordan protested. "These things are much too expensive."

"Too late now!" Billy laughed. "What size are you? Eight? I sure hope so."

Jordan nodded her head. "Wait, let me do it! You'll mess them up." She took out a pleated white tennis skirt and a blue-trimmed cotton V-neck sweater and folded them neatly on the kitchen table. Next came the knit slipover shirt, tennis shoes, and cotton socks.

"Your racquet's in the car," Billy added. "It's the same kind Alice Marble used to win the U.S. Open in '38, '39, and '40."

"Don't imagine I'll be winning anything, but I'll try to be a good student for you. Maybe I can get the ball over the net a few times."

"Land sakes! Look at all them pretty clothes!" Annie shuffled into the kitchen wearing a faded and tattered man's bathrobe.

"Morning, Miss Annie," Billy said quickly.

"Look, Annie, aren't they beautiful?" Jordan picked up the clothes from the table and held them in front of her.

Annie glanced at the clothes while she poured some coffee into her china cup. "Looks like you'd get enough of white, wearing that nurse's uniform all day."

Jordan smiled at Billy. "They're for tennis. Billy's going to show me how to play today."

"Why don't you sit down," Annie nodded to Billy. "You look stiff as a soldier standing there."

Billy sat at the big table as Annie poured coffee into another mug and set it in front of him. "How you been feeling, Miss Annie?" Billy asked. "Jordan said that you'd been sick."

"Tolerable."

Billy shifted uneasily in his chair. "Annie, I'm real sorry about hitting you with—"

Annie laughed loudly, cutting Billy off as she sat down across the table from him. "Thought you looked bothered about something. That was seven years ago, besides, it's one of my fond memories."

"I don't understand." Billy sipped his coffee with a puzzled frown.

Annie looked into his young, sincere face. "Only time I remember anybody apologizing to ol' Annie since we lost all our money. Yes sir, it was a rare experience."

118

Somehow, a barrier fell in those moments, allowing a healing flow of warmth to enter the room. Annie talked about the old times, about her growing up in Liberty, with Billy listening intently, obviously enjoying the stories and occasionally joining in himself. Jordan merely listened to the two of them, feeling, for the first time, something like a sense of family.

Glancing at his watch after a few minutes, Billy finally said, "We'd better be going. Don't want to lose my favorite court."

Jordan changed quickly, and they headed across town in Billy's Cord to the country club in the affluent Pine Hills community. Songs played on the radio; Jordan recognizing "I'll Get By" with the first few notes. "I think Dick Haymes is better than Frank Sinatra," Jordan sighed, gazing out the window at the quiet Saturday morning town.

"Me too," Billy agreed. "That's my favorite song. I thought all the girls liked Sinatra better than anybody though."

"Not all of us. Billy, would you do me a favor?"

"Name it."

"Would you not drive so fast?"

Billy glanced at Jordan with a quick smile and eased off the accelerator. "Sorry. Guess I do push it a little sometime, most of the time as a matter of fact. Must be my way of letting off steam or something."

Pulling into the almost deserted parking lot, Billy grabbed his tennis bag and headed for the last court next to a stone wall covered with ivy. "This is my favorite court," he said. "The wall reminds me of a castle. Sometimes I pretend I'm jousting instead of playing tennis, or swinging a battle axe instead of a racquet."

Jordan smiled warmly at him, beginning to feel a little more at ease in such opulent surroundings. "I believe there's something of the romantic in you, Billy Christmas."

"Don't tell my father that," he laughed, flushing slightly. "He'd disown me for sure."

At that moment, General Logan Christmas sat in the clubhouse reading the *New York Times*. He wore sharply creased gray slacks, a white shirt, and a navy cashmere cardigan. Having arrived late the previous night from Washington, he had gotten up at dawn, as was his custom, and walked over to the club for an early breakfast. As he watched his son giving a tennis lesson to the striking girl with the flowing blonde hair, the waiter approached and stood at his table.

"Morning, General, suh," Isaac Paul said in his easygoing way. In his mid twenties, he had grown up working around the club and knew it better than his own home. Short and stocky with ebony skin and a perennial smile, he had proven himself quietly and inconspicuously efficient, as well as unfailingly taciturn. He had a job for life.

"Morning, Isaac." Christmas nodded toward the court next to the wall. "Do you know that lovely girl my son's instructing? It certainly isn't the one his mother and I have chosen for him, but then young men will have their flings, won't they?"

"Yes sir, they sho' will." Isaac glanced at the court uneasily, then looked at his shoes. "That's Lisa Jordan Simms with young Billy, General. She ol' Annie's niece."

Christmas's eyes narrowed in anger, his lips drawing thin and pale as he glared out the window at his son.

"You want yo' usual breakfast, General?" Isaac knew he would not be eating now.

Logan Christmas folded his paper neatly, slapped it sharply on the table, and marched out of the room.

* * *

Billy was whistling "I'll Get By" as he flopped onto his bed, staring at the ceiling, but what he saw was the morning sunlight striking Jordan's hair as it swirled in a shimmering, golden cloud about her face. Even though her tennis strokes were awkward, as all beginners' are, there was a certain grace in her movements and a healthy sensuality that was as unaffected as her laugh.

"Do you enjoy making fools of your mother and me?" Logan Christmas stood woodenly at the foot of Billy's bed, his arms folded across his chest.

Stunned by the sudden intrusion, Billy sprang from his bed. "What are you talking about?"

"That . . . that common girl I saw you with!" Christmas spat viciously. "How could you bring her to the club? Do want us to be the laughingstock of this community?"

Billy's eyes blazed at his father. "She's got more class than any-body I know!" he breathed hoarsely.

The General stiffened as if struck across his back with a riding crop. "I'm not interested in your opinions! I absolutely forbid you to see her again!"

"I'm not a child anymore, Father!" Billy shot back. "I'm ca-pable of making my own decisions."

"You're not capable of making your own bed! From now on you will be seen strictly in the company of your own kind, people of background and breeding." Christmas spun around and left the room before Billy could collect his thoughts.

Billy stormed into the bathroom, stripped off his tennis clothes, and flung them against the walls and onto the floor. He stood under a cold shower for five minutes, gradually beginning to calm down. *Why do I let him get to me like that? Nothing I do is good enough for him. I oughta be used to it by now.*

Slipping into a pair of tan slacks and pulling on a light tennis sweater with his college logo, Billy sat on the bed and put on white socks and scuffed brown loafers. He went out the back door where his mother sat on the patio in a wrought-iron lawn chair, reading.

"Where are *you* off to in such a hurry?" Agnes closed her book, a finger marking her place and gazed with concern at her son.

"Nowhere, Mother. Just going for a ride." Billy snatched the car door open.

"Anything wrong, son?"

"No ma'am. Everything's the same as it always is." Billy climbed into the car and screeched down the driveway as the pow-erful engine roared to life.

Calming himself, Billy eased off the accelerator and cruised smoothly along the quiet, shady streets of the town. *Well, I guess it could be worse. What if I had been brought up like Jordan. No mama, no daddy, raised by ol' Annie with most of the town making fun of them. She certainly seems to have come through it all right though. Something sure changed in her life this last year or so. She doesn't even seem like the per-son she was in high school.*

Passing by Lyle Oliver's house, Billy thought about all the ex-citement Lyle was having in some far-off exotic part of the world. As he glanced at the banner hanging in the front window, Billy felt a sudden coldness in the pit of his stomach. He pulled the car over to the curb, switched off the engine, and sat there shaking, as the impact of what he had just seen hit him harder than any blow he had taken before.

Billy forced himself to look again at the star, willing with all his strength that it would be blue, but the star was gold, as gold as the lost, endless summers of childhood. He remembered a poem that he and Lyle had discussed for Leslie Gifford's English class—"Nothing Gold Can Stay"—and he wondered how long the gold star would remain in the window and how many other windows in his country would bear witness to their sacrifice with their stars of gold.

Billy sat for a long time in his car on the side of the street. The school bell rang and children skipped and ran and giggled their way down the sidewalks to their mothers' hugs and their dogs, waiting for play. As the red sun dipped behind the distant bell tower of the Methodist church, he started the engine and idled along the streets in a daze.

J.T. Dickerson ambled out of the front door of the office that had become his home, since most of his law practice had drowned in a sea of moonshine. He sat down on the front stoop, took a silver flask from his inside coat pocket, and turned it up.

Parking his car at the curb, Billy got out and walked over to the stoop and sat down next to J.T. "Can I have a drink of that, J.T.?"

J.T. reached inside his jacket and flicked the flask to Billy in one smooth, quick motion.

"Uhh!" Billy grunted, snatching the silver flask from the air with one hand just before it hit the sidewalk. "What's the matter with you?"

J.T. grinned mischievously, his teeth showing a thin, dull film of neglect. "Good reflexes. I could have used you back in high school. Earl Logan was the best running back in the state, but there wasn't a decent pair of hands on the whole team. Only way anybody caught a ball was that soft touch I could put on my passes."

Billy took a long swallow from the flask and felt it burn all the way down. "Hhhhh!" he breathed out hoarsely, shaking his head. "What *is* this stuff?"

"Moon Mullins's best," J.T. expounded. "Aged in genuine

hickory barrels since last Tuesday. That's why it's so smooth. Notice how easy it goes down?"

Leaning back on a post of the stoop, Billy took another swallow, a small one this time. "How long has it been since you said anything that made any sense, J.T.?"

"Well, you must remember, Billy, I'm a lawyer, so the answer to your question would of necessity predate my passing the bar exam," J.T. pontificated with exaggerated sincerity. "I believe it was as an undergraduate in Professor Arnhardt's modern German literature class. He asked me what Hesse meant by, 'I have already died all deaths, and I am going to die all deaths again'—the first two lines of his poem, "Alle Tode"—to which I adroitly replied, 'Beats me, Professor.'"

Billy chuckled softly, taking another swallow of the bootleg hooch, finding that it seemed to have lost some of its bite.

J.T. took the flask and finished it off. "Yes, young Bill, I believe that's probably the last time I said anything that made sense."

"Let's get some more whiskey." Billy had a warm feeling in his stomach and a silly grin on his face.

"Capital idea!" J.T. agreed readily. "Just inside my modest lodgings, if you please."

Billy followed J.T. into a small, dusty reception area that led to what appeared to be a law library. There were countless volumes scattered about on the table, chairs, and floor—novels, books of poetry, plays, history—incongruously, the law books were neatly arranged on their shelves and looked untouched. "J.T.!" Billy called out. "Don't you ever read your law books?"

J.T. stopped in the doorway leading into the kitchen. "Too confusing. Inhibits my courtroom repartee."

In the kitchen, J.T. dug inside a cluttered cabinet under the sink and produced a corked bottle of clear whiskey. He refilled his flask and, after wiping it out with his shirttail, poured a water glass full for Billy and stepped out the back door.

Billy walked down the three concrete steps to a walled garden. The bricks were overgrown with ivy, reminding him of his favorite tennis court. A three-tiered fountain, topped by a figure of a Greek water bearer, held a green, scummy liquid that had once been rainwater. Five once-white, wooden lawn chairs were randomly spaced about the brick area surrounding the fountain.

J.T. arranged two chairs next to a wicker table and plopped down in one of them. "Take a load off, young Bill. You look like a man carrying a boxcar full of woe on his shoulders."

Billy sat down, taking a swallow from his glass and placing it on the table. As he looked about the garden with its ruined landscaping and the office drifting into disrepair, he could almost hear the echoes of better days.

"Something on your mind?" J.T. mused. "You ain't exactly been a regular at my place."

"Just this," Billy smiled, lifting his glass and taking a swallow.

"Jordan's a nice girl, isn't she?"

Billy glanced at J.T. with a shocked expression. "How did you know about that?"

"Saw ya'll together a time or two—this morning in fact. Jordan looked good in that tennis getup." J.T. gazed up at the smattering of fleecy clouds drifting lazily toward the sun. "I once found myself in a dilemma very much akin to yours."

"I'm not in a . . ."

"Billy, Billy! Ol' Annie's niece and the General's son. That's a dilemma to the third power." J.T. smiled at Billy and lifted his flask. "There lived in Liberty a beautiful blonde of humble origins named Ellie . . ."

"Debbie's mother?"

"The same." J.T.'s mind drifted like the clouds back into the past. "Enter the dashing young quarterback whose parents wanted someone more suitable for his exalted station in life, someone of quality and breeding."

"What happened?" Billy asked eagerly, leaning forward in his chair.

"Look about you, young Bill, at the sad remnants of what happened. I'm beginning to think I may have made a wrong decision somewhere along the way."

Billy thought of J.T. as a young man like himself torn between emotion and family loyalty. His mind could not rid itself of images of Jordan that filled him with a bittersweet ache. And he remembered Lyle and all the years he had known him, and the pain became all bitter with none of the sweetness.

J.T. glanced at Billy's empty glass, got up, and went into the kitchen. "'I drink a liquor never brewed,'" he muttered as he returned, filling Billy's glass to the brim from the bottle.

"What'd you say?" Billy slurred the question, lifting his glass from the table.

"Just a little Emily Dickinson. Maybe that's what I'm looking for. 'A liquor never brewed.'" J.T. lifted his flask in a toast to Billy. "But for now this'll do just fine."

Billy awakened in darkness, his head hammering with pain—his mouth dry as cotton. For a panic-filled moment he couldn't remember where he was or how he got there. Then he noticed J.T. still sitting next to him in his chair, mumbling to himself.

Standing shakily to his feet, Billy spoke softly, feeling that his head would crack like an eggshell at any moment. "J.T., I got to be going. Thanks for the drink."

J.T. stared into the darkness, muttering under his breath to some ghost from the past.

When Billy got home his father was pacing in the driveway at the rear entrance where he always parked. Billy got out of the car, aware of what he must look and smell like.

Logan Christmas glared with disgust at Billy. "If you aren't a sorry excuse for a son! This is the last time . . ."

Billy bowed his head under the tirade, going directly to his room as his father followed him step for step.

"Things are gonna be a lot different for you from now on, young man!" Christmas snapped from the foot of the bed as Billy sprawled across it.

That's for sure! Billy thought as he felt himself falling into a dark, dreamless slumber.

The next morning Billy stood in front of the Marine recruiting office. *This is exactly where I was standing when I came here with Lyle. Well, no time like the present. I know the Marines have room for at least one more jarhead.*

Two weeks later Billy Christmas was on a bus bound for Parris Island and feeling some anxiety about what lay ahead of him. *Oh, well,* he thought confidently, *how bad can it be?*

9

APRIL IN PARRIS

Marcell Duke! You're the last person I expected to see here!" Billy almost yelled as he stepped off the bus at Parris Island in the dead of night. "Why aren't you at college?"

"Why aren't you?" Duke shot back with a big grin.

"Joined the Marines!"

"Me, too!" Duke sat on a bench against the wall of the station platform, dim lights shadowing the hollows of his darkly handsome face. Eight or ten other recruits bound for boot camp slouched along the benches near him. "Daddy didn't want me to go in the service till I finished college, so I just got up and walked out of English 101—went down and joined up. He oughta get my letter tomorrow. Wish I could be there to see his face when he opens it." Marcell grinned broadly as the realization hit him. "The General's son—a private in the Marine Corps. I bet that made him real happy."

"Oh yeah! He hasn't stopped laughing since I told him I was joining up." Billy dropped his small bag on the bench and sat down. "You hear about Lyle?"

"Yeah." Marcell folded his arms across his chest and leaned back against the wall. "Saw the gold star the last time I was home. Couldn't get it out of my mind. Maybe I thought I could take his place or something. I don't know. Anyway, here I am."

A green flatbed truck with high wooden rails and a canvas top pulled up in front of the depot, stopping abruptly with a metallic screeching of its brakes.

"You waitin' for an engraved invitation?" said a pie-faced young marine sitting behind the steering wheel of the truck.

The men along the benches looked at him, then at each other, speaking in confused undertones.

127

"I believe ever bunch gets dumber," the driver said in a tone of exasperation. "Git on the truck!"

The men piled into the back of the truck. It sped off before they could all find seats, sprawling some of them across the floor. When, somewhat battered from the bouncing ride to the base, they spilled out of the back, Sergeant Sullivan stood there to greet them. In all, some two hundred men stood scattered before him in ragged rows at the edge of the street, exhausted and bleary-eyed from travel.

Sergeant James A. Sullivan was five feet, ten inches of bone and muscle with a mouth like a sewer. Blasphemy and obscenity flowed from his lips as easily as sonnets from Shakespeare's quill—and he dearly loved his job as drill sergeant.

"I got one thing to tell you before we get our little Sunday school picnic started," Sullivan crooned sweetly, his eyes like buckshot in his craggy red face. "Give your hearts to Jesus, boys, 'cause *all* the rest of you belongs to me."

"This is *not* a nice man!" Marcell whispered to Billy, leaning toward him as they stood among the ragged ranks of men.

"You!" Sullivan bellowed, pointing to Marcell.

Marcell found something interesting to look at on the ground.

The next thing Marcell knew he was somehow propelled airborne through the ranks of startled men. It happened so quickly, he didn't realize that Sullivan, two inches shorter but twenty pounds heavier than Marcell's two hundred, had lifted him by his collar and the seat of his pants, hurling him easily to the front of the group. Stunned, Marcell dropped to the pavement on his hands and knees. Getting to his feet, he dusted himself off and grinned uneasily at the sergeant.

"Don't just stand there, dimwit!" Sullivan roared, his big-knuckled hands on his hips. "Take over!"

Marcell's face went blank. He glanced at the ragtag gaggle of men massed under a slice of moon hanging like a pale, bright scimitar above their heads. "I, uh, don't know what you mean."

Sullivan rushed toward Marcell, stopping abruptly, his face two inches from Marcell's. "Run the show!" he roared. "You ain't got time to listen to me. You must know everything *already!*"

Two other drill sergeants appeared miraculously next to Marcell, flanking him on either side.

"Where you from, slimeball?" one sergeant bellowed into Marcell's ear.

"Liberty," Marcell mumbled.

"Liberty?" the other one bellowed. "Where's that, Idaho? What state, you idiot?"

The three sergeants verbally bludgeoned and badgered Marcell for a full two minutes, ushering him, on the brink of tears, back into the ranks. Then they were among the men, splitting them quickly into three training platoons of sixty men each. A few stragglers were left standing by the curb to await the next arrival of recruits.

Marcell and Billy ended up in Sullivan's platoon, much to their chagrin. His sharp, nasal Boston accent raked their backs like a cat-o'-nine-tails as he marched the men to the mess hall. In its dimly lighted warmth, they pushed metal trays along the serving line manned by sleepy and disgruntled "boots" on KP duty. Sullivan disappeared through a door marked "Mess Sergeant."

"Cold pork and beans and spam! Ecchh! I thought the food at Liberty High was bad!" Marcell sat next to Billy at one of the long tables in the clatter and clamor of the mess hall.

"If the rest of Parris Island is anything like this, I'm gonna apply for a transfer to the Army," Billy added, stirring the congealed sauce and beans with his heavy fork. "Tomorrow!"

Their mostly uneaten meal over, the men marched under the stinging snap of Sullivan's cadence to the quartermaster sheds where they would leave the majority of their civilian identity. Stripping down on the concrete floor in the chilly, cavernous shed, they squatted like Neanderthals before a fire in some dank cave. Naked, they were pitifully defenseless, depending solely on the Corps for protection, identity, and the companionship of their own kind.

The men of the darkling sheds descended on them like wraiths wielding measuring tapes. They were pelted and deluged with shoes, socks, pants, shirts, underwear, caps, belts, and coats. Then each received a number. Billy Christmas no longer existed; 352537 replaced him and he had no purpose, no reason for existence apart from the Corps.

One final vestige of individual personality remained, and in five smooth strokes of a barber's clippers it disappeared into the all-encompassing green chaos of the Corps.

"Forwarrrrd . . . Harch!" In the mind-deadening, cadence-calling, shoe-polishing, gun-cleaning bellowing discipline of the Parris Island "boot," bereft of sleep and sanity, marching became the single cord that bound the separate parts together. March to the mess hall, march to sick bay, march to the drill field where the art of marching was perfected. March to draw a weapon . . . the rifle . . . the piece . . . never, never a gun.

"What's this on my gun?" With his dark, heavy eyebrows and thick black eyeglasses, Kelly Parrino, from Chicago, looked like a young Groucho Marx, minus the mustache. But his voice, lifted in song, was more like Dick Haymes's. Always quick to learn the proper way to salute or mop a deck, and with that wonderful singing voice brightening the barracks before lights out, even Sullivan's contempt for all boots was moderated in his case. But Parrino had spoken the forbidden word, the supreme blasphemy.

"Gun!" Sullivan screamed in his face. "Gun? Is that what you called this weapon?"

"Yes sir!" Parrino cowered before the sergeant, holding his newly issued M-1 Garand covered with cosmoline.

Sullivan smiled benignly. "*Gun* is *not* a Marine word. It's a *civilian* term of endearment. You're in love, Parrino."

Sullivan marched the men to the wash racks to scrub the cosmoline from their weapons, then to chow, and finally to the barracks to bed them down for the night.

"How's your sweetheart doin', Kelly?" Marcell lounged on top of his blanket in his skivvies, gazing at the M-1 nestled on Parrino's pillow as he tried to get comfortable on the narrow cot next to his weapon.

Undaunted, Parrino patted the heavy wooden stock of the weapon. "Oh, she's a *hot* number, this one is. *Especially* when I get her loaded. I'm gonna enjoy sleeping with her for a week."

"You think them Japs are as mean as the newspapers say they are?" Albert Jackson, a sleepy-eyed boy from Missouri asked the barracks at large. His brown eyes were wide with anxiety. His slim face was taking on some color from the Carolina sun. It also took on some large, widely spaced freckles, which earned him the nickname Spots.

"Ask the men in the Philippines," a stocky Wyoming cowboy answered, sprawled on his bunk, hands behind his head. "They got

Luzon, Bataan's next. Corregidor can't hold out much longer. From what I hear, they don't place the same value on life that Americans do."

Marcell propped himself up on one elbow. "Y'all can't be serious, can you? You sound like you're afraid of 'em. They're little bitty people. Hardly any of 'em more'n five feet tall."

"I think they may be a little bigger than that." Billy sat on his bunk next to Marcell, rubbing his short bristly hair. "Anyhow, when you're shootin' at each other the gu—excuse me, Kelly—the *weapons* make everybody just about the same size."

"Well, I ain't scared of none of 'em," Marcell boasted loudly. "Can't wait to get my hands around one of them little yellow necks after what they done at Pearl Harbor!"

Sullivan stood in the shadows next to a square ceiling support just outside his quarters at the end of the barracks, his massive arms folded across his chest. "I'm glad you feel that way, *Hero*," he growled, his hard eyes holding a mica glint, " 'cause it's a sure bet you're gonna get your chance when you ship out."

Over the barracks, an uneasy silence descended heavily on the men who sat or lay on their bunks. Their eyes were fixed on the drill sergeant with something like a pale foreshadowing of the "Stare," that peculiar metamorphosis of the eyes seen only in men who have been too long in the company of death. Sullivan flipped the light switches on the wall, casting the high-ceilinged room into murky darkness, and silently disappeared into his quarters.

* * *

"Today you start to learn what being a Marine's all about. The only reason we feed and clothe you." Sullivan paced before the men as they stood in the chilly, damp dawn in front of the barracks, their weapons struck and packs on their backs. "Today you go to the rifle range. You will remain there until you become a *Marine! Some* of you might as well tell the real world good-bye!"

Having learned absolutely nothing from his first experience, Marcell turned his head ever so slightly and whispered to Billy, "You think they'll brand us like a herd of cattle?"

Sullivan's voice boomed in the still morning air: "Duke! Front and center!"

Marcell cursed under his breath and stepped forward, standing at attention before the red-faced sergeant.

"They're all yours, Hero," Sullivan crooned politely, his right hand beckoning toward the platoon, doing their best to stifle their laughter. "Take them to the rifle range."

"But I don't know . . ."

"Oh, but you do, Hero!" Sullivan growled. "You know *every-thing* about the Corps."

Marcell tried out a shaky command voice, "Platoon! Ten . . . hut! Column right . . . harch!" And promptly marched the men into the barracks wall.

The men stacked up on each other, stepping on heels and tromping feet until there was only a writhing mass of bodies.

"Stop!" Marcell screamed, but the bedlam continued.

"At my command. Platoon . . . halt. Fall out!" Sullivan spoke calmly. "Fall in!"

When the men were in formation again, Marcell moved to step back into ranks.

"Not yet, Hero!" Sullivan bellowed. "This ain't the rifle range. They're all yours."

Muffled groans spread among the ranks.

"Platoon! Left flank . . . harch!" Marcell shouted, trying to imitate Sullivan.

Half the men marched along the road while the other half marched directly into a wide drainage ditch with a foot of water and two feet of mud.

"I mean, column left . . . march!" Marcell shrieked, running around in front of them. "Wait a minute! No! Get outta the ditch!"

"At my command. Platoon . . . halt." Again Sullivan spoke in a calm level voice.

The four rows of men in the ditch stood thigh deep in mud and water, some glaring quickly at Marcell. Two men had one foot on a metal culvert, the other in the ditch. The remainder stood in the street.

"As you were, Hero!" Sullivan barked.

Marcell returned to his position in the ranks, standing in the mud and water next to Billy.

"Platoooon! Forwarrrd . . . harch! Lefflank . . . harch! Columnrite . . . harch! Thrip . . . faw . . . yah leff, thrip . . . faw . . . yah leff. Ya leff . . . rite . . . leff."

On the dusty six-mile march, Sullivan ran through his repertoire of cadence calls with the whole platoon doing the rousing echoes in perfect unison.

"I got a gal who lives on a hill."
I got a gal who lives on a hill.
"She won't kiss me, but her sister will."
She won't kiss me, but her sister will.
"Sound off."
One, two.
"Sound off."
Three, four.
"Bring it on down."
One, two, three, four, one, two, THREEFOUR!

The platoon arrived at the rifle range in the heat of the day. They were assigned to six-man tents and then marched out to the windy, bright sand dunes to learn the three shooting positions: standing, prone, and sitting. The first two were relatively simple: a double-jointed contortionist would have had trouble with the third.

Billy held the stock of the rifle in his left hand, looped the sling around his left arm, and sat cross-legged in the sand, but, try as he might, he could not get his right shoulder around enough to touch the butt of the weapon. Suddenly, he felt a tremendous pressure on his right shoulder, thinking his back would snap in two, his shoulder moved gradually forward until it rested against the rifle butt. He was now in the sitting position.

"You're welcome," Sullivan growled, pressing both hands on Billy's shoulder. "Thought you'd never do it, didn't you?"

The next morning, after the three basic positions were learned, Sullivan formed the men up in front of their tents. "Today we use live ammo. *Real bullets . . . thirty caliber,* for those of you who haven't learned anything yet," he announced, glancing at Marcell.

Marcell's jaws tightened, but he had learned to keep his mouth shut as long as Sullivan was in sight.

Sullivan paced in front of the platoon, holding a .30 caliber cartridge between his thumb and forefinger. "I'll tell you one last time.

Always keep your weapon pointed down range until the gunney tells you otherwise. *Whatever* you do, *don't* shoot any sergeants! It'll make 'em mad, and they might hurt you."

On the firing line, the men lay prone on either side of the range officer, each with two eight-round clips next to him.

Billy held the M-1 lightly in his left hand, the stock nestled against his right shoulder.

The command came with a roar: "Lock and load!"

Inserting the clip into the weapon, Billy slapped it home.

"Ready on the right! Ready on the left! Ready on the firing line! . . . Fire!"

The earth seemed to rise up with the deafening roar of the firing line. Billy forgot all about the precise Marine instructions as he snuggled the stock of the M-1 beneath his chin, lapsing unconsciously into the shooting patterns of his youth. He could almost see a rabbit, its white tail flashing when it bolted from a thicket as he emptied the first clip, ejected it, slammed the other home, and fired the final eight rounds.

With his ears ringing, Billy watched Sullivan striding directly toward him. *Oh, no! Here it comes!*

As Sullivan leaned over Billy, his face red with rage, mouth opening for a tirade on the Marine way of shooting, he glanced at the target. His eyebrows raised an eighth of an inch before he could stop them. Without a word, he stood up and stormed toward another intended victim.

The platoon learned bayonet fighting, with its block-parry-thrust technique, and pistol shooting during their five days at the rifle range, but shooting for "record" took first place in the Marine hierarchy of values. Three men in the platoon failed to qualify, and, true to Sullivan's word, they were conspicuously absent on the march back to the barracks.

"Them 'dogfaces' and 'swab jockeys' better take a wide berth around me! I'm finally a real Marine!" Spots lounged against the wall of the barracks the next afternoon, smoking a Camel, trying to squint his eyes like Clark Gable. "Got through the worst they could dish out!"

"Maybe, maybe not," Marcell lit up a Lucky Strike, preferring the Bogart scowl.

Billy lay prone in the newly risen April grass, chewing on a pale green stem. "Don't leave us in suspense, Hero. What kinda top secret information did you pick up?"

Marcell still flinched at the sound of his nickname, but it was as much a part of him now as his propensity for getting into trouble. "While I was H.Q. runner this morning, I heard Sullivan talking to somebody in the C.O.'s office. There's a place called New River out in the boondocks where the First Marine Division is forming up. From there you get a one-way ticket to the South Pacific."

That night the platoon, along with several others, stood at parade rest beside a long green file of idling trucks. Sullivan ran them through the manual of arms one final time, their hands popping their weapons with confidence and precision.

Sullivan paced in front of them for the last time, hands behind his back. Several times it looked as though he were about to speak, but he never did. Finally the order came.

"At ease! Fall out! Climb aboard, *men!*" Sullivan boomed.

Marcell turned his head toward Billy. "He called us *men!*"

"You got a hard head, Hero," Sullivan smiled.

"He smiled, too!" Marcell beamed. "Where we going, Sarge?"

The smile left Sullivan's face, and Billy thought he actually saw a trace of sorrow in the eyes. "New River!"

Billy kept his eyes riveted on Sullivan, standing there by the side of the road, hands behind his back. Then he was lost in the darkness and there remained only the roaring of the truck and the overwhelming silence of the men.

* * *

They arrived in darkness, confusion and shouting and lights flashing all along the railroad siding as they formed ranks almost without thinking. Above the shadowy, rushing figures of the officers and NCO's, above the yelling and the chaos, above all, the overwhelming immensity of New River impressed itself upon the men as it seemed to stretch endlessly under the ebony span of sky.

"You'd think the Marines couldn't move if it wasn't dark," Parrino grumbled as they moved toward a lighted Quonset hut. "I can't figure it out."

Spots marched beside him. "Maybe it's to get us used to the night. I hear the Japs always attack at night."

Parrino glared at him in the darkness, sliced by the random, swinging beams of the flashlights. "That's just what I wanted to hear, Spots. I feel much better now."

Billy stood in line outside the hut until an NCO called his name. He stepped into the crowded room and seated himself in front of a scarred wooden desk beneath an oil lantern.

"Christmas, huh? What's your first name—Mary?" The corporal seated behind the desk wore a buck-toothed grin and thick glasses over his bovine eyes.

Billy glanced quickly around, hoping no one else had heard the comment, but Marcell sat at the desk to his left with a grin bigger than the corporal's, and Billy knew there was no help for it; he would be "Mary" for the duration.

Giving the corporal his serial number, rifle number, and the endless, repetitious information that all armies accumulate, Billy noticed a man sitting to his right who had not been in their training platoon. He looked to be in his late twenties, ten years older than most of the recruits. His gray eyes stared through round, gold-rimmed glasses beneath wavy brown hair that appeared absurdly ornamental among the "skinheads" of the other men.

"First Marines," the corporal said matter-of-factly to Billy as if unaware of the import of those two words. "Tell the sergeant. He'll be just outside the door."

Billy stepped into the night and walked over to three sergeants standing off to the side of the several groups being formed from the men filing out of the huts. Smoking and talking in their easy camaraderie, they looked impervious to the fears Billy saw on the faces of the recruits, as if the stripes themselves held some mystical power.

"First Marines!" Billy said a little too strongly.

A dark, razor-faced sergeant pointed to one of the groups, and Billy took his place among them. Hero, Spots, and Parrino were the only others from their training platoon assigned to that group. Finally the older Marine with the gold-rimmed glasses walked from the lighted hut and took his place among them.

At a command from the dark sergeant, they climbed aboard a truck and quickly found themselves bouncing through the potholes along the muddy roads lined with rows of darkened huts stretching endlessly into the night. The vastness of New River made it seem like an unearthly region under a sky of strange new stars.

"I'm Sam Dalton." The man with the gold-rimmed glasses bumped along next to Billy. "Where you from, son?"

"Liberty." Billy mumbled into the near-darkness of the truck. "Liberty, Georgia. How 'bout you?"

"Someplace you never heard of, I bet," Dalton grinned, his white teeth gleaming in his tan face. "Van Horn, Texas. Dry, windy, desolate. That pretty well describes it."

"I've never been west of Montgomery, Alabama," Billy remarked, staring at the truck splashing along behind them. "You're kind of . . . old to be in this bunch, ain't you?"

Dalton laughed, his warm brown eyes crinkling at the corners. "I was in the Corps ten years ago, served my hitch, and got out. Then Pearl Harbor came along, and here I am again."

It was then Billy noticed the gold cross shining in the darkness. "Are you a preacher?" he asked, pointing to Dalton's collar.

"Chaplain," Dalton corrected. "I got permission to go through boot camp with the men."

"You mean you didn't have to?" Billy was amazed.

Dalton smiled, looking out into the night. "I heard a sermon when I was a boy that stayed with me through the years. The preacher said that if a man wants to be a shepherd, he's got to walk among the sheep, touch them, smell like they do, or they won't follow him."

Billy thought about the chaplain's statement. "Makes sense to me. You gotta be a little nuts to go through all this when you don't have to though."

"There may be something to that," Dalton laughed. "Anyway, when we leave New River, I'll have to go back to Regimental H.Q. No fun at all working around all that brass. I spend as much time as I can away from there."

"So you can be with the sheep," Billy suggested.

"You *were* listening."

"I like them glasses." Marcell peered around from the other side of the truck. "My grandma's got a pair just like them."

Dalton smiled, taking off the glasses and cleaning them with a green handkerchief. "I hope her eyes aren't as bad as mine."

Parrino tapped Dalton on the shoulder. "Hey, Granny. Would you hear my confession tonight?"

10

A HOUSE WEARING A
SAILOR CAP

*Y*eee . . . haaah!" Marcell burst through the door of the squad hut, gasping for breath. "We bombed Tokyo!"

Spots jumped off his bunk. "Is the war over? Did the Japs surrender?"

Marcell lit up a Camel and dropped onto his bunk. "I seriously doubt that, Spots. All I heard was that some Colonel Doolittle took a squadron of B-25's right over Tokyo and let 'em have it. Imagine what those Japs must be thinking! How would we feel if they bombed Washington?"

"Well, if it ain't gonna end the war, it ain't worth talking about," Parrino grumbled. "Anybody wanna go to the slop chute? We ain't got any beer for tonight."

Billy swung his legs over the side of his bunk. "I could use some cigarettes."

"You could use a pacifier is what you could use, Mary," Parrino taunted. "You've been smoking three days and ain't even learned how to hold one yet. You look like a bear cub playing with a stick."

"Yeah, well you might as well have a stick as that M-1," Billy scowled back at Parrino. "I saw your scores at the rifle range. The only thing the Japs have to worry about is your mouth. You might talk 'em to death."

"You think you're such a hot shot since you scored sharpshooter on the rifle range," Parrino shot back. "You still make twenty-one dollars a month just like the rest of us."

"I think y'all better turn in early tonight." Sam Dalton, wearing his inscrutable half-smile, stepped into the barracks from the doorway where he had been listening.

"What's up, Granny?" Marcell asked, unlacing his boots.

"Tomorrow we go to the boondocks." Since they had come in on the truck together, Sam Dalton had adopted this squad as his own, keeping them abreast of the goings-on. He was a chaplain for the men, spending very little time at headquarters, unlike the others. None of them came to his Sunday morning services, but this only deepened his parental attitude toward the little group, seeing them as the strays that he had to gather into the fold.

"How far is it?" Spots asked nervously, the way he always responded to most changes in his routine.

"Don't know for sure, but it'll be a long way to pack machine guns and mortars."

Billy lit a Lucky Strike, his eyes watering as he tried to let it dangle from his lips. "How long we stayin' out there, Granny?"

"Beats me. One thing I know, we'll be training for beach landings."

Two hours later, the platoon sergeant, a lanky towhead from the mountains of Kentucky, formed them up in front of the huts. "All right, here's the straight," he scowled, trying to appear fierce but merely giving the impression that he was bothered by irregularity or some similar affliction.

"This comes right from the general," Marcell whispered to Billy. He had become more proficient at his whispered commentaries and was seldom caught.

"We're moving out to the boonies at first light," the sergeant continued. "Enlisted men will fall out in full marching gear. Check your mess gear, shelter halves, and tent pegs."

Marcell kept his head straight, using only the corner of his mouth. "Them NCO's love to say *enlisted men*, don't they? Must make 'em feel important."

"Shut up in the ranks, Hero!" the sergeant snapped. "Leave your sea bags in the huts. You'll be living out of your packs."

That night Billy lay on his bunk next to the tiny window. Lights out had sounded and Parrino and Marcell had gone outside for a smoke. As they sat against the hut near the window, the mood struck Parrino and he began to sing "I'll Get By."

Billy lit a Camel, but the sting of the smoke in his lungs caused him to cough hoarsely. He put it out and flipped it into the butt can near the door. Lying back on his pillow, he listened to Parrino's smooth baritone, the lyrics telling of that certain bittersweet joy and heartache between young lovers.

Suddenly, Billy could almost feel the leather grip of the Cord's steering wheel that morning when he drove Jordan across town to teach her to play tennis on his favorite court next to the ivy-covered wall. Parrino's voice became that of Dick Haymes on the car radio as they drove past the ancient white houses with their wide front porches, flower gardens, and broken sidewalks, with the pale sunlight flashing in the crowns of the live oaks.

Then they were walking onto the manicured grass of the tennis court, and Billy again saw Jordan gracefully moving around the court, losing himself in the sensual choreography of her movement. He drifted within a misty world of music, movement, and grace.

"All right, let's hit it! Move! Move! Move!" The lights glared down on cursing, coughing, scuffling men rising to an unwanted early dawn and dragged Billy from his dreams.

The battalion traveled a narrow dirt road through a pine forest. Somewhere ahead, through this primeval-looking growth, lay the boondocks. As the sun rose overhead, dust billowed up from the road in red clouds and settled onto their faces and their light green dungarees, now rapidly darkening as the sweat poured from their bodies. The clank and clatter of equipment and the roaring of jeep and truck engines shattered the silence of the woods.

Billy trudged along next to Marcell, his leather rifle sling creaking as if he were astride a saddle. "Wonder how far we got to go? I'm 'bout dead of thirst."

Marcell wiped the dust-reddened sweat from his forehead with the back of his hand. "They got to give us a break pretty quick. A camel couldn't make it much further."

Billy gazed at Dalton ahead of him, straining under the load of a mortar base plate, at the slight thickening around the stomach, absent from most of the younger men, and at the cross, gleaming on his collar. "Look at Granny," Billy coughed as a jeep sped by, smothering them with a red cloud. "Packin' that base plate just like one of the enlisted men when he could be ridin' in a jeep."

"He's pretty tough for a rabbi," Marcell mumbled through the dust. "Old too. He must be close to thirty."

"A rabbi's a Jew, Hero," Billy smiled. "If Granny was a Jew, he'd have a Star of David stuck in his collar, not a cross."

"You seen one preacher, you seen 'em all," Marcell mumbled, taking his helmet off and brushing the sweat from his soaked GI-cropped hair. "I'm waitin' for Granny to pass the hat any day now."

"Look!" "What's that?" several men in the front ranks asked over the clamor and clank of the battalion.

Billy could barely make out sunlight glinting on the surface of water and landing craft pulled up along the shoreline. He remembered they were called Higgins Boats. They had come to the Inland Waterway that curved and bent its way through the pine forests in this part of North Carolina.

"This is beautiful!" Spots took his helmet off, standing on the bank of the canal as sweat poured down his slim face. "It's like something out of a movie."

"It's gonna be a Frankenstein movie for you if you don't get in that boat!" one of the sergeants bellowed, walking up behind Spots. "Everbody get aboard!"

The Higgins Boats glided through the thick pine forests on the dark, mirrored surface of the canals. Birds sang in the treetops and flitted through the shadowed woods, flashing blue and red and yellow as the sunlight caught their wings. From a distance came the incessant rat-tat-tatting of a woodpecker as it hammered against the side of a lightning-struck pine.

"What's that sound?" Spots stood up, looking anxiously ahead through the thick underbrush.

The boatswain sat behind his wheel, a look of sadistic pleasure on his plump face. "Time to see what you're made of, Gyrene. You're about to meet the briny deep."

Minutes later, half the men in the boats were leaning over the gunwales, vomiting into the ocean as the boats wallowed in the deep troughs of the groundswell. The boats circled in the capping waves, awaiting the command to begin the initial amphibious training of the First Marine Division.

Billy turned his pale, wet face toward Marcell, who was wiping vomit from his mouth and nose with his shirt sleeve. "Hero, the

Japs can't be any worse than this. I believe I'd rather be shot than put up with this ocean much longer."

Marcell held to the gunwale of the churning boat with one hand, the other cradled his M-1. As he started to speak, his eyes went wide. Snatching off his helmet, he threw up in it.

At that moment, the boatswain gunned his engine, the boat flattening out as it picked up speed and headed for the beach. When the boat leveled out, the churning motion ceased, and looks of relief crossed the faces of the men.

"Down!" A sergeant yelled.

Billy crouched below the gunwale as the cold spray stung his face, the roar of the engines drowning out all sound as the boats fanned out into an assault line and hurtled toward the shore. Then came the scraping sound of the keel against the bottom.

"Up and over!"

The men lurched and stumbled out of the boat over the ramp that dropped down at the bow. Some fell under the weight of mortars, machine guns, and ammo boxes as they leaped into the shallow water. Then they were on the beach taking firing positions against an imaginary enemy dug in at the edge of the real woods. After the silent battle was over, they marched, sand sticking to their saltwater-soaked dungarees, to their new camp.

Billy saw that a glade had been formed in the woods by clearing away the underbrush. "This is great!" he commented cheerfully. "Someone actually did the work for us. Look at this camp! Reminds me of the boy scouts."

"Let's get our tent pitched before it rains." Marcell broke out his shelter half, fished Billy's half out of his pack, and began fitting them together.

Billy gazed upward at the dark wall of clouds moving in from the sea and at the jagged lightning, flickering across the sky like faulty wiring. "I'll get us some pine needles for a mattress."

When camp had been struck and the men had gotten hot chow from the pyramidal galley tent, they sat around under the trees eating and talking of training and of where they would be going at the end of the training. Then the storm hit with sheets of cold rain sweeping in from the sea and the wind bending the tops of the pines.

Lying on his dark green blanket with the sharp, clean scent of the pine needles filling the tent, Billy dug through his pack and found a letter that had arrived just before they left the base.

"Who's it from?" Marcell asked, blowing smoke rings at the tent's angled ceiling.

"Just Gloria." Billy slit the envelope with his bayonet, leaning back against his pack.

"*Just* Gloria! Sounds like a real exciting romance," Marcell grinned through the blue-white smoke.

"My parents *approve* of her *and* her family, don't you know," Billy trilled in a fake British accent. "Top drawer, bloody good sport, and all that rot."

Marcell turned on his side. "Well, she's good looking enough. I might approve of her."

"Trouble is, you approve of all of 'em. Always had any girl you ever wanted."

"Not quite."

Billy's eyes narrowed, as he stared at Marcell over his letter, his face clouding over.

"Don't look at me like that. We might as well clear the air right now. . . . I never intended to hurt Jordan Simms." Marcell took a final drag, stubbed out his cigarette, and lay back, watching the smoke clouds gathering in the peak of the tent. "Guess I just couldn't stand her because she never would give me the time of day. I thought if I had her alone for a few minutes, she wouldn't be able to resist me. But, somehow, my charm always seemed to escape her. I just figured there must be something wrong with her. No offense."

"Forget it. That was two and a half years ago." Billy unfolded his letter.

"Well, I heard you'd started dating her," Marcell said to the smoky ceiling.

Billy looked out at the rain plopping into puddles in the dim lantern glow of the camp. "Only a time or two. She's just another girl."

"That's what I hoped you say, partner," Marcell chuckled. "Love 'em and leave 'em."

Billy opened the letter and read it in the dim smokey light.

Dearest Billy,

I miss you terribly and think of you every day. When will this horrible war be over so you can come home and we can be together? I'm so tired of the same old college routine day after day. I can only have three gallons of gas a week for my car since rationing started. We usually meet down at the malt shop after classes and talk and play the jukebox. There's so many boys enlisting these days that getting a date is almost impossible. Of course I'm not interested in that anyway. If only you were here!

We went to see *Wake Island* last night with Brian Donlevy and William Bendix. I don't like war movies, but I just feel like I should see some since you're in the war and all. I also read *For Whom the Bell Tolls* and thought about you the whole time. There's a boy in it who reminds me so much of you, and he's in love with this girl, Maria, who's had a really bad time in the war. But the ending is so sad—well, I just can't think about it.

Oh, Billy, I'd just die if something happened to you. I had a long talk with Daddy the last time I went home. Oh, by the way, he's back in the Navy in Washington now and got promoted to admiral. Well, anyway, he says when you finish boot camp, he could get you into the Officers' Corps in the Marines—if that's what you want—or in the Navy. Daddy thinks the Navy would be best for you, and so do I. You'd be on a nice clean ship instead of walking around in that awful mud or sand or wherever it is they send you.

Now, Billy, when you finish your Marine camp and get home, we'll all get together and make plans for you to be an officer. Wouldn't that be nice? Daddy talked to the General, and he's all for it. Just between you and me, I think he'd rather you go to West Point, but I guess he's just about given up on that.

Here's a picture of me to put on your nightstand or dresser or whatever it is you have. I love you so much. I'll be waiting for you when you get home.

All my love,
Gloria

Billy folded the letter and put it away.

Marcell turned over, his back to Billy and mumbled sleepily, "She still love you?"

Billy ignored the question. "Didn't the sergeant say we'd get some liberty to go home before we shipped out?"

"Yeah. Three or four days," Marcell yawned. "Why?"

"I think I'm gonna use that time to see some of San Francisco. Who knows? I may never get another chance."

"I'm with you, buddy," Marcell murmured into his pillow.

* * *

Those Carolina spring days were filled to the brim with constant training provided free of charge by the U.S. Marine Corps. They also cut into the dream time with night exercises and guard duty. The men clambered up and down wooden structures draped with cargo nets and built to look like the side of a ship until their breaths came in ragged gasps and sweat poured in rivulets from their lean and hardening bodies.

The men in the Philippines had given the foxhole its name, and the Marine D.I.'s were determined to perfect it as an art form. Foxholes were dug, redug, and modified until the men could dig them in their sleep. Mired in boredom, they marched in blazing sunlight . . . in howling, drenching storms . . . in the midnights of those endless, glorious, innocent days of youth.

They endured the tedium of lectures and inspections and the fine points of military courtesy. They threw themselves mightily into their weaponry and the care and knowledge of their ordnance, knowing that this was as vital as any friendship. And they learned to sleep in wet blankets in the dripping forests or on the raw baked earth at the bottom of a shallow foxhole.

Then there were the nights off.

"Lets go find a juke joint." Marcell sat on a bed of pine needles staring up at a huge white moon rising out of the sea.

"I'm done in," Spots admitted, swallowing the last of the clear liquor from the bottle they had been passing around. "We spent so much time in them boats today, I can still feel the waves."

"A what?" Parrino sat up with interest, cleaning his black-framed glasses with a sock.

"Juke joint," Marcell repeated. "You'd call it a bar or a tavern up in Chicago."

"Well, what're we waiting for?" Parrino said eagerly, getting to his feet. "Where is it?"

"There's one about a mile down that dirt road out on the highway." Billy looked up from his dog-eared copy of *You Can't Go Home Again.* "It's called The Red Horse Saloon."

Parrino was elated. "I like the sound of it. Might be a pretty nice place."

Ten minutes later Billy, Marcell, and Parrino stood at the intersection where the dirt road led out of the pine forest onto the highway. Across the highway, thick with cars and pickups and military vehicles, their horns blaring and lights glaring, stood the Red Horse Saloon.

Parrino's face dropped. "It's awful!"

"I love it!" Marcell beamed.

The Red Horse stood in a rutted, dusty parking lot that had been part of an open field six months before. Constructed of tarpaper-covered sheets of plywood and a tin roof, it was surrounded by a barbed wire fence on three sides to keep the cattle away from the paying customers. Camel, Lucky Strike, and Pabst Blue Ribbon signs were plastered over the front of the building and completed the decor.

With Marcell leading, they threaded their way through the rushing traffic and parked cars, entering the open doorway of the Red Horse. Three men in white shirts with their sleeves rolled up tended the long bar that ran the length of the opposite wall. Crude wooden tables crowded with sailors and marines were scattered about on an uneven plank floor. To the left, a jukebox glowed softly, with Helen Forrest trying to make herself heard above the clamor as she sang "I Had the Craziest Dream."

"There ain't a woman in the place!" Marcell moaned loudly, gazing about at the bedlam.

"Maybe not, but there's plenty of booze. And not that rot gut we've been drinking either." Parrino straightened his shoulders and swaggered through the maze of tables to the bar.

"Better'n nothin', I reckon," Marcell remarked, his bulk dwarfing Parrino as he followed him.

They stood at the bar drinking bourbon and chasing it with tall, brown bottles of beer. The biggest sailor Billy had ever seen pushed his way to the bar and crowded against Parrino who stood on the other side of Marcell. Wearing his dress whites, the man looked like a small whitewashed house wearing a sailor cap. He stood at least six feet, five inches, and, with his considerable paunch, weighed close to three hundred pounds.

"Gimme a water glass and a bottle of whiskey," the sailor growled at the closest bartender.

Billy smelled trouble in the air like the sharp scent before a storm. He looked over his shoulder at the table of five sailors where the giant had been sitting. *Please, keep your mouth shut, Marcell! Just this one time.*

The giant sailor reached for the mangled cigar in his mouth, bumping Parrino with his elbow and causing him to spill his beer. "You know, you look a lot like Groucho Marx," he rumbled down at Parrino, "except you're a lot uglier."

Glenn Miller's "In the Mood" began playing on the jukebox.

Marcell knocked off his shot of bourbon, lit a Camel, and tossed the box of matches on the bar in front of the giant. Leaning forward, he smiled sweetly into the sailor's face. "How'd you like to carry your teeth around in that match box, Lard Belly?"

At six feet and two hundred pounds, Marcell was by no means the biggest in their company of 180 men, but after the first punch anyone threw at him, he was never challenged again. Almost as quick as Billy, who was an inch taller and weighed thirty pounds less, Marcell had never been truly tested, but then he had never faced a Goliath like this before (nor did he have a word from God or a slingshot and five smooth stones).

Billy saw the sailor's eyes go flat and dark. His face giving nothing away, the huge man flung Parrino onto a nearby table with his right arm, throwing a left straight at Marcell's face in almost the same motion. Marcell ducked as the man's massive fist caught him a glancing blow just at the hairline, knocking him ten feet backward, where he landed in a heap on the floor.

As the brute rushed in for the kill, a blur of rolling motion from the floor left Marcell crouched, knees bent slightly, legs spread just enough for balance directly in front of the astonished sailor. It was too late for him to stop the charge! A look of disbelief crossed the man's face as Marcell exploded from his crouched position, his right fist crashing into the sailor's open mouth. The sound was sickening. The sailor's lips came apart in a splatter of blood and teeth popped loose from the gums with the noise of snapping twigs.

Billy watched the force of Marcell's blow actually lift the sailor from the floor as he crashed onto the rough planks, lying as motionless as a corpse. Marcell stood over the man, a black gleam in his eyes as though he were about to draw a sword and behead his fallen enemy. Then the five sailors from the giant's table moved across the saloon toward the three marines in their salt-encrusted, faded dungarees. Billy downed his shot glass of whiskey and turned to face them.

* * *

"I don't know why he made such a fuss," Marcell complained, stanching the flow of blood from his left eye with a sock. "He can have another wall built on the front of his joint for practically nothing. It ain't like we tore up the Stork Club."

Billy trudged along the dirt road through the pine forest, supporting Parrino, whose eyes were almost swollen shut. "Well, I hope he don't find out what company we're in. I ain't interested in spending my liberty in the brig."

A week later the three friends sat in a dining car as a train rattled along over the trestle spanning the Royal Gorge. Far below them, the Colorado River leaped and tumbled in a reddish-white froth on its way to the Grand Canyon.

"It's all downhill now," Parrino remarked, peering down at the rushing torrent. "Yamamoto might as well pack up his chopsticks and head back to Japan after what we did to him at Midway."

Billy cut into his steak, savoring it as he talked with his mouth full. "There might still be a little fightin' left to do."

"You're right, Irish." (Marcell's new name for Parrino since he learned that the Chicagoan's mother was Irish.) "Them Japs won't be so cocky now." Marcell agreed, sipping a little bootleg mash he had smuggled onto the train. "Those Marine pilots sure blew their carriers out of the water."

"I think the Navy pilots helped a little," Billy mumbled through the steak.

"Maybe so," Marcell suggested with a sigh, feeling the liquor go down. "Don't really matter. The Japs are short four aircraft carriers and a lot of other ships. We'll run 'em clear back to Tokyo now."

A shadow crossed Parrino's face. "You know, the sergeant said those islands in the South Pacific are just swarming with Japs. You think we'll have to take them all?"

Billy laughed, reaching for Marcell's whiskey. "I don't think so, Irish. We might leave one or two for the Army."

San Francisco was a three-day blur of Chinatown bars and jukeboxes playing Tommy Dorsey and Harry James tunes.

The morning their ship left for the South Pacific, Billy stood on the fantail gazing upward at the burnished span of the bridge gleaming in the sunlight. He wondered how many men would pass under the Golden Gate on their way to the war and how many would return.

11

MELBOURNE

A stadium! They're gonna bed us down in a stadium?" Parrino marched along in front of Billy into the Melbourne Cricket Stadium. "Is this any way to run a war?"

Billy glanced about him at the huge horseshoe-shaped structure that surrounded a circular field of grass. The seats had been taken out and bunk beds stood row upon row to the top of the stadium where a high roof partially overhung it, providing some protection from the elements. "Well, it's right in the middle of town. We could be stuck way out in the boonies like the others."

Parrino gave Billy a thoughtful glance, then broke into a grin. "You could be onto something there, Mary. I just may quit complaining for an hour or two."

After cleaning up in the stadium bathrooms, the men wasted no time in hitting the town. As Australia had been fighting in Northern Africa and Malaysia for two years, there was a distinct shortage of young single males in the city, and the men of the First Marine Division did their best to assuage the loneliness of the "sheilas," the Australian counterpart of babe, chick, dame, and bobbysoxer.

After such close proximity to so many men on the long voyage, Billy decided to take off on his own that first night. Feeling a need for the open air, he strolled through Yarra Park, which surrounded the cricket grounds. Coming to a lake, he strolled along its shore under a sky he had never seen before, a sky stretched like a black velvet curtain above the underside of the world.

A few marines had found their sheilas already and were walking hand in hand along the cinder paths or across the grassy areas on the way to a pub or a restaurant or a more private rendezvous.

Finding a bench under a gum tree, leafless now in the June of the Australian winter, Billy sat down and breathed in the sharp, fresh air. The lake stretched before him like a dark mirror, glimmering with the cold, tiny flames of the stars as they gathered around the bright moon.

An unexpected sadness settled over Billy as, for the first time in months, he found himself alone. No growling, cursing sergeants. No half-drunk friends with too much life in them and too little time to spend it. It hit him with an almost physical impact just how very far away Liberty, Georgia was from this strange land that provided only a temporary reprieve from the battles that would soon take place on the beaches, in the steaming jungles, and most of all in the hearts and minds of the men of the First Marine Division.

The first pangs of homesickness hit Billy so hard he felt he could not bear it. He folded his arms over his chest, leaning forward as he gazed out over the star-bright lake. Movement to his left caused him to look at the shoreline where a young woman knelt next to the water. She appeared to be throwing something into the water. Just then, three ducks paddled toward her, barely visible in the dim park lights.

Billy couldn't take his eyes from the girl and, after a few minutes, she stood and walked in the opposite direction along the water's edge. Watching her graceful movements, a sudden picture leaped into his mind. He saw sunlight flashing in a cloud of blonde hair as Jordan Simms glided across the grass surface of the tennis court, the short white skirt bouncing about her legs.

Without realizing it, Billy sprang from the bench and raced along the shoreline toward the girl. Slowing to a walk, he called out, "Jordan . . . Jordan Simms!"

Jordan whirled around at the sound of Billy's voice and stood transfixed at the water's edge. "Billy! Is it really you?"

Billy felt the heavy sadness lift from his heart and vanish somewhere beyond the light. He hurried toward Jordan, feeling a joy and lightness in his whole being.

"What are you doing here!" they both exclaimed simultaneously, then they were in each other's arms, embracing, laughing.

Stepping back, Billy held Jordan at arms' length, unable to stop grinning. "You first."

Jordan took a breath, her left hand resting lightly on her breast. "Well, I joined the Navy. They sent me to San Diego for a few weeks' training, and here I am . . . a Navy nurse!"

"You really do something for that uniform!" Billy smiled. "Almost makes me want to transfer to the Navy."

Jordan blushed, glancing away across the lake. "I heard you joined the Marines."

"Yeah," Billy boasted. "If you're gonna fight a war, might as well do it with the best in the business."

"It's so good to see you, Billy!" Jordan beamed. "This is such a coincidence!"

"Well, it looks like half of Melbourne is American. By the time MacArthur gets ready to invade the islands up north, half of Liberty might be down here." *I believe she's the prettiest girl I've ever seen. Maybe it's just being around a bunch of ugly Marines so long.* "How about a drink?"

"I, I don't drink, Billy." Jordan brightened, "But they have places called milk bars here. You can get ice cream and malts."

"Well, OK," Billy mumbled. "I just hope nobody from the company sees me in a *milk* bar."

A short walk from the park and they were in a district of small neighborhood businesses. Billy gazed up at the neon sign above the plate glass window. "Well, the sign says Alfie's, but it kinda reminds me of Ollie's back home."

Inside, they sat at a booth, drinking chocolate malts and listening to "Boogie Woogie" by Jimmy Dorsey.

"You know, it's been so long since I've had a malt, I forgot how good they are," Billy smiled, chocolate froth coating the end of his nose as he sat the glass down.

Jordan glanced at him and laughed softly.

"What's the matter?"

"Here, lean over," she smiled, using her napkin to wipe the ice cream from his nose. "You look more like a little boy than a big, bad Marine. Reminds me of all those years we went to school together."

Billy blushed slightly. "We've known each other for a long time, haven't we? Strange we'd get together like this on the other side of the world."

"Maybe not so strange," Jordan mused.

"What do mean?"

She looked into Billy's eyes, a darker blue than her own. "There were so many things that kept us apart in that little town. Down here we're both on our own."

Artie Shaw's "Stardust" came on the jukebox as Jordan and Billy talked of what had happened in their lives during the last six months and of the upcoming invasion somewhere to the north.

"Well, I have to be going," Jordan finally said.

"How 'bout us gettin' together tomorrow," Billy said quickly.

"It's Sunday. I always go to church."

Billy narrowed his eyes in thought. "I've got it! Sam's preachin' in the park near the stadium. We can go there if you want. It'll be short and we can have the rest of the day together."

"Who's Sam?" Jordan asked, sliding out of the booth.

"He's our chaplain." Billy took Jordan's arm and walked her toward the front door. "He's not like most chaplains. Usually the only time you see 'em, they're hanging around the headquarters tent or ridin' by in a jeep. Sam's one of the guys. Toughs it out just like we do."

"Sounds like a fine man," Jordan remarked as they walked along the busy street.

"Only chaplain I know that the men respect," Billy added, taking Jordan's hand in his. "You'll go then?"

Jordan felt the gentle pressure from Billy's hand. "Sure. I couldn't say no to a man who's fighting for the world's freedom, could I?"

*   *   *

'Twas grace that taught my heart to fear
And grace my fears relieved
How precious did that grace appear
The hour I first believed

Jordan and Billy stood side by side on the grass in a grove of eucalyptus trees near the Cricket Stadium. A gathering of about twenty Marines had showed up to hear Sam Dalton preach. As they sang the last verse, Billy didn't join in, listening, enraptured, to Jordan's rich, clear alto.

"You've got a beautiful voice," Billy whispered as the song ended. "Did you take lessons?"

Jordan leaned close to him. "Yes. In that little white church of Wash's on Sunday mornings."

Dalton opened his brown leather Bible that lay on a crudely built wooden pulpit. Looking over his small flock he began to speak in a soft voice that somehow carried well beyond them. "This is a time of darkness in the world, and I fear my friends that greater darkness is yet to come. America has sent us to this land to battle the forces of oppression, to make an end to those who would take away the freedom of the peoples of this world. At the end of the service I'll pray for each of you, that God will give His angels charge over you to protect you, but now I want to speak of a different kind of battle.

"In Ephesians six, verse twelve, Paul writes: 'For we wrestle not against flesh and blood, but against principalities, against powers, against the rulers of the darkness of this world, against spiritual wickedness in high places.' There is a battle going on for the souls of mankind that is being fought on a spiritual battleground and the stakes are eternal."

As the winter sun climbed a cloudless sky, Dalton walked about the grove, speaking almost conversationally to the men who had settled themselves on the dry grass under the trees. He used Scripture after Scripture to illustrate how the powers of sin and darkness brought spiritual death and eternal separation from God.

"I've painted a pretty bleak picture for you, haven't I?" Dalton said solemnly, nearing the end of his message. Then his face brightened like the sun rising out of the sea. "But praise God, the *final* victory is ours! And that victory is in Jesus Christ! He came into the world 'to give light to them that sit in darkness and in the shadow of death.' He is our only hope, but—*Glory to God!*—He is enough!

"Salvation is a gift from God. You have only to reach out and receive it." Dalton quickly turned the pages of his Bible. "Again in Ephesians we read, 'For by grace are ye saved, through faith, and that not of yourselves: it is the *gift* of God.'"

Dalton closed his Bible and stood before the small gathering under the trees. "'That is, the word of faith, which we preach; That if thou shalt confess with thy mouth the Lord Jesus and shalt believe in thine heart that God hath raised him from the dead, thou *shalt* be saved.' Jesus said, 'Him that cometh to me I will in no wise cast out.'

"I've done my best to give you the gospel. The Holy Spirit will have to do the rest. Any of you who want to accept Jesus Christ as your Savior can come forward and do it right now."

As if it were planned, Jordan began to sing, "'Softly and tenderly Jesus is calling, calling for you and for me . . .'"

Billy thought that he had never heard anyone sing so sweetly. He glanced at Dalton, holding his Bible against his chest, head bowed in prayer. Billy sensed a battle raging inside himself. The song continued and, as he began to take the first step across the glade, he felt a wall of darkness come against him like a solid, living thing. He trembled, feeling drops of sweat trickling down his face in spite of the coolness of the morning.

As Jordan sang the last verse of the song, Billy watched a short, stocky Marine with straight black hair walk across the glade. He began to speak as Dalton placed his hand on the man's shoulder and leaned forward to listen. After he had prayed with the man, Dalton turned him toward the group, placing his arm around his shoulder.

"This is Billy Nightwolf and he just got saved." There were a few "Praise God's" and "Hallelujahs," and several of the men clapped their hands.

When Nightwolf had returned to his place, greeted by a few hugs and handshakes, Dalton again opened his Bible and laid it on the pulpit. "'I will say of the Lord, He is my refuge and my fortress: my God; in him will I trust. . . . Thou shalt not be afraid for the terror by night; nor for the arrow that flieth by day; . . . A thousand shall fall at thy right hand; but it shall not come nigh thee. . . . For He shall give his angels charge over thee, to keep thee in all thy ways.'

"I'd like to pray for each of you now if you'll come forward," Dalton said, extending his arms toward the men.

As they lined up, Dalton placed his hands on each of them in turn, praying for their safety.

"Come with me, Billy," Jordan urged, taking him by the arm.

Billy looked around for an escape route out of the glade. "I don't know, Jordan. We never did anything like this in our church back home."

"Come on. There's nothing to be afraid of."

"Afraid?" Billy protested. "I'm not afraid!" He took Jordan by the arm and led her to the back of the line.

Billy stood with his head bowed, as he had seen Jordan do, while Dalton put both hands on his head and prayed, crying out to God to protect him and keep him safe. Billy could not understand it, but he felt something happening to him as Dalton prayed. He could almost feel a powerful current run through his body from Dalton's hands, and it frightened him, but he resolved firmly within himself that he wouldn't say anything about it.

"You've got a beautiful singing voice," Dalton complimented Jordan after Billy had introduced the two of them. "You must have had a lot of training."

Jordan smiled, glancing at Billy. "No, but I did sing at a little church back home."

Billy could see that Dalton and Jordan hit it off right from the start, and it began to irritate him in spite of his respect for his chaplain's unique qualities. "You 'bout ready to go, Jordan? I'm gettin' hungry."

"Would you like to have lunch with us, Sam?" Jordan beamed. "I'm sure Billy wouldn't mind—would you, Billy?"

"Uh, no, I guess not."

Sam shook his head. "No, it would be an imposition. You young people go ahead and have fun."

"You heard what he said, Jordan." Billy grabbed her by the arm, leading her out of the glade.

"Now, Sam," Jordan insisted, "you've got to come with us or we'll both be insulted. Isn't that right, Billy?"

"Uh, yeah, Sam."

The three of them stopped at a kiosk near the lake and bought meat pies and dishes of "icy cream," eating on a bench while they watched the "Yanks" parade through the park with their newly found girlfriends. Then they visited Captain Cook's cottage in Fitzroy Gardens. The house had been dismantled in England, shipped to Melbourne and reconstructed in the park. Lastly, they made the trip out to Phillip Island, a natural zoo for a large colony of koalas.

After Sam had taken his leave, Billy walked Jordan back to the hotel where most of the nurses were being quartered, which turned out to be fairly close to the stadium. From across the street, Billy could see that the dimly lighted lobby was crowded with men of all branches of the service. They were either dropping off or picking up their dates for the night. The window of the hotel bar was slightly ajar, and they could hear the unmistakable voice of Dick Haymes singing "I'll Get By."

"You don't have to go in just yet, do you?" Billy took Jordan's hand, sitting on a bench just off the sidewalk under a huge oak.

Jordan sat down stiffly. "I really should. There's so much work to be done tomorrow."

"Beautiful song, isn't it?" Billy slipped his arm around Jordan's shoulders.

She eased a few inches down the bench. "It sure is. Remember the day you gave me the tennis lesson? It was playing on the car radio when we were driving to the club."

"I remember."

The music drifted faintly to them from across the street. Billy placed his left hand softly against the curve of Jordan's face and turned her toward him, kissing her firmly on the lips.

Jordan pulled away quickly, standing up from the bench. "Don't do that!"

"We've known each other all our lives!" Billy was furious as he got to his feet. "I'm not gonna hurt you! It's a natural thing to do. What's wrong with you?"

Jordan clutched herself with both arms, turning away. "I don't know! . . . Nothing! . . . I have to go now." But she hurried across the street and disappeared into the hotel lobby without looking back.

Well, that's it for me. Fightin' a war oughta be enough, but I gotta hook up with some nutty girl on top of that! As Billy stormed down the street he failed to notice the sheilas giving him the eye. What he saw was a cascade of blonde hair and deep blue eyes that held some meaning he desperately needed.

The next morning Billy sat in the lobby of Jordan's hotel, waiting to take her to an early breakfast. He saw Jordan every night that week except one, when he pulled guard duty. On Saturday night she kissed him very tenderly on the lips in the hotel lobby. *I believe the glacier is melting a little around the edges,* he thought as he leaped happily over all five steps of the hotel entrance onto the sidewalk.

* * *

"Are you sure this girl's good lookin'?" Billy sat on his bunk in the mildly cold morning air, shining his shoes. He enjoyed sleeping in the open stadium under the star-crowded sky, but he hadn't adjusted to having winter in July.

"You think Dorothy Lamour's good lookin'? You think Hedy Lamarr's good lookin'?" Marcell looked in a mirror he had hung from the top rail of his bunk, combing his glossy black hair.

"That doesn't answer my question, Marcell."

Marcell slipped his comb into the waistband of his pocketless dress blue trousers. "She's pretty, Billy boy. She's pretty."

"Where we goin'?"

"I thought we'd slip on down to the beach at St. Kilda. There's hardly anyone there this time of year and," Marcell winked at Billy with a licentious smile, "there's plenty of cheap hotel rooms."

"I don't know, Marcell," Billy mumbled, gazing out over the expanse of winter grass far below on the stadium floor, toward the ocean sparkling in the blue distance. "I keep thinking about that 'beauty' you fixed me up with in high school for the homecoming dance. Of course it was real easy to find her in the gym after the game—'cause everybody around her had turned to stone."

Marcell chuckled, remembering the look on Billy's face in the gym that night which seemed like a hundred years ago. "Well, if you'd rather go to the chaplain's preachin' with your little Eskimo, Jordan Simms, that's fine with me."

Billy remembered the spiritual storm that had ripped through him the previous Sunday. "No thanks. One of Granny's sermons'll do me for a long time."

"Tell me something, Billy boy," Marcell frowned solemnly, suppressing a grin. "When you take Jordan back to the hotel, do ya'll shake hands or just rub noses?"

Billy threw a shoe at him.

At that moment, Jordan was walking along the Sunday-quiet streets of Melbourne toward the glade where Sam Dalton conducted his services.

"I'm so glad you could make it, Jordan," Sam greeted her warmly. "Where's Billy?"

"I have no idea," Jordan shrugged, clutching her Bible with both hands. "I expected him to pick me up this morning, but maybe he had guard duty or something."

Sam asked Jordan to lead the singing, and when the service was over they walked to the railway station to hire a horse and carriage. Soon they were clattering along the streets to have lunch at one of the restaurants on the Yarra River that ran through the center of town. A band of five or six Marines, disheveled and still half-drunk after their night on the town, paraded by them along the sidewalk, singing. Lifting their bottles high, they made up in volume what they lacked in harmony. "You'll come a-waltzing, Matilda with me . . ."

"That's an Australian song," Jordan remarked. "Why don't they sing an American song?"

Dalton smiled as he watched the Marines unconsciously keep in step to the beat of the song, their left foot striking the ground harder than their right. "The war's still young for us, Jordan. We don't have our own marching songs yet. Lyrics like, 'Just to show all those Japs, the Yanks are no saps,' or 'I threw a kiss in the ocean' don't exactly rouse the fighting spirit of the troops."

"I never thought of it that way," Jordan laughed. "There are some pretty love songs though."

"There sure are," Dalton agreed, feeling a kind of warmth at the sound of Jordan's musical laughter. "Songs like 'I'll Be Seeing You' and 'You Made Me Love You.'"

"And 'I'll Get By,'" Jordan added. "But they were all written before the war."

After lunch, they visited the botanical gardens along the Yarra and then caught a tram back to Jordan's hotel. They walked across the crowded lobby to the elevator, feeling the sense of urgency that seemed to permeate the entire city, a collective urgency born of war that made every moment something to treasure, for every parting could be that dreaded and final farewell.

"Jordan, are you sure Billy won't mind my seeing you like this?" Dalton shifted about uneasily on the carpet.

"Why should he?" Jordan answered cryptically. "He's never been serious with me. We're just hometown friends."

"Well, I have this idea. There's a resort area north of here in the Victorian Alps. It's only an hour away, and I thought we might drive up one day and spent the night at the lodge—separate rooms of course. I hear the scenery's beautiful." Dalton smiled nervously, his gold-rimmed glasses glinting in the dim light from the elevator.

"I'll have to think about it," Jordan mused. "No, I *don't* have to think about it at all. They can spare me for two days. Let's go tomorrow. Can you get off?"

Dalton's face seemed to light up the dim hallway where they stood. "As you can see, my services aren't exactly standing room only. There aren't a whole lot of the men looking for spiritual guidance while they're on the loose in Melbourne. I expect my work will pick up when the shooting starts, but right now it's just plowing through paperwork that really isn't important."

Jordan laughed softly. "Sam, I'm not your commanding officer. You don't have to convince me."

"I, I see what you mean," Dalton stammered.

"Sam?"

"Yes?"

"You never did answer my question."

"Oh, that's right, I didn't. Yes, Jordan, I *can* get off."

The next morning they drove into the Victorian Alps north of Melbourne in a jeep Sam had borrowed from the motor pool. They stayed at a lodge in a small valley at the bottom of a ski slope. The first day they tried skiing, walked the hiking trails through the eucalyptus forests that covered the mountainside, and sat before a roaring fire that night drinking hot chocolate.

"It's been such a lovely day, Sam. Thank you so much." Jordan sat next to him on a huge sofa before the stone fireplace, the flickering firelight dancing in the clear depths of her eyes.

Sam took Jordan's hand in his, feeling her tremble slightly. "Are you comfortable being with me, Jordan?"

Jordan turned quickly toward him. "Yes. Of course! Why do you ask?"

Drawing his right leg up on the sofa, Sam faced Jordan with a look of concern on his face. "It's just that in these last two days I've noticed you seem, well, almost afraid every time I touch you. Even now, holding your hand."

Jordan gazed out the tall window where the moonlight poured like spun silver down the mountainside, giving it an almost lunar quality. She felt the pangs of betrayal flooding over her from the lost, dark years of her childhood. "It's—it's not you, Sam. I . . ." Jordan glanced at him and slipped her hand out of his.

"Jordan, I'm a man who has come to care for you a great deal in this very short time," Dalton said softly. "But I'm also a pastor, and I've done my share of ministering to those who have been bruised."

Jordan remembered hearing the phrase long ago in the little clapboard church that sat in the field next to Annie's, *To set at liberty them that are bruised.*

"From what you've told me of yourself, I gather your childhood was a difficult one. You've been hurt very badly by someone—maybe more than one."

Jordan stared into the flames.

"Look at me, Jordan." Sam gazed into Jordan's eyes, seeing the sadness and the pain . . . and something even deeper. "You believe the blood of Jesus Christ has the power of salvation, the power to give us eternal life, don't you?"

Jordan had a puzzled expression on her face. "Why, yes, of course. I'm a Christian!"

"Well, then, you should also know that it has the power to *heal.* And not only blind eyes and crippled bodies, but emotional wounds too. In that beautiful fifty-third chapter of Isaiah it says, 'By his stripes we are healed.'" Sam held Jordan with his eyes. "That's what Jesus meant when he said, 'he hath sent me to heal the brokenhearted . . . to set at liberty them that are bruised.'"

Jordan's eyes were bright with the beginning of tears. "But you don't know what he did to me!" She looked quickly around the huge room, embarrassed at her outburst.

"Don't worry, there's no one around except the night clerk," Sam said, pointing to the reception desk a hundred feet away. "*Whoever* hurt you, you *have* to forgive them, Jordan."

"My *father!*" Jordan blurted out before she could stop herself. Then the tears came and she put her head in her hands, her body wracked with sobs.

This was the thing that Jordan couldn't face, the thing that had driven her away from any man who took more than a casual interest in her. She had buried it deeply within herself, but it had found itself in fertile soil. Untended, it had grown monstrous—this saurian shape in the dark—with a lethal, insidious intent.

Jordan struggled up from the plush sofa, hurrying almost blindly across the slate floor to the fireplace. She couldn't speak the unspeakable, couldn't talk to anyone about this. *How could anyone understand that my own father—Oh, Jesus! I'm so tired of being this way! Please take this terrible thing out of my life! Jesus—help me!* Jordan wept as the flames crackled softly in the fireplace.

Sam knew that the battle had reached a decisive moment for Jordan, and he knew that the only one who could help Jordan at this time was the Lord. He prayed that His Spirit would find Jordan reaching for His help now and find the healing she needed.

The night clerk noticed the woman crying at the fireplace and thought, *Another wartime separation. Happens every night.*

Gradually, the weeping abated. Jordan returned to the sofa and wiped her tears away with the handkerchief Sam offered. She told him in subdued tones, broken by more tears, of how her father had abused and abandoned her. "I know now that I've hated him all these years."

Sam took both of Jordan's hands in his own. "You've got to forgive him, Jordan, then the healing can begin. Like salvation—it takes place in the heart."

Jordan bowed her head, asking God to forgive her of her hatred for her father. As she let go of the bitterness, forgiving him for all that he had done to her, she felt the terrible burden of the years lifting—felt the hatred dissipating like a vapor—truly felt the healing begin in her heart.

* * *

Billy sat in a brown leather wing chair in a remote corner of the hotel lobby. He had spent a great deal of time waiting in this lobby over the past two days, smoking one cigarette after the other, reading a newspaper or simply dozing. Mostly he thought of Jordan, of where she could be for two whole days. He tried not to think of the day and night he had spent at St. Kilda's beach with Marcell and the two sheilas.

Finally, just after 9:00 P.M. of the second day, Billy's patience was rewarded. He watched Jordan and Sam Dalton walk hand-in-hand across the crowded lobby to the elevator. Jordan took her overnight bag from Dalton as they spoke briefly *and intimately,* Billy thought.

Then she kissed him on the lips and turned to enter the elevator as he strode happily across the lobby and out the door.

Billy slammed his newspaper on the floor. Hurrying over to the stairs, he took them two at a time and assumed a position in front of Jordan's room on the third floor as she left the elevator.

"Billy, what in the world are you doing here?" Jordan dropped her bag on the floor next to her door, fumbling in her purse for the key.

"Where have *you* been for two days?" Billy almost shouted before he could stop himself. Embarrassed, he continued with forced control. "I don't have to ask *who* you were with. I assume you and the *chaplain* were discussing some particularly stimulating points of theology."

Jordan glanced at Billy, her eyes blazing. "*What* I do and *who* I see is none of your business, Billy Christmas. You didn't bother showing up at *all* Sunday."

Billy had lost ground, but he tried to fight his way back into the battle. "Oh, yeah!" *Great retort, Billy. You'll be drooling and wetting your pants next.* He stood in the hallway, breathing as though he had played a hard-fought set of tennis.

"Is there anything else?" Jordan asked calmly. "Or am I allowed to go to bed now?"

"What's that thing on your bed?" he asked, pointing to the tattered Raggedy Ann doll that rested on the pillow.

"A doll," Jordan explained as if to a child.

"Oh, well."

"Are you finished now?"

Billy cleared his throat, taking a deep breath. "I'm sorry. I shouldn't have acted like that."

Jordan's face relaxed in a smile. "He's a fine man, Billy. He was so worried that you would be upset, but I assured him that we were just old hometown friends. I was right, wasn't I?"

"Well, I just, uh . . ."

Jordan took Billy's face in her hands and kissed him deeply and firmly on the mouth. "Good night, Billy" she said sweetly, enjoying the expression of total bewilderment on his face. "Call me tomorrow."

Billy stood rooted to the spot, his mouth slightly open for several seconds. Then he shook his head and came out of it. "Yeah," he mumbled to himself as he half-stumbled down the stairs. "That's a good idea. I'll call you tomorrow."

Jordan thoroughly enjoyed her two suitors for an entire week. She realized, however, that she could only care for Dalton as a friend. Finally, when she told him after church, she was deeply saddened to see the pain in his eyes.

"I'll never be able to repay you for what you've done for me," Jordan said as they walked by the river.

Sam stopped, watching a black swan glide over the surface of the Yarra. Holding to her hand, he leaned over and kissed her on the cheek. "You're a treasure, Jordan Simms," he smiled as they continued along the edge of the wind-rippled water.

Three days later, Jordan awakened at four o'clock in the morning to a loud pounding on her door. Trying to rub the last of the heavy sleep from her face, she put on a robe and opened the door.

Billy stood there out of breath, his pack on his back and M-1 slung over his shoulder. "I had to see you! We're pullin' out!"

"I, I don't understand," Jordan mumbled, still half-asleep. "Pulling out for where?"

Stepping into the room, Billy shut the door. "I don't know where. We just got the word two hours ago. But the scuttlebutt is the invasion's on—the Solomons. The whole stadium's like a madhouse. Marines everywhere heading out for the docks!"

"Oh, Billy, you can't be leaving like this!" Jordan was abruptly and completely awake. "We, we've just begun to know each other."

Billy dropped his rifle on the bed, taking Jordan in his arms and embracing her with a breathless urgency. She held him tightly around his waist, feeling the rough straps and buckles pressing against her.

"Jordan, I don't know how long we'll be gone," Billy said solemnly as he stepped back, holding her by the shoulders. "This war may last for years. I don't even know myself anymore. It seems like the whole world is racing toward some terrible end. All I know is that I had to see you one more time before I left."

Tears brightened Jordan's deep blue eyes. "I can't stand to see you leave this way, Billy. We need more time. We just haven't had enough time *together*. It's not *fair!*"

Billy pulled Jordan close, kissing her with a compelling desire to draw the moment out, to make it last for years, or to compress years of living into this solitary moment, as he clung desperately to Jordan, realizing for the first time how very much he loved her. "I've got to go," he breathed hoarsely.

"No! Not yet!" Jordan held him tightly, pressing her face against his chest.

Embracing her once more, Billy pulled away. "I have to! There's no more time!" He grabbed his M-1 from the bed.

"Billy! Billy!" Jordan took his face in her hands, kissing him with a fierce and final passion.

Billy looked deeply into her eyes once more as if trying to print her image inside him, as a keepsake to take off to war, then he spun and left the room.

Jordan stood in the doorway, calling out, "I'll pray for you every day, Billy." But all she heard was the thundering of his boots down the stairwell.

Part 3

12

THE ASH DUMPS OF HELL

*A*t seven o'clock, August 7, 1942, Billy stepped through the open hatch onto the deck of the ship that had brought them to the Solomons. In the murky dawn, he saw only a few small fires glowing along the slow curve of Lunga Bay. From below decks, the sound of the bombardment had led him to believe that the whole island would be engulfed in flames. But Guadalcanal awaited them intact, its scattered fires flickering and smoldering in the gray morning like the ash dumps of hell.

Billy stood next to Marcell, with the grinning specter of death that prowled the beaches and lurked in the jungles binding them together as brothers. The bombardment had begun to lift now. From behind them, across Sealark Channel, they heard the sharp crackling of small arms fire as the Marine Raiders engaged the enemy on Tulagi and Gavutu Islands.

"Third platoon! Over the side!" the sergeant barked. "Git down them nets!"

Rolling in the tidal swells, the ship seemed to be in league with the enemy as it added another peril to the landing. Billy clung to the cargo net, snaking down it as it swayed in and out, banging him against the side of the ship. As he clutched the swinging net, his rifle muzzle bumped his helmet, knocking it forward over his eyes. Pushing the helmet back from his face, he saw below him the Higgins Boats wallowing in the slate-blue troughs of the channel.

The cargo nets ended three feet above the Higgins Boats. Billy tried to time his jump so that he would land inside the boat as it rolled toward the ship, clanging against its steel hull. A missed jump would tumble him between the boat and the side of the ship where he would be crushed or drowned. With other Marines descending on him like circus monkeys, one even tromping on his hand, he leaped. Stumbling under fifty pounds of equipment, he hit the deck clumsily, but he had survived the first obstacle. Now, all he had left to face were a few thousand Japanese and a million bullets.

Holding to the gunwale, Billy looked around him. Sealark Channel was thronged with American vessels. Higgins Boats flocked to the mother ships. Marines scrambled down the nets into them as they moved out into the continuous circling patterns with the others. Then the command came and the boats fanned out into attack line.

"Down!"

Billy ducked below the gunwales, feeling the boat swing around with the others until it pointed toward the shore. The engine revved up, the hull vibrating with its power as they roared toward the beaches of Guadalcanal.

The assault had begun. It marked the beginning of the first major American offensive in the Pacific.

The salt spray stung Billy's face as he crouched below the gunwales of the boat, lost in the metallic growl of the engine. He had prayed the night before for God to keep them all safe, to help his family, to let him see Jordan again. And he tried to pray now, but all he could think of was the beach and what waited for him there.

Billy could see himself flung across the sand among dozens of shattered and bleeding bodies, firing blindly at the groves where the Japs were ripping them to pieces with the intensity of their fire. He prayed he would make it to the towering palms where there would be cover. Every muscle tensing with an animal-like fear, he listened for the plop of mortars, the chattering of the light Japanese machine guns. *Oh, God, don't let me die in the water, sloshing around like so much garbage! Please, let me make it to the trees!*

The hull of the boat abruptly crunched on the sandy bottom, lurching to a stop. Billy sprang over the side into the hip-deep water, his legs churning toward the shore. The simple, delicate patterns of the palm fronds swung above him against a thin gray sky. Everything became a blur of motion as he waited for the sudden impact of the bullets to drive him into the sandy bottom.

Breathless among the palm trees, Billy lay prone, realizing that he had survived the water and the beach. All around him men were scrambling for the safety of the trees, grunting as they hit the ground. Breathing heavily, eyes wide with fear, they aligned themselves into battle positions.

But there was no battle. The Japs were gone!

Billy saw Marcell, lying next to him, peering ahead into the trees, his M-1 against his shoulder. Behind them the landing craft scrunched into the sand and unloaded their human cargoes. Wave after wave swept into the long curve of Lunga Bay to face only the palm trees waving lazily in the morning breeze.

Marcell turned his head slowly toward Billy, a sardonic smile on his lips. "Them Japs must have heard there was a couple of 'ol boys from Liberty, Georgia, comin' after 'em. They probably won't stop runnin' 'til they hit Tokyo Bay."

"Move out!" someone shouted from up the beach. The men formed staggered squads, plodding off through the coconut groves.

The sun came out. As Billy glanced back at the white glare of Red Beach, he heard the high whine of aircraft and the hammering of antiaircraft guns. The Japs weren't whipped just yet.

"C'mon! Get the lead out!"

They sweated through the long stretches of kunai grass, crossed and recrossed rivers, climbed and slipped and finally blundered like members of a defunct carnival into the jungles.

"I think the lieutenant's lost as a goose!" Marcell sat against a vine-covered tree in the deep jungle shade.

Billy lit a Camel, coughing as the smoke curled from his nose. "I think the whole company's lost. Every time I see an officer with a map, he keeps turning it around like he don't know which way's up."

Jackson slouched over to where Billy and Marcell sat smoking, his green twill shirt and trousers soaked with sweat. "Anybody got any water? I ran out two hours ago."

"Why certainly, Spots," Marcell smiled helpfully, pointing behind him. "Me and Billy just filled our canteens at the fountain on the other side of this tree."

"I've got maybe a cup left," Billy said, unhooking his canteen and tossing it to the thin-faced boy from Missouri.

"Thanks, Billy. You're a pal." He turned the canteen up, draining it in three swallows. "That's the best water I ever had in my life."

Angered that Spots drank the last of the water, Billy watched the young man smile wearily. Abruptly Jackson's left eye disappeared, replaced by a gaping crimson hole, the sharp crack of a rifle ripping the air as he dropped in a crumpled heap at the foot of the tree.

Time skidded to a halt. An absolute and terrible silence smothered the jungle for a fraction of a second—then bedlam. The men dove, jumped, and scrambled to places of safety behind trees, in the underbrush, or in a tangle of vines. Some stared wildly about them, trying to locate the sniper. Others merely clung to the ground as though some invisible force were trying to drag them off the face of the earth.

"Take cover!"

The belated command rang out in the gloom, as useless as the one that followed.

"Corpsman!"

Instinctively, Billy and Marcell had grabbed Jackson, dragging him behind the tree where he had fallen. Even as he struggled with the limp form, Billy knew it was hopeless. He lay beside the lifeless body, its one eye staring in eternal wonder toward the canopy of the trees, to somewhere beyond the spinning planet and the high cold glittering of the stars.

The company was bloodied. Their innocence and youth and dreams of glory lay crumpled and lifeless in that quiet jungle glade. They realized they were still only civilians dressed up like soldiers—children playing war—but they would grow up quickly.

They moved out through the jungle in the relentless heat toward some unknown destination. Climbing the muddy hills, the men cursed as they sought secure footing in the slime that seemed to be spread over slick concrete. On the opposite side, they would slide, the tripods for the machine guns and the base plates of the mortars banging against their weary bodies, bruising them as they cursed breathlessly. In the early afternoon, a shower gave them a brief respite from the merciless sun that turned the jungle floor into a steam bath.

Night moved in upon them in a wave of impenetrable darkness. They set their guns up on the perimeter of a hill as a slow rain began to fall. Sitting under the dripping trees, they ate cold

C-rations out of their packs. Their homes and families had become little more than hazy dreams. Cold and wet, on the backside of the world, they waited for the faceless enemy.

Billy listened to the murmuring sibilance of the jungle. "You think they'll hit us tonight?"

"I don't think an owl could find us, black as it is," Marcell whispered back.

"Poor Spots, dying like that. He never hurt anybody. Didn't have a mean bone in his body." Billy gripped the damp stock of his M-1, straining to hear the sounds of small men, stalking them, their bayonets seeking American flesh.

"Yeah," Marcell mumbled. "I reckon there ain't no good way to die, is there?"

"It's us or them, Marcell." Billy spoke after a long silence. "That's all there is to it. Like ol' Ridgeway used to tell us in the locker room, 'Show me a *good* loser, and I'll show you a *loser*.' It's just like the football field—except one loss is all you get here." Billy espoused the philosophy of nineteen-year-olds suddenly disenchanted with war.

In spite of the fear, the day's marching, the slogging up and down those muddy hills in the smothering heat had siphoned away their wills, and the men lapsed into a comalike sleep.

The second day was a repeat of the first, except no one was killed. At dusk, with the sky glowing in shades of pink and orange and rust, they came out of the jungles onto the long slopes of the kunai fields that led down to the coconut groves.

In the middle of the night Billy awakened to see the heavens on fire—he thought of the great Battle of Armageddon. The whole island seemed bathed in a wavering red light. Planes roared through the dark skies above the light. The men cowered on the hillside, open and vulnerable in the eerie red glow.

"We're done for, Billy," Marcell remarked almost casually. "And I'm too tired to care one way or another."

Billy stared at the glowing skies. "I don't think so. Those planes are flying too slow to be fighters or bombers. It's got to be some kind of reconnaissance mission."

In seconds the thunder of heavy naval guns shook the island. Out toward Savo and Florida Islands, huge flashes of red and white lighted the black expanse of Sealark Channel. As the cannonading continued, Guadalcanal trembled beneath the men—threatening to break apart and crumble into the sea.

At dawn they gathered their sodden equipment, slogging down through the kunai fields toward the palm groves. They walked onto a beach of desolation and despair. Across Sealark Channel, where the American Fleet had been, all the way to Florida Island, the water was clear of ships—except for smoking and burning wreckage.

A force of Japanese cruisers and destroyers had swept through Savo Sound, surprising the American warships. The glowing lights of the previous night were flares dropped by seaplanes serving as the eyes of the enemy armada. The American heavy cruisers *Quincy, Vincennes,* and *Astoria* and the Australian heavy cruiser *Canberra* were sunk. Other ships were heavily damaged.

"Where's our Navy?" Parrino ran up behind Billy and Marcell, unbelief dulling his eyes behind the black-rimmed glasses.

Billy slumped against the base of a palm tree, just beginning to stare, his eyes slightly sunken in their sockets, a tinge of dark circles under the eyes. "Halfway to Australia I imagine . . . the ones the Japs didn't blow to pieces."

"We're on our own now, Irish." Marcell lit a Camel as the sea breeze whipped the smoke away. "I never had much faith in them swab jockeys anyway."

Parrino became agitated. "You know what this means? No supplies. No reinforcements!"

Billy glanced up at him. "Sit down, Irish. We're all in the same boat now." He looked at the mangled ships of Sealark Channel, soon to be renamed Iron Bottom Sound. "No pun intended."

The last of the reinforcements to escape the Japanese armada were trudging up the beach. The sun had dropped behind the hills. In the purple twilight the men were cast in silhouette against the darkness gathering over Florida Island, their forms looking as if they had been cut with tin snips.

Billy felt like one of these shadow-figures, insubstantial as the thin violet light settling over Guadalcanal. Cut off from the world, he saw himself exiled for some crime he had yet to commit.

The bombers awakened them the next morning. "Condition red!" someone yelled down the beach. At a dizzying height above the swaying palm fronds, the slim silver bombers sailed in a perfect V against the blue curve of the sky. They were bound for Henderson Field, which gave the island its military value. The earth shook from the explosions as they dropped their lethal cargo.

"You know, if it wasn't for the Japs, this would be like a tropical vacation." That afternoon after the first bombing, Marcell drank from one of the quart bottles of Japanese beer the squad had found in a log warehouse. Wrapped in little straw skirts, the bottles were much smaller than the balloonlike bottles of sake found with them.

Sitting in the shade of the palms next to Marcell and Parrino, Billy watched the caravans of Marines passing along the beach from the storehouse. Like conquerors of some oriental marketplace, they pushed their plunder of cases of beer and bottles of sake in rickshaws, their heads awash with false security.

Billy held his huge bottle of sake between his legs, rolled back, and let the cool rice wine slide down his throat. "I believe there's some ships comin' for a visit."

"Must be Jap ships," Parrino offered, slurring the words. "Ours all went home. Left us flat!"

The shells roared overhead on the way to Henderson Field as the Japanese navy shelled the island with impunity.

"I think we're gonna have to build some bunkers," Billy remarked matter-of-factly, taking another huge swallow of sake.

"Capital idea," Marcell agreed, as the shells exploded on the airfield. "First thing in the morning."

Fortunately for the Marines, the liquor ran out before the Japanese mounted an offensive. On the same morning they drank the last of the beer and sake, an officer from headquarters came by with a work party confiscating the flour, sugar, peaches, and spam the individual squads had taken from the stockpiles they found on the beach. After the battalion galley began operation, the men found themselves subsisting on a bowl of rice in the morning and another at night.

*　*　*

"This ain't a river, it's a sewer!" Marcell stood on the steeply sloping bank of the Tenaru River, staring down at its stagnant, scum-covered surface.

Parrino unlimbered his entrenching tool and began digging his gun pit. "They're supposed to attack tonight, Hero. You might wanna do your river survey some other time." With the death of Albert Jackson, Billy Nightwolf had teamed up with Parrino as his assistant gunner and helped him dig the pit for their .30 caliber water-cooled machine gun.

"Why don't we give 'em a hand here, Marcell," Billy asked, walking over to where Parrino and Nightwolf were digging in the soft red earth. "We need to have this machine gun ready for tonight. Besides, we can use it for a bomb shelter if we make it big enough. Them Jap planes are gettin' thicker every day."

Without answering, Marcell took off his faded dungaree shirt, revealing his tanned barrel chest, and went to work.

"First time I ever saw you go to work without a fuss," Parrino remarked over his shoulder to Marcell, his thick glasses clouding over with perspiration. "Took a whole army of Japs to make you do it though."

Piling shovelfuls of red dirt along the riverbank as a breastworks, Nightwolf glanced up at Marcell. "Don't worry, Hero. I won't let them ol' mean Japs hurt you."

"I ain't worried, Tonto," Marcell replied to Nightwolf, piling his dirt alongside the Indian's. "I know you'll kill 'em all for their scalps so you can buy yourself a wife."

They worked on the west bank of the Tenaru which ran north, almost emptying into Iron Bottom Sound. It was blocked by a forty-foot-wide sandbar that fronted on the sound. An attack could be expected across this narrow sand bridge, so the men furiously dug their gun pits just north of it. Another squad was fortifying the bridge. The only other alternative for the Japanese offensive was a frontal assault directly across the river from the no-man's-land of coconut palms on the east bank.

By nightfall the ten-by-ten pit, five feet deep, yawned behind its earthworks. Roofing it with coconut logs would have to wait until the next morning.

A pale moon hung in the sky as Billy and Marcell lay on their ponchos behind the mound of red earth between Parrino's gun pit and the sand bridge.

"You think they'll come tonight?" Marcell asked, cupping his cigarette in his hand to hide the red glow.

Billy glanced to his right at the shadows that were Parrino and Nightwolf standing in the pit behind their machine gun and then to his left at the emplacement guarding the sand bridge. "Who knows? I'd just as soon they come now and get it over with. This waitin' around is givin' me the heebie-jeebies."

As if in reply to Billy's spoken request, the sound of trucks wheeling into the coconut grove across the river rumbled through the dark.

"They're driving in there like it's a grocery store parkin' lot!" Marcell shouted.

At that moment, Parrino opened up with his machine gun, piercing the darkness with its clattering fire. The gun at the sand bridge answered, and from behind them came the flat *whump* of the heavy mortars, crunching loudly as they hit the grove. Thirty-seven-millimeter antitank guns fired point blank and the seventy-five-millimeter howitzers roared their destruction across the river. The sharp crackling of rifle fire up and down the lines punctuated the heavier weapons.

Billy lay behind his low mound of earth, staring at the shadowy, dreamlike figures approaching the riverbank. His hand felt numb on the M-1, the trigger finger frozen and useless. Suddenly from the darkness among the shadows, a machine gun opened up on him in a long vicious burst, its white light slashing the night like an acetylene torch. The heavy slugs ripped into the dirt behind him. Shrill unearthly screams rose from the riverbank as the Japanese charged.

Reality hit Billy with the shock of cold water. He settled into his firing position as comfortably as if he were in the woods around Liberty, pouring round after round into the ranks of screaming men slogging through the river at him. Fear no longer prickled his neck or lay like a stone in his chest. War had come to him, and he would do his job. The roaring inferno of battle disappeared, all that remained were the rifle's heavy stock and long barrel and its reassuring tap against his shoulder each time he squeezed the trigger.

Something changed. Billy realized the river was empty of men, except for those lying twisted and crumpled in the water. In a white flash of light, the gun pit at the sand bridge to his left exploded. The hammering of the machine gun stopped.

"Marcell, we gotta get that machine gun goin' again!" Billy shouted above the din.

"I'm with you!" Marcell barked, scrambling up and sprinting along the bank of the Tenaru behind Billy.

Parrino, swung his gun downriver, spraying the sand bridge with a lethal barrage as the Japanese tried to gain the other side.

His lungs burning, breath rasping in his throat, Billy saw that one Japanese soldier had made it across the bridge and into the pit. As he tried to turn the machine gun toward the Marines along the riverbank, Billy stopped, raising his rifle in one motion, and emptied an eight-round clip at the soldier. Three of the slugs struck him, flinging him backward into the bottom of the pit.

Billy leaped behind the gun, slipped the spindle back into the tripod socket, and clamped the gun back in place. As he swung the gun toward the sand bridge, he saw a hideously grinning Japanese above him raise his bayonet to drive it into his chest. In a blurred movement, Billy glimpsed a dark, bulky figure swinging an M-1 by the barrel like a baseball bat, its heavy wooden stock shattering the skull of the Japanese soldier like an eggshell as it hit with a sickening thud.

Marcell stood above his fallen enemy, rifle raised for another blow, and then leaped in next to Billy, his Rebel yell rising above the din of battle. "Yeeeehaa! Give 'em hell, Billy Boy!"

Grabbing one of the light green boxes that held the 250-round belts of .30 caliber ammo, Marcell placed it in the feed position. Billy pulled back the bolt on the gun and rammed it home.

Billy stared down the barrel of the machine gun at the black, howling figures only yards away. Pressing the trigger of the gun, he felt it jump and buck under his hand. The handle slammed against his fist as Marcell fed the belt smoothly through the breech. The acrid smell of the hot steel barrel filled the pit as Billy swung the gun from side to side, raking the ranks of the enemy like a scythe through a wheat field.

The dark, screaming men kept coming, but they churned slowly through the deep sand, bodies piling up like cordwood in front of the gun pit as it spat its deadly fire at them. In an instant that seemed frozen for eternity, Billy saw the moonlit face of a boy in front of his gun sights. No more than fourteen, his smooth, beardless face was a mask of terror as he charged, his bayonet glinting in the pale light. For half an instant, Billy hesitated with a mindless grief—then pressed the trigger.

Suddenly, four scrambling shapes from the sea, silhouetted against the open bay, drove toward the two Marines, their rifles firing. Billy swung his gun toward the men as smoothly as the forehands he hit on the tennis court, hammering them into the sand.

Silence hit Billy like a dropped curtain. No longer did the dark hordes swarm toward him. Firing died out along the lines as the sun glowed redly behind Savo Island. Bodies lay piled up along the sand bridge—scattered among the palm trees across the river—crumpled and sodden at the water's edge.

They saw the shattered remnant of the Japanese forces running beyond the groves toward the ocean. The Marines were walking their mortar rounds in—dropping them to the rear of the Japanese and moving them steadily closer so they were forced into the American lines to be annihilated.

Light tanks crossed the sand bridge, crushing the tumble of bodies. Infantry followed in a sweeping movement that would drive the few remaining Japanese into the ocean.

Billy sat in the pit beside the machine gun, numbed by the carnage around him. He watched a group of enemy soldiers flee down the beach from the scorched grove, throwing themselves into the water to escape the blood-crazed Americans. They swam out into the channel, their heads bobbing darkly on the sun-bright water. The Marines lay on their bellies in the sand and shot them like turtles.

13

THE CEMETERY

Near the sea, with the palm fronds rustling softly in the breeze, they walked toward the cemetery which lay west of Koli Point. The sun—so huge and red and shimmering it looked as if it would set the ocean to boiling—had dropped beyond Cape Esperance across from Savo Island, its last rays suffusing the rippling waters of Iron Bottom Sound with hues of violet and pink.

"How many men you think are buried here?" Marcell stood with his back to the sea, gazing out across the cemetery.

Billy looked at the few rough crosses that leaned above some of the graves. "Who knows? Most of 'em were buried with nothin' to mark their graves . . . unless their buddies just happened to be there."

Dogtags were nailed to some of the crosses. Others bore tin plates from the mess gear, scratched with brief epitaphs: "A real friend." "He died like a man." "Our Buddy." "We'll miss him."

"Look at this one, Billy," Marcell murmured, pointing to a verse scratched on a piece of battered tin. It hung from a tilting cross made of a piece of orange crate.

> And when he gets to Heaven
> To St. Peter he will tell:
> One more Marine reporting, sir—
> I've served my time in Hell.

"I've heard that before somewhere," Billy said softly, kneeling beside the grave.

Marcell stared at the crude marker. "Who wrote it?"

"I don't know. One thing for sure though, he sounds like a Marine."

They walked on into the cemetery until they came to a grave whose surface had been leveled and brushed clean. Pressed into the earth were bullets with the round brass ends exposed. They formed the words *Albert "Spots" Jackson.*

Billy and Marcell sat on the dusty ground next to the grave, elbows resting on their knees, looking out over the coastal plain that held the cemetery. It reached in a long sweeping flatness to the distant hills. The brass epitaph gleamed dully in the fading light. Behind them, from the direction of Florida Island, the drone of a single airplane carried on the wind.

Billy gazed at the darkling hills. "You could bury thousands of Marines between here and those hills."

"Yeah," Marcell grunted. "We might be short on a lot of things. Burying room ain't one of 'em."

"Neither is that Japanese rice," Billy added. "I'm gettin' sick of that wormy stuff twice a day."

"Remember how we complained about Spam back at Parris Island? What I wouldn't give for a piece now. Fried up with some of them powdered eggs." Marcell lay back, hands behind his head, staring at a small gathering of clouds scudding across the deep blue sky.

Billy rubbed his flat stomach. "While we're wishing, how 'bout a thick rib eye, medium rare, with a baked potato and lots of fresh baked bread?"

Marcell didn't speak for a long while. "We ain't never gettin' off this island, Billy Boy."

Billy looked closely at his friend. His eyes were rounder, the circles beneath them darker, the tendency to stare more pronounced. It was the same for everyone he knew—and himself. "What're you talkin' about? Sure we will."

Marcell stood up, shambling back toward the sea.

Billy fell in beside him. "We'll never get off this island? That's crazy talk."

"You think so? Them Jap cruisers and destroyers sail into Iron Bottom Sound every day and shell us like they own the place. Their planes bomb us two, three times a day and every night." Marcell reached the beach, sitting down where someone had begun a rudimentary castle in the sand and abandoned it. Like most things on the island, except for the bomb shelters, it was left unfinished.

Billy sat in the sand beside him. "It could be worse. We coulda been with the Raiders up at the battle on Bloody Ridge. All we've had is a few night skirmishes."

Marcell glanced at Billy with his big, round, dark eyes. "Yeah, and the shelling and the bombing every day and night!"

"Stop it, will you?"

Marcell hung his head, staring at the ruined castle. "You see what's happening, don't you?"

"What are you talkin' about?"

Marcell pointed toward the sand castle standing at the edge of the incoming tide. "The Japs are gonna wash us away just like the ocean's doin' to that little castle. Every wave makes it crumble a little more. Every day we lose a few men to the shelling from those battleships or to their bombers. Every night it's an attack or the bombs—more Marines dead. Some of us going nuts. I heard one or two blew their brains out."

Billy stared out to sea, unable to respond to Marcell's litany of despondency for it carried in it the irrefutable weight of truth.

"We're eatin' that crummy Jap rice 'cause our supply ships can't get to us. Half the time our airplanes can't get off the ground cause they ain't got gas. The Japs got ships, planes, and plenty of men. I heard a lieutenant say this mornin' they was unloadin' three more troop transports down at Taivu Point. They don't care how many men they lose; they don't think about life the same way we do." Marcell stared at the sand castle slowly succumbing to the tide.

"They've got to have feelings like us, Marcell. They're men, too. They don't want to die any more than we do," Billy remarked, feeling a chill at the back of his neck.

"You think so?" Marcell rubbed his stubby beard with his thumb and forefinger. "You remember that night at Hell's Point, how they kept comin' at us across that sand bridge like there was a thousand geisha girls waitin' for 'em on the other side. Some of 'em was smilin'—not even firin' their rifles."

Billy looked at Marcell's gaunt face, at the hollow staring eyes, and tried by force of will not to look like that himself—like Marcell —like all the other men.

Marcell stared across the open channel at the dark bulk of Florida Island. "It's got something to do with dying for the emperor. Supposed to be a great honor. Gets 'em to Shinto heaven quicker, something like that."

An image flashed in Billy's mind—his father's paneled study and himself as a twelve-year-old poring over a stack of books. "I remember reading an old Japanese sayin' in one of my daddy's military books at home. I can't quote it, but it said something like, life is heavy as a stone, but death is lighter than a feather."

"That's exactly what I'm talkin' about. Maybe they ain't all crazy, but most of 'em run after death like we run after women." Marcell's eyes narrowed slightly. "I knew we was in big trouble when I saw 'em run straight into your machine gun that night—smilin'."

"Only thing I remember is a horde of screamin' men comin' at me . . . and those long bayonets shining in the moonlight," Billy said flatly. "Except for one. I saw his face. He was just a kid."

"What happened that next night in the river is what bothered me."

Billy remembered, hoping Marcell would let it drop.

"I can still see them crocodiles eatin' the Jap bodies. Hear their bones crunching with every bite." Marcell's eyes were bright with dread. "Whatever happens, Billy, don't let me end up like that."

Finally Billy could take it no more. "Marcell, you're gonna have to stop this. It ain't doin' either of us any good."

"You're right. Must be this malaria gettin' to me."

Billy reached over, touching Marcell's forehead. "You're burning up. You better get down to sick bay."

"What for?"

"'Cause you're sick."

"All they'll do is give me some aspirin. If I get real bad, they'll stick me in a tent with a bunch of strangers. They won't take me off this stinkin' island. They won't send me home. Nobody ever leaves here. What's the use?"

Billy glanced at the waves breaking over the mound of sand that no longer had any resemblance to a castle. "Maybe you're right."

"I know I'm right," Marcell murmured against the sound of the waves. "If I'm gonna be sick, I'd rather stay with my friends. Nobody leaves this place."

Billy's hope withered in the face of logic. "Not even in a pine box," he muttered, gazing back at the cemetery, its tilting crosses dark against the last rays of the sun that lingered on the tops of the hills. "We got our own cemetery."

* * *

"Well here he comes. I guess we'll get the scoop now." Nightwolf lay back against the combination bomb shelter-gun pit, watching the slim Marine in green utilities, wearing a helmet covered with camouflage netting, labor up through the fields of kunai grass toward them. On his back he carried a pack made from a blanket.

Billy dropped his pack in the shade of the gun pit and stretched out on the ground.

"Well, what's the deal?" Marcell demanded, trying not to stare at the pack.

"No reinforcements far as I can tell. I don't know if the Japs are sinking all the transports, or MacArthur just ain't got the men yet." Billy lit a Camel, inhaling deeply.

"I bet 'ol Dugout Doug is laid up at the officer's club in Melbourne talking about what grand times they all had in France in 1918. They called that one the war to end all wars, didn't they?" Marcell asked sarcasticly. "They need to put a Marine in charge of this show."

Parrino looked up from his carving. He had used his bayonet for the past week to carve scraps of coconut logs into grotesque figures that resembled trolls or gargoyles. "I thought after the Marines took an island, the Army would come in and relieve us so we could go someplace else. That's what they told us."

Billy smiled sardonically, letting the cigarette smoke curl up from his nostrils. "What they told us ain't what we've learned, Parrino. All that was before the Canal."

"What bothers me is they never let us know anything," Nightwolf commented. "Wouldn't surprise me if we ended up like those poor devils in the Philippines."

Parrino looked at Nightwolf, his eyes glazed with fear. "I'd rather be dead than get captured by the Japs. I heard they got ways of torturing a man that—" Parrino shuddered and returned to his carving.

"I'd like to know why the Navy hasn't sent some PT boats in here to stop that shelling every night." Billy rubbed his shoulder where the pack had cut into it.

"Yeah," Marcell agreed, "and what about the production back home? Where's the P-47's and that new F4U or whatever the navy calls their new fighter these days? The Japs rule the skies here."

After a few more criticisms of the military and civilian leadership, an uneasy silence fell among the disgruntled Marines.

Finally, Nightwolf's curiosity got the best of him and he nodded at Billy's pack. "What'd you bring back?"

"Take a look."

Untying the pack, Nightwolf unfolded the blanket, spreading the plunder out on top of it. It contained three bars of Lava soap, a pack of Gillette razor blades, four pairs of white cotton socks, four green t-shirts, and two Hershey bars. "You struck gold."

Marcell's hollow eyes grew even wider. "Where'd you get all this stuff?"

"The officers got their own supply tent. The guard's daddy just happened to be in my daddy's outfit in France in the last war. Told me his daddy thought General Logan Christmas was the finest officer West Point ever turned out." Billy flicked his cigarette butt into the tall grass. "How could I disagree when he gave me all this?"

They had left the green and malevolent Tenaru two weeks before, moving out into these fields. Digging gun pits twice the size of those on the river, they roofed them with a double thickness of coconut logs and a layer of dirt. Then they planted grass on the roof, which took root quickly. From a distance the whole thing looked like a small hill.

Six feet deep or more, the pits offered relief from the blistering heat. With some Japanese rope and logs driven into the ground, they made beds that kept them dry and warm when the cold rains struck. It was a paradise compared to the Tenaru. With their fortifications and their broad field of fire spreading before them like a vast wheat field, their greatest fear was a direct hit from a bomb or a battleship.

After Billy's swag had been sorted and divided—the two Hershey bars shared equally by the four of them—they lay in the grass waiting for the night.

Billy took a Camel from his watertight tin, lit it, and slipped the top back on the tin. He carried two Colt .45 automatics in a webbed belt slung low on his slim hips, three hand grenades in his baggy trousers and a bayonet in a sheath strapped between his shoulder blades. After the battle at Hell's Point, he had discarded his M-1 in favor of a Thompson submachine gun. With his heavy black handlebar mustache and a red bandanna tied around his forehead, he looked like a blue-eyed Mexican bandit.

Save for the pistols, Billy's arsenal lay neatly stacked on his bunk inside the gun pit. "Anybody remember what a woman's skin feels like?" he asked, the cigarette dangling from his lips.

"What's a woman?" Marcell asked solemnly.

"You know, they're soft and white and don't have beards," Parrino answered, carving his demons.

"Nightwolf ain't got a beard. Is he a woman?" Marcell's expression remained deadpan.

"Don't know. I never looked." Parrino glanced at Nightwolf, who fathomed no humor in the conversation.

Billy turned his haunted eyes toward the darkening sky as a white sea bird sailed over the fields of long grass. "I'd just like to hold a woman. At least once more."

"What do you think they're doing back in the States?" Nightwolf asked, sitting cross-legged, his natural resting position.

"My people are probably sitting down to a big spaghetti supper. The whole family comes to Mama's, and we've got a big family." Slivers of wood fell into the growing pile between Parrino's legs. "What I wouldn't give for a big plate of Mama's spaghetti."

"Venison, that's what I'd like to have," Nightwolf mused, staring at Parrino's carvings. "Fresh out of the mountains and cooked over an open fire."

"You know what I'd like?" The hollows of Marcell's face were thrown into shadow by the failing light.

"Ollie's. You'd like to go to Ollie's," Billy smiled behind the trail of blue-white smoke rising in front of his face.

"You got it," Marcell grinned crookedly. "Get my hands around one of them thick chocolate malts, sit in that last booth by the jukebox with one of my Liberty girls, and listen to Glenn Miller."

"No malts for me," Parrino mumbled, polishing a wooden figure. "Give me a whiskey sour over at Apollyon's Bar and sit me down at that poker game in the back room. Man, that's living! I've won more money in that game than you guys have ever seen."

"What about you, Billy?" Nightwolf asked, "What do you dream about?"

Billy spread his arms expansively in front of him. "Who could ask for more than this? Fresh air and bombings—an ocean view and shelling from Jap battleships—a dry place to sleep and suicide attacks at night—why, it's a dream come true!"

Marcell's eyes narrowed with concern for his friend. Billy flicked his cigarette at him and lay back on the grass laughing. He was joined by Marcell and Nightwolf. Parrino stared at his carvings, arrayed before him like a miniature army.

From the hilltop, Billy gazed out at the waters of Iron Bottom Sound. In the rose-colored afterglow he saw the shadowy bulk of a Japanese battleship enter the strait between Cape Esperance and Savo Island. "Better enjoy the last of the fresh air, boys. Big Bertha's headin' into the sound. It's gonna get real noisy around here tonight."

Marcell stood up and looked out to sea. "Probably means the banzai boys'll hit us about 2:00 A.M. when the shelling's over. All that screamin' gives me the creeps."

"Me, too." Nightwolf shuddered, staring at Parrino's figures. "Not as bad as those things you carve though, Irish. What are they supposed to be anyway?"

Parrino lifted one of the hideously scowling figures, rubbing it with his forefinger. "I don't know. Just things I see inside my head." He gathered up his figures and slipped quietly into the gun pit.

Two minutes later, the blast of a .45 pistol thundered out of the gun pit. Billy leaped to his feet, stepping into the shelter in one smooth motion. Something crunched under his boot as it hit the coconut log threshold. Moving his foot quickly, he stared down at the white curve of a skull fragment, bits of skin and dark hair still clinging to it.

* * *

"Hey, Christmas! The lieutenant with his right ear lobe missing stood outside the gun pit, his bright hair almost as red as the sun glowing just above the western treetops.

Billy stepped out from under the shelter of coconut logs eating from a can of Spam with his bayonet. "Yes sir."

"One of the regimental scouts got killed yesterday. You scored 'Sharpshooter' in boot camp. You get to take his place."

"Yes sir."

"Jap transports are landing at Kokumbona. We don't know how many yet, but we think they may be planning to cross the Matanikau and build up for an offensive somewhere around Grassy Knoll." The lieutenant tugged at his short ear. "See if you can verify any of this. Get us some numbers if you can. Don't risk your position by shooting anybody unless it's a general."

"Yes sir."

The lieutenant swung away down the hill, turning back when he had gone no more than twenty yards. "Two more things. You leave at first light and bring a backup with you. Gives you twice as good a chance at getting the information back."

The next morning, in the dripping coolness of the rain forest, Billy and Marcell sat under a giant tree, its foliage, along with a million others, casting the jungle into perpetual gloom. With sound cushioned by the thick vegetation and the decay of the forest floor, the effect was that of being inside a huge cathedral. Striated light from far above could have been filtered through green stained-glass windows.

"How much further?" Marcell whispered, as though he were actually in a church.

Billy looked at his crumpled map. "I can't make heads or tails of this thing. Shouldn't have slept through map reading back at New River, I guess."

"Why didn't you bring your M-1?" Marcell glanced at the Thompson leaning against the tree. "That ain't exactly a sniper's weapon."

Billy blew three smoke rings into the clammy air. "I feel safer with it. Especially in these jungles. More firepower. What's the chance of us seeing a general anyway? If we do, I'll just use your M-1."

"Let's find some Japs, get a count, and get outta here," Marcell murmured, glancing furtively around him. "This place gives me the willies."

"I'm with you." Billy shoved his cigarette butt into the soft earth and slung his Thompson on his shoulder.

"Billy?"

"Yeah?" Billy had taken one step, glancing back at Marcell.

"Next time you see Jordan, tell her I'm sorry, will you?"

"Sure thing," Billy replied, perplexed at the request.

At the top of the next hill, Billy crouched down behind a stand of heavy ferns next to a tree and signaled for Marcell to be quiet. A quarter of a mile below on the valley floor, a large contingent of Japanese soldiers were assembling. Light tanks and artillery stood in neat ranks at the opposite end of the valley. Closer to them, men gathered in small groups around their cooking fires.

"Looks like three or four battalions down there," Billy whispered, as Marcell slid down beside him.

Marcell stared transfixed at the valley. "Must be eight, nine hundred troops."

"Give me those glasses!" Billy whispered urgently.

Taking the heavy binoculars from Marcell, Billy trained them on a small group of men walking slowly among the troops toward their end of the valley. "Tell me what you see!" he demanded, handing them back to Marcell.

"Some high-ranking Jap. Might be a general."

Billy took the glasses back, taking another long look. "That's got to be his adjutant, prancin' around him like he was a little struttin' Buddah. Good chance we've got a general down there."

"You gonna drop him?" Marcell asked, taking the glasses and peering down into the valley.

Billy smiled thinly, reaching for the M-1. He lay prone on the hilltop, breaking the ferns back out of the way to get a clear line of fire. Estimating the distance, he adjusted the sight of the M-1 and steadied himself in firing position. Taking a breath and holding it, Billy centered the front sight on the Japanese officer and squeezed the trigger.

The report of the rifle thundered across the valley. Instant bedlam broke out below, like someone had kicked over an ant nest. Soldiers grabbed their weapons, some looking frantically around, others running about in all directions.

"Did I get him?" Billy ran slightly ahead of Marcell through the gloom of the rain forest back toward their own lines.

Marcell still breathed easily. "The little adjutant stepped in front of him to light his cigarette just as you fired. Looked like you nailed him right between the shoulder blades."

Billy saw a flash of yellow light in the darkness off to his left. A sudden pain seared the left side of his neck, and he tumbled to the jungle floor, rolling in the leaf mold. A screaming figure from the shadows lunged toward him, a malevolent light glinting from the upraised bayonet.

Trying to scramble backward, Billy saw that it was too late. Abruptly, the man with the bayonet jerked and thrashed like a berserk puppet as three thunderous reports crashed in the narrow glade.

"You all right?" Marcell stood above Billy, his .45 automatic still pointing at the Japanese soldier who lay crumpled and twisted in the sodden leaves.

Through the burning pain, Billy felt a warmth, gushing at the side of his neck. "I think so."

Marcell folded his handkerchief, applying a pressure bandage to the side of Billy neck where the bullet had passed through. Taking Billy's bandanna, he tied it snugly in place. "That too tight?"

"No. It's OK."

"Thank God it missed the jugular." Marcell helped Billy to his feet, handing him the Thompson. "Can you walk?"

"Yeah. We gotta get out of here."

The flat *whump* of a heavy mortar sounded in the distance to their rear, then another, and another. They ran on through the dripping forest, the crashing of the exploding mortar rounds ahead of them.

"They're walking the mortars back toward us," Billy shouted in sudden realization. "We've got to get around the flank." He moved at right angles from the approaching explosions, shattering the jungle, the shrapnel singing through the trees around them like angry wasps.

Billy glanced back at Marcell and saw him smile as he had done a hundred times, trotting back to the huddle after a plunge through the line. The world flared unbearably bright. He felt himself lifted from the earth, floating among the bright and shimmering stars, and the stars became the pain that burned him with their cold fire.

Gradually Billy opened his eyes. The black mold of the forest floor, then the green leaves came into focus. He felt his back was on fire, but he lifted himself into a sitting position. He heard a terrible moaning. At first he thought some enormous tropical worm was devouring his friend. Then he realized Marcell's intestines were slithering and sliding out of his open body cavity, shining pinkly in the dim light.

"I'm cold, Billy," Marcell moaned. "So cold."

Billy slid over to him. He took off his utility shirt, then his t-shirt. Lifting Marcell slightly, he struggled to get his t-shirt on him, pushing the intestines back in and holding them in place with the t-shirt. Next he put his utility shirt on Marcell, backwards, buttoning it tightly to hold his stomach together.

"Billy, help me . . . I'm so cold."

Billy held his friend's head in his arms, speaking softly to him. "It's OK, partner. You're gonna be just fine. I'll get you back."

Sitting there until the erratic blurring of his vision stopped, Billy struggled to his knees, using all his strength to ease Marcell over his shoulder. He could feel the intestines sliding around under the double layer of cloth. Staggering a few yards, he had to lower his burden to the ground and rest.

Billy lost track of time. He no longer knew he struggled through the jungles of Guadalcanal. The only thought left him through the heart-stopping effort and the pain was that he must get this friend of his childhood to a place that lay somewhere in front of him where everything would be all right. Unconsciously, he held to his course by keeping the angling shafts of sunlight in the same position to his right.

Stumble a few yards . . . gently place his burden on the ground . . . gasp for breath, the damp air burning in his lungs like the shrapnel in his back . . . reach for a strength somewhere in his deepest being . . . lift and stagger a few more yards.

Voices! He heard voices as if someone were speaking over the sound of a softly breaking surf. Arms lifting him, moving through the soft green light.

"Tell HQ . . . eight . . . maybe nine . . . hundred Jap troops . . . other . . . side . . . mountain . . . tanks . . . artillery . . . missed . . . general . . . save . . . Marcell . . . ," was all he could say before he passed out.

Billy awakened at the edge of the rain forest. He lay on a stretcher on the ground. Two men, one short and lean, the other bulky, stood a few feet away like green angels. Marcell lay on a stretcher next to him, his head cradled by Sam Dalton's arm.

"I'm afraid to die, Preacher" he moaned. "It's so black out there . . . so *dark!*"

Dalton lowered his head very close to Marcell's face. "Listen to me. You don't have to be afraid."

"Oh, God! It's too late for me! There's nothing I can do!"

Sam spoke softly. "That's right. It's already been done for you."

Marcell's eyes held Dalton's with a desperate plea.

"Do you know the story of the thief that hung on the cross next to Jesus?"

Marcell moved his head in answer.

"There was nothing the thief could do, except trust Jesus. And that's all he needed. Jesus told him, "'Today shalt thou be with me in Paradise.' He's one man we know for *sure* made it to heaven."

Dalton propped Marcell's head carefully on a rolled blanket. Kneeling so he could look in the dying man's face, he took his hand, holding to it firmly.

"Jesus died for you Marcell. He loves you so much. There's nothing you can do to stop him from loving you."

The strain and the dark horror began to drain slowly from Marcell's face as Dalton spoke.

"Jesus wants to save you, Marcell. To give you eternal life. The Bible tells us, 'For God so loved the world, that he gave his only begotten Son, that whosoever believeth in him should not perish, but have everlasting life.' God made it very simple for us because He loves us so much."

Marcell took a shallow breath, shuddering as he released it.

"Marcell, do you accept Jesus Christ as your Lord and Savior right now?"

Billy saw Marcell squeeze Dalton's hand and nod his head slightly. He struggled to sit up.

Dalton took him gently by the shoulders, easing him back down on the stretcher. "It's all right. I understand. You don't have to worry anymore, my brother. You're in the arms of Jesus now."

Billy saw the fear leave Marcell, saw it vanish almost as a living thing into the very air. He had changed. In those few moments he had been given a peace that was unmistakable. The glimmer of a smile on his pale face and a certain light that had come into his eyes shouted it to the world.

Dalton held both of Marcell's hands in his own, sitting with him as the darkness moved in from the sea. Billy felt himself drifting away from the two men beside him, could see them fade. The last thing he remembered was the pale gold light of the setting sun as it shined on the face of his friend.

14

UNDER THE SHADOW OF THE ALMIGHTY

*B*illy awakened, glancing next to him for Marcell, listening for the sound of his friend's labored breathing, looking for the pale gold radiance he had seen in his face, seeking the comfort of that light he had seen shining in the darkness. His friend was gone. The light in the room was a thin gray pallor.

A double row of gray, metal-framed beds stretched away from him toward an open door. Through it he saw sailors in their blue dungarees and light blue shirts, as well as men and women dressed in white, bustling back and forth in a corridor.

The room itself had gray walls and a white ceiling and round windows on one wall. Some of the men occupying the beds were swathed in bandages—still as mummies. Others smoked cigarettes, read magazines, or talked among themselves. They seemed so different from those hollow-eyed, gaunt-faced men he had been with on the Canal.

The room was pungent with the smell of antiseptic and disinfectant and something else, something very sweet that had an underpinning of decay and corruption as if gallons of perfume had been poured on the Japanese corpses that lay along the Tenaru after the battle at Hell's Point. He placed his hand on the wall next to his bed. A faint vibration came through it—the throbbing of engines. The hand resting on the wall didn't belong to him. Clean and pale, free of caked dirt under his fingernails, it held no smell of cordite or oil. It belonged to a stranger.

Just then, Jordan stepped into the room, seeing that Billy had regained consciousness. She leaned against the door frame, gazing at the face she had called to mind so many times over the past four months as she worked—as she prayed. Even with the terrible loss of blood, some of the tan from that blazing sun of the tropics remained. The cheekbones were more pronounced, the eyes seemed darker and held a strange, staring brightness. Jordan could not imagine what had given them such an extraordinary appearance.

Quickly, Jordan left the room, going directly to the galley. She set a tray with a bowl of clear broth, a glass of orange juice, and a half-cup of steaming coffee. As she reached the door of the ward, she stopped again, staring at Billy. *Thank you, Jesus! Oh, Lord, thank you for protecting him and bringing him safely back to me!*

When Jordan reached the end of the aisle, she stood at the foot of Billy's bed holding the tray. He had his eyes closed, his hair a rumpled black mass against the white pillowcase. She took the few steps to a chair that stood against the wall and sat down.

Billy dreamed he smelled coffee, the dream fading and the smell becoming stronger as he slowly opened his eyes. He thought he had drifted from one dream into another as he stared at Jordan's deep blue eyes and the generous mouth, curving slightly into a smile. The anemic gray light through the porthole brightened as it struck the cascade of honey-colored hair, giving her face a luminous quality.

"If you think you can get rid of me by hiding out in those jungles, you're mistaken, Billy Christmas."

"Jordan! It really is you!" Billy struggled to sit up. "I thought I was dreaming."

"Here, let me help you." Jordan placed the tray on the chair and helped Billy to sit up in the bed, propping a pillow behind him.

"Where am I?"

"You're on a hospital ship with a lot of wounded men bound for Sydney."

"But . . . how did you . . ."

"I'm a nurse, Billy. This is where the work is." *It's also where I knew you'd be if you got wounded.*

Billy lifted his right hand, holding it out as if in supplication. "How . . . how long have I . . . ?"

Jordan took his hand. "Three days. They brought you out to the ship that night after you were hurt."

Something seemed to click behind the bright hollow eyes. "Marcell . . . did he . . ."

Jordan looked down at the pale hand she was holding. A jagged scar ran across the top from the knuckle of the little finger to the inside of the wrist.

"Jordan?"

"They didn't bring him to the ship, Billy."

Billy looked away to the porthole where the gray light drifted like smoke. He saw again the Marine cemetery by the sea and the coastal plain beyond, sweeping cleanly toward the distant blue hills. The tilting crosses bore their crude markers in final tribute to those that lay beneath them. *I hope someone was there with Marcell. To build him a cross. Someone to write how we felt about him.*

"Billy . . . are you all right?" Jordan squeezed his hand slightly, concern furrowing her smooth brow.

"What? Oh . . . yeah."

"You sure?"

Billy touched the stitched wound under his left eye, the heavy bandage on his neck, felt the tight wrappings encircling his body from the shoulders to the waist. "Am I, you know . . . gonna be OK?"

Jordan smiled. "You're going to be just fine. The bullet went through your neck cleanly, no permanent damage. The shrapnel raked your back pretty good. They took a few pieces out, but none of it went in very deeply."

"Guess I was lucky, huh?"

"Something like that," Jordan replied. "You'll have a pretty nasty scar under your eye. You could think of it as a keepsake from Guadalcanal, or a badge of honor, like a Prussian dueling scar."

Suddenly, Billy saw with precise clarity the church service in the little grove in Melbourne where Sam Dalton had prayed for him, for all the men. "Maybe it was more than luck, Jordan."

"I know it was, Billy," Jordan almost whispered, her eyes growing bright. She quickly wiped a tear from the corner of her eye before it could fall. Composing herself, she continued. "You lost a lot of blood. That was the main problem. Now it's time to get a little food in you so you can start getting your strength back." Jordan placed the tray on his lap, the legs resting on the bed on either side of him.

"Jordan, could I have just a little sip of that coffee first? It's been so long."

"One sip, then you have to eat something." Jordan held the cup to Billy's lips, watching him savor the hot coffee. Then she stood by his bed, spooning the hot broth into his mouth until he had finished the bowl. "I'll leave the juice here on the table next to the water. Drink some when you feel like it."

"Jordan . . ."

Jordan had picked up the tray, preparing to leave. "Yes?"

Billy glanced at her, then down to the clean hands he was beginning to recognize as his own. "I thought about you a lot . . . especially right before an attack or when the shelling got bad. It just seemed to give me something to hold on to."

Jordan set the tray down, placing her hands on his. "Oh, Billy! It's so good to have you back safe." She looked about the room at the other men, then bent over the bed, putting her arms around him. Billy placed his hands on her back, gently moving them up to touch the softly falling waves of her hair.

Some of the men had noticed.

"Hey, Dollface! You never nursed me like that."

"Ohhhhhh . . . I'm dying! I'm dying! For a kiss, that is!"

"Hubba, hubba!"

Jordan straightened up quickly, color rising into her face. She grabbed the tray and hurried down the aisle and out the door to the shouts and whistles of the patients.

* * *

Billy leaned on the rail at the bow of the ship, watching a pair of blue dolphins knife gracefully through the blue-green water, shimmering wetly in their silent parabolas. The sun had just cleared the seam between the sky and the sea, fading the deep violet sky to a mild blue.

Regaining his color, Billy had also put on four pounds. His skin where the wounds were healing felt as if it were being drawn tightly across his body, but the itching was becoming more bearable.

As he sipped coffee from a heavy white mug, Billy pulled his gray cotton robe close to his chest against the morning chill and the sea wind. "Beautiful, aren't they?"

Jordan had just stepped out of the hatchway and stood next to him. "Yes. I wonder why they stay so close to the ship?"

Billy stared at the dolphins, seeming not to hear the question. "I just heard some good news from the radio room."

Turning toward her, he smiled, the morning light casting the left side of his face into shadow. "I could use some of that."

"Remember the sea battle I told you about off Savo Island—the one not long after we headed back south?" Jordan shuddered as she spoke, remembering the star shells exploding in a shower of red brilliance against the night sky and the orange flashes of the giant tracers, and, finally, the terrible rocking concussion of some great ship exploding. "I thought we were done for."

Billy put his arm around her shoulder, pulling her close and kissing her cheek.

"Well, we won," Jordan smiled weakly. "They're calling it the Battle of Guadalcanal, and it's turned the tide against the Japanese. Reinforcements and supplies are going in every day now."

Billy glanced back to the north in the direction of the volcanic and mountainous island called Guadalcanal. He saw gaunt faces, hollow men squatting in muddy gun pits in a downpour, eating cold, wormy rice from wooden bowls. "Thank God!" Eyes shining with tears, he turned away from her.

"The worst is over for them now, Billy." Jordan stood next to him gazing down at the dolphins slicing through the sun-bright sea.

Billy turned toward Jordan, the strange hollow darkness still in his eyes. "We thought nobody remembered us back in the States. Thought they'd never heard of Guadalcanal."

Jordan looked at his haunted face, letting him talk out the pain and the emptiness.

"The day I came to—when you brought me the broth—well, after you left, an ol' Navy chief stopped by to see one of his buddies in the bed next to me. He asked me how it was on the Canal. I didn't think he'd even know the name of the place. He was shocked. 'Are you kiddin'?' he said. 'Everybody's heard of Guadalcanal! The First Marines! You guys are heroes back in the States!'"

"He was right," Jordan smiled. "But that's nothing compared to the way the Australians feel about the First Marines. You saved their country for them."

Billy looked into Jordan's eyes. A different kind of light had come into them. "Jordan, I want to accept Jesus Christ as my Savior."

"Just like that!" Jordan blurted out. Then put her hand to her mouth. "Oh, I'm sorry! I didn't mean . . ."

"No, you're right. It does seem 'just like that.' But I've been thinking about it ever since Melbourne, that day we went to Sam's service in the park next to the stadium. I grew up in church, but it was just boring words, you know, like a history class."

"Billy, this is wonderful! We'll go to church when . . ."

"Shhh!" Billy held his finger to his lips. "I've been readin' a New Testament somebody had in the ward. I don't need a church for this."

"Well, that's true, but . . ."

Billy put his finger to his lips again.

"Sorry! I'm just so happy!" Jordan exclaimed.

"I believe that when Sam prayed for me, for God to protect me, that's what got me through. I should have been killed a dozen times, but God kept me alive. One time I thought I could see an angel standing . . . the shelling was so bad . . . I don't know, maybe it was just flashes from the explosions.

"What I did see for sure was Sam Dalton coming out in the gun pits, the jungles . . . wherever men were bleeding and dying . . . bringing them the hope of eternal life in the gospel. I guess the closest I'll ever come to seeing Jesus in this life is in the face of that good man.

"Anyway, I'm going to confess Jesus as my Savior. I read in the twelfth chapter of John where a lot of the chief rulers believed on Him, but they wouldn't confess him 'cause they didn't want to be put out of the synagogue. Well, I don't care about the synagogue. Jesus said if we don't confess Him before men, He won't confess us before His Heavenly Father. So here goes."

"Billy, do you believe in your heart?" Jordan's face was full of wonder and concern.

Billy smiled at her, and she saw the answer that was already in his eyes.

Closing his eyes, his head bowed, Billy began: "Jesus, I confess you as my Lord and Savior before Jordan here, and I'll never be ashamed of You before anybody. I ask You to forgive me for all the things I've done wrong and make me the man You want me to be."

"Thank you, Jesus!" Jordan threw her arms around him, hugging him tightly.

Billy stumbled against the rail.

"Oh, I'm sorry!" Jordan reached out to steady him. "I forgot you were so weak."

"You're more dangerous than the Japs," Billy laughed.

Jordan hugged him again. "How do you feel now?"

"You mean about being saved?"

"Yes!"

"No different. Well, maybe a little."

"How?" Jordan asked eagerly.

"I don't know. Maybe I expected the clouds to open up and there'd be a choir of angels singing the 'Hallelujah Chorus.' I feel, well . . . almost invulnerable."

"Invulnerable?"

"Yeah. You know, like nothing can hurt me. I just feel *good!*" Billy looked into Jordan's eyes, his face radiant, then out toward the east where the sunlight filled the sky and sparkled like blue-green jewels on the water.

* * *

"I thought you'd be happy, son." Colonel Stratford Briggs sat in a nondescript wooden chair next to Billy's before a bank of windows in the hospital lounge. Forty-two years old, he was six feet of whipcord and bone with eyes like flint and hair going gray around the temples. "Anyway, I'm afraid you don't have much choice in the matter."

Billy held in his lap the orders he had taken out of the brown manila envelope. He knew they couldn't force him to become an officer against his will. "I don't mean to sound ungrateful, sir. It's just that I never had any desire at all to go to Officer Candidate School. I guess I'm more the enlisted type."

Briggs smiled tightly. "I think you're officer material posing as enlisted."

Gazing out the tall windows of the lounge, Billy watched the columns of Marines embarking at the docks below onto one of the

Liberty ships for their trip north to the Solomons and beyond. Their weapons were slung, packs strapped on their backs. He knew they may have to live out of those packs for months at a time, as he had done. "Lying around here makes me feel like a slacker."

"This is no time for personal feelings, Christmas. We desperately need good officers in the Marines. Almost none of the junior officers coming out now have any combat experience."

Billy continued to stare out the window where the hills rolled back from the sea with the glare of the afternoon sun glowing redly on the roofs of the houses. He heard again the sound of Marcell's voice moaning for help as his guts spilled out onto the dark corruption of the jungle floor.

"Are you listening to me, son?" Briggs leaned forward in his chair, looking into Billy's face.

"Yes sir."

Briggs took a pack of Camels from his inside jacket pocket, shook one out and offered it to Billy.

"No, thanks."

Lighting his cigarette, Briggs leaned back and blew a thin blue-white stream of smoke toward the high ceiling. It wavered and vanished in the dark air above them. "You mind if I call you Billy? I don't see the need to stand on military courtesy here."

"That's fine, sir."

"I've read your file, Billy. You've got one year of college, but more importantly you proved your courage and initiative under fire. It's that experience we need in our officers."

Billy shifted in his chair, rubbing his lower back through the coarse robe with his right hand. "Sir, I think I need to be back with the company where I can do some good."

Briggs placed his hand on Billy's shoulder and bore in. "That's exactly my point. As an officer you can use your experience to help out a whole company, not just a squad. A hundred men instead of eight or nine. Why, think of the lives you might save! These new officers do the best they can, but they make terrible blunders until they get some combat time under their belts."

For the first time, Billy looked at the colonel with interest. "Maybe you're right. We all saw some mighty big mistakes from some of those green shavetails."

"Tell you what," Briggs said, sure of his victory now. "You're gonna be laid up for another month or two anyway. We'll just give you some liberty Stateside with your folks, and when your convalescence is over, you'll go straight to OCS."

"When can I get out of this place?" Billy asked, watching the last of the Marines walk up the gangplank onto a Liberty ship.

Briggs shook hands with Billy, stubbing his cigarette out in the metal ashtray that stood next to his chair, and stood up to leave. "I'll talk to the doctor. Maybe a week or two."

"Thank you, sir." Billy started to get up.

"Don't bother," Briggs said quickly. He rubbed his right temple with three fingers. "I guess it's all right if I tell you. Your buddy, Marcell Duke, is gonna be awarded the Silver Star for his actions at Hell's Point."

Billy smiled, remembering, and murmured, "That's great! His folks'll be so proud."

"Yours hasn't been approved yet—but I'm sure it's just a matter of time."

Startled at the unexpected news, Billy glanced up at Briggs, unable to say anything.

Briggs grinned back. "That oughta make the General happy. One more thing, Billy. Don't be too anxious to get back into this little fray. You'll see a lot more action. Guadalcanal's only the first. Tokyo's still three thousand miles away." His heels clicked smartly on the polished tile as he turned and left the room.

* * *

Billy sat stiffly in the passenger seat of the jeep threading its way through the streets of Sydney. The scenery that morning in the Blue Mountains west of the city had been spectacular, but now he was tiring, his strength unexpectedly fading in this first outing since he had entered the hospital.

"Weren't the mountains beautiful? I'd like to go sometime in the winter when there's more snow." Jordan had exchanged her stiff white nurse's uniform for a pair of tan slacks and a white blouse.

"Well, if we don't make it back, we could always go to the

mountains of north Georgia. They kinda remind me of these." Billy noticed Jordan glance quickly at him.

Jordan took a deep breath, stretching her arms out against the steering wheel of the jeep. "Billy, I don't want to cause any problems for you with your family. I know how they feel about me, like a lot of the . . . other people do."

"Other snobs, you mean," Billy laughed. "It's all right to say it, Jordan. That's what most of the Pine Hills folks are." Billy seemed to ponder something for a moment. "Maybe I should say it's what *we* are. I was born and raised with 'em."

"Billy, I don't care if you're rich or poor as a church mouse," Jordan remarked. "Everything's fine here, but what happens when we get back home? I'll never be accepted in your world."

Billy stared at Jordan, remaining silent, content to watch her glossy, blonde hair blowing about her face.

They were passing Manly Beach with its sunbathers stretched out on the sand, others frolicking in the surf. Children were making beach sounds in their play while a little black terrier ran among them yapping. The sound of the waves barely rose above the traffic's din as they hummed along the open road.

After a sixteen-mile drive east from the city toward the Pacific, passing the beautiful old homes located on bays and inlets along the sloping shoreline, they reached the "Heads." These three headlands, reaching like giant fingers out into the sea, guard the entrance to Sydney Harbor.

Jordan and Billy stood together on North Head next to the navy jeep Billy had managed to procure from the motor pool. They had spoken very little during the drive except for an occasional comment on the scenery or a particularly lovely home.

I guess he's trying to figure out how to get out of this relationship gracefully now that he's going to officer school back home. "You remember when we crossed the Sydney Harbor Bridge?" she remarked, not waiting for an answer. "Right next to it is Sydney Cove. That's where the first British settlement was founded in 1788. Did you see the wharves? Joseph Conrad wrote about them in his memoirs. Don't you find that interesting?"

Billy looked away from the boundless windblown stretch of the Pacific, a glimmer of a smile at the corners of his mouth.

"You're awfully quiet, Billy."

Gazing directly into Jordan's blue eyes, he thought of the brightness she had brought to the shadowed places of his heart. "I've been trying to decide whether we should have a big wedding or just a simple ceremony. What do you think?"

Jordan was thinking of how empty her life would be after Billy left. Her eyes grew wide as his words sank in.

"Your mouth's open, Jordan," Billy laughed.

She quickly closed it. "What wedding?"

Billy got down on one knee, taking Jordan's left hand in both of his. "Will you be my wife, Lisa Jordan Simms?"

Jordan went into Billy's arms as he stood to his feet. He held her for a long while, till the quiet weeping stopped . . . and afterwards. Brushing Jordan's tears away with his fingertips, he stood back from her, holding both of her hands. "You're going to make a beautiful bride, Jordan Simms. Every man in Liberty's gonna be jealous of me."

Jordan smiled into his eyes, her mind flooded with memories: Billy in the first grade, sitting rigid as a little soldier in his desk; passing by her window with his family in the big black Cadillac; sweating in the afternoon sun after splitting stove wood the day he apologized to Annie. "I'm so happy, Billy. I love you so much."

Billy took her in his arms again, feeling the smoothness of her cheek against his neck, her hair blowing silkily about his face. "I think I've loved you for years, Jordan. Just never had the gumption to tell you. Always trying to do what my family expected of me." Taking her face in his hands he whispered, "Well, those days are over. You're first in my life from now on."

As Billy kissed her, Jordan knew that all the old pain, all the fear of being touched, all the dark memories that had haunted her down through the years had vanished like shadows in the sunlight of God's love for her and in the love she felt for Billy. Desire rose in her like gentle waves, then spreading outward with a warm tingling sensation.

Then their lips parted, leaving Jordan breathless. "My goodness! I've never felt like that before!"

Billy kissed her on both cheeks. "I'd marry you now if we had a preacher here."

They walked hand in hand to the steep precipice that dropped to a rocky shoreline far below. Standing in the wind, they gazed north toward the Coral Sea and Guadalcanal.

"I thank God every day that He kept you alive, Billy," Jordan whispered, her arms around his waist.

"We're both in His care now," Billy said with conviction. "'Under the shadow of the Almighty.' That's one of my favorite passages. It's from the ninety-first Psalm."

Jordan closed her eyes, pressing close to Billy.

He glanced down at her as the sea breeze swirled her pale hair in a shimmering dance of light about her face. "I think maybe God kept me alive in those jungles so I could take care of you, Jordan."

Turning their backs to the wind and the sounding sea, they walked back to the jeep.

"You know," Jordan said, climbing into the jeep, "it's strange how God works in people's lives. We grew up in the same town and we get together like this on the opposite side of the world."

"Guess it doesn't matter what town we were living in," Billy mused. "We didn't get together till we started walking the same path."

The next morning Billy awakened to an orderly telling him that he had an urgent phone call. He hurried down the hallway to the nurses' station, picking up the telephone that sat on the counter. Glancing at several nurses bustling around in the glare of fluorescent lights he took a deep breath.

"Hello."

"Billy, I just got word that Annie's very sick. The Red Cross got me a flight back to the States."

"What's wrong with her?"

"They just told me that she's terribly ill. It sounds like she may not have much time left."

"How long have you got?" Billy tried to keep his mind clear through the cobwebs of sleep that still clung to him.

"My plane leaves in ten minutes," Jordan said breathlessly. "I'm at the airfield now."

"Can I see you? You can't just leave like this!"

"I don't want to. I just don't have any choice. Annie needs me now. She doesn't have anyone else."

"I know. I'll pray for you to have a safe trip."

"Oh, Billy! I'll miss you so much!"

Then she was gone, and Billy walked back to his room. Sitting on his bed, he thought of the long days without Jordan, determined that he would regain his strength quickly and leave this place where the hollow-eyed men with their terrible wounds were flooding in from the north.

15

HIS FACE DID SHINE AS THE SUN

*J*ordan stared at Annie, asleep in the hospital bed, her face ravaged by disease. The thin, papery skin—yellow as butter—looked as if it had been stretched directly over the skull. Her stomach, swollen to three times its normal size, was that of a woman in the last stages of pregnancy. *Ascites* and *paracentesis* Jordan thought automatically, remembering the terms for accumulation of fluid that was causing the extreme swelling and the process by which it was siphoned off. She had seen patients in this last stage of cirrhosis before.

Taking a bottle of Jergen's lotion from the nightstand, Jordan poured some into her hand and gently rubbed it with her fingertips into the dry, flaking skin of Annie's face, hands, and thin, reedlike arms. Then she sat in the chair next to the bed staring at her, listening to the shallow breathing, quietly sibilant in the gloom. Memories seemed to hang like ethereal tapestries in the sterile air.

"How long have you been here?" Dr. Simmons touched Jordan gently on the shoulder.

For some reason, the smell of his foul cigar brought her comfort. Standing up, she embraced him, then motioned for him to come into the hall.

Jordan blinked in the brightness of the fluorescent lights. "I came in on the bus about two o'clock. What time is it now?"

"My, my, Jordan! What a pretty girl you turned out to be! Even in that military garb," Simmons observed, around his cigar. "It's about six now. Let's eat and you tell me all about the war."

"I better stay with Annie."

"You'll follow the doctor's orders," Simmons growled, tossing his cigar into the trash. "Besides, the nurse gave her a sedative at four o'clock. She'll sleep awhile longer."

They were the last customers in the hospital cafeteria. At Simmons's insistence, they got suppers of chicken-fried steak, black-eyed peas seasoned with ham hocks, cornbread, and peach cobbler.

"I couldn't eat all this if I stayed here the rest of the night," Jordan smiled, tasting the peas.

Simmons wolfed down a thick slab of the steak. "You just leave it on the plate, young lady. I'll see it don't go to waste. I'm hungry as a wormy hound. Been on the go since five this morning."

Jordan had forgotten how good Southern cooking was—even in a hospital. She enjoyed her food, knowing conversation would be impossible until Simmons's voracious appetite was sated.

When Simmons had finished his meal, Jordan pushed her bowl of cobbler over to him.

"You always were a thoughtful girl, Jordan Simms." He finished the cobbler in less than a minute.

"I hate to see a man just pick at his food like that," Jordan remarked with a smile.

Simmons leaned back in his chair, rubbing his ample belly. "Now if I could just talk somebody into getting me a cup of coffee, I'd be happy as a pig in mud."

Jordan smiled and walked over to the huge silver coffee urn at the end of the serving line. Through the swinging doors, she saw two black women mopping the kitchen floor. They wore red kerchiefs around their heads. She filled a heavy white mug with the coffee, which at this late hour had the consistency and color of hot macadam, and took it back across the empty, darkened room to the table.

Spooning sugar into his coffee, followed by a liberal dollop of cream, Simmons stirred it well and took a sip. They spoke for a few minutes about the war and about Jordan's work in Melbourne and on the hospital ship.

Simmons placed the cup on the table, holding it with both hands and looked directly into Jordan's deep blue eyes, shadowed by the dim overhead light. "Annie's not gonna make it this time."

Jordan was stunned. "But . . . she's been sick before. She . . ."

"Jordan, you're a nurse—a mighty good one. And you had time to observe her."

Jordan made an effort to will her emotions out of the equation. She knew it was too late for things like vitamins and a salt-free diet. The disease had almost run its course. All that could be done was to make things bearable. Drain the fluid that would continue to painfully distend her stomach, keep the dry, cool skin clean and moist. Alleviate the symptoms. There was no cure.

Simmons waited to let Jordan work it out for herself. "Annie loves you more than you'll ever know, Jordan. I'd stop by and see her pretty often after you left. You're just about the only thing she ever talked about. If I hadn't let myself drift into a state of near apostasy, I'd say it was God who put you with her."

Jordan's eyes grew bright with unshed tears. "I never should have left her."

"We talked about that, too," Simmons remarked in a solemn tone. "You did just what she wanted you to do."

"I don't understand. I thought you said she missed me so much," Jordan frowned.

"You need an old bachelor like me to tell you how mothers are? And that's how she came to think of herself, as your mother." Simmons sipped the sweet, tan coffee. "It's the hardest time in a mother's life when she has to let her child go out into the world. But for Annie, it was also one of the happiest—to see you as a nurse—making a good life for yourself. She was so proud of you, Jordan."

"She never told me any of this." Jordan felt an almost desperate need to go awaken Annie so they could talk.

"Well, Annie never was much of a talker, long as I knew her," Simmons mused, cradling the warm mug. "Especially about the things that meant the most to her." Simmons pulled his gold pocket watch out, glancing at it. "Let's go. The nurses are probably waking her up to give her a sleeping pill about now. Maybe you'll get a chance to talk to her for a few minutes."

Annie sat in a chair next to the bed when Jordan and Simmons entered the room. Pain burned in the lines of her face. She had a fresh sheet draped over her body. A nurse of about fifty with short

211

gray hair, glanced at Simmons, then took a huge syringe from a metal cart next to the chair, inserting it into Annie's distended stomach through a fold in the sheet.

"That's Ouida Stewart," Simmons murmured. "Excellent nurse."

A muted cry escaped Annie's lips. Stewart attached a length of tubing to the syringe and began siphoning off the fluid into a graduated glass receptacle that she had placed on the floor, monitoring it carefully. An expression of relief and gratitude replaced the pain in Annie's face as the smothering pressure was eased.

Simmons whispered into Jordan's ear. "I've a few rounds to make. Be back later to take you home."

Jordan watched Annie relax as the cloudy fluid drained into the bottle. When the procedure was completed, she helped Stewart get Annie back into the bed. After speaking with Ouida a few seconds, the nurse left and Jordan sat by Annie's bedside.

"Annie?" Jordan spoke softly as she took the dry, brittle hand in hers.

For the first time since Jordan had entered the room, Annie opened her eyes. They were glazed with pain and held a black despair in their cloudy depths. "Jordan! Is that you, baby?"

"It's me, Annie." Jordan stood up and sat on the side of the bed, bending forward, so Annie could see her better.

"Oh, baby, it's so good to see you!" Annie tried to sit up higher in the bed.

Jordan eased her gently back down. "Let me help you." She cranked the head of the bed up and adjusted Annie's pillow behind her back so she could see and talk more comfortably.

A single tear gleamed in Annie's left eye, spilling softly over and down her withered cheek. "I didn't think I'd ever see you again."

"Oh, you hush!" Jordan admonished gently. "I've come back to take care of you. We'll have lots of time."

Annie's faded eyes held a timeless knowledge of mortality as she spoke. "I wish we did, baby. But my time's about up. And I don't even know why I was placed here on this earth."

Jordan squeezed her hand and smiled. "I think one reason was to take care of me, Annie. Nobody else wanted me."

"You'll always be my baby, Jordan. I wish we could be together forever." She held to Jordan's hand with surprising strength, as if it would keep her from slipping away.

"We can be, Annie," Jordan whispered close to her face. "We can be together forever. Jesus made it possible."

Annie looked away, toward the window where the amber glow of a street light burned the darkness. "Not for me, baby."

"Oh, yes, Annie. Especially for you. Jesus was poor just like you, and He loves you so much He died for you. He's there holding His arms out right now." Jordan tried to keep her voice calm and steady.

Annie turned back to Jordan, trembling with grief. "You don't know what I've done!"

"It doesn't matter, Annie. The Bible says, 'There is none righteous, no, not one. For all have sinned and come short of the glory of God.' God will forgive anything if we only ask Him."

"I killed someone, Jordan!" Annie sobbed. "My own baby!"

Remembering how Sam had let her talk through her guilt and pain that night in the Victorian Alps outside Melbourne, Jordan patted Annie's hand gently, remaining silent.

"I got pregnant not long after Harold and I were married. He didn't want a child. Said he'd leave me if I didn't get rid of it."

Jordan wiped away the tears from Annie's face and kissed her on the cheek.

The sobs were subsiding as Annie continued in a hoarse whisper. "I loved him so much, Jordan! I didn't want to lose him. So I did it."

There was quiet in the room except for the ticking of the radiator near the window.

Annie took several shallow breaths. "When I woke up after . . . I knew then exactly what I'd done. I murdered my own child! I felt so . . . so empty. And I never felt like a woman again after that."

Oh, Jesus, help Annie! Help her to come to You so You can save her and take away this awful pain. Jordan sat next to Annie, holding her hand, rubbing it tenderly.

"I can see now that's why I always dressed like a man . . . acted like a man," Annie murmured, gazing back through the years. "After what I did, I didn't think I had the right to be a woman anymore. What chance have I got to make things right now?"

Jordan softly stroked Annie's cheek. "You can't make things right, Annie. That's why Jesus came—to make things right for all of us. Only His blood can cleanse us from sin, save us, and give us eternal life."

Annie lay very still, her eyes wide. Jordan had spoken to her of Jesus before, but this time she listened to the words!

Taking a small New Testament from her coat pocket, Jordan thumbed through the pages. "Jesus said, 'He that heareth my word, and believeth on him that sent me, hath everlasting life.' Turning further toward the back, Jordan read: "'Whosoever believeth that Jesus is the Christ is born of God. . . . And this is the record, that God hath given to us eternal life, and this life is in his Son. He that hath the Son hath life; and he that hath not the Son of God hath not life.'"

Annie smiled weakly. "I remember the first verse I ever learned in Sunday school down at the Baptist church. I was just a little girl, about the same age you were when you came to live with me. 'For God so loved the world, that he gave his only begotten Son, that whosoever believeth in him should not perish, but have everlasting life.' That was such a long, long time ago, but I still remember it."

"That's it, Annie. The gospel. The good news of Jesus Christ. All we have to do is believe it."

Turning toward the window, Annie spoke softly. "I blamed God for all those hard years . . . for all the loneliness and the poverty and for being made fun of by just about the whole town. All the time, I was doing it to myself, punishing myself for that terrible thing I did all those years ago." Closing her eyes, Annie's breathing grew quieter.

"Annie!" Jordan checked her pulse. It was weak, but steady. *I guess it's just exhaustion.*

Jordan sat with Annie in the darkened room, thinking of all the times Annie had pulled her around Liberty in the little wagon: to school or to the store or as she gathered plunder in the back alleys and forgotten byways of the town. Foremost among her memories was the day Annie had given her the little lamp with the shining angel as she sat in the wagon at Three Corners Grocery.

Simmons came and drove her out to the house, saying he would pick her up the next day and take her back to the hospital.

Jordan prayed for Annie far into the night, kneeling by the bed next to her bright angel of the lamp as he stretched his arms out over her.

* * *

Jordan awakened to the sound of knocking on the kitchen door. Hurriedly, she threw on a robe and went downstairs. Standing on the back porch were J.T. and Wash.

"Come on in." Jordan unhooked the screen door. "It's seven o'clock in the morning. What are you two doing out?" She glanced at Wash's ice wagon parked at the bottom of the steps.

J.T. had on khaki's, his Harvard sweatshirt, and an old pin-striped suit coat. He had slicked his hair down and stuck a piece of toilet paper to the side of his face where he had cut himself shaving. "Wash was already in Annie's room when I went to visit her this morning."

Jordan noticed two extraordinary things about J.T. He had obviously been up for an hour or two but hadn't had anything to drink yet, and he wasn't entertaining her with his witticisms. She felt a chill enter the pit of her stomach as she turned to Wash.

Wash stood there in his overalls and red flannel shirt, a steadfast look in his eyes. "Miss Annie's with Jesus now. We thought you'd like to hear it from us and not a call from the hospital."

The color drained from Jordan's face. She felt faint as she pulled a chair out and sat at the table. Then the full meaning of Wash's words hit her.

"You all right, Miss Jordan?" Wash stepped to the table, placing his hand on her shoulder.

Jordan gazed into Wash's dark eyes with a grave intensity. "You said that Annie's with Jesus. Don't you know . . ."

"I mean just what I said, Miss Jordan. I was there with her before she died."

J.T. pulled out a chair, sitting at the long table next to Jordan. "Listen to him, darlin.'"

Wash sat down across from them. "I got to the hospital about fifteen minutes 'til six o'clock so I could see Miss Annie before I started my rounds. I know she wakes up real early sometimes. Well, anyhow, when I walked into that room I felt it!"

215

Jordan glanced at J.T., then back to Wash. "What do you mean you 'felt it'?"

Wash smiled at both of them, his dark face almost glowing. "I felt the presence of Almighty God! It was so powerful in that little room. Ain't many times I felt it like that! You know what I mean, don't you, Miss Jordan?"

Jordan nodded her head, a gentle light coming into her eyes. J.T. shifted uneasily in his chair.

"Well, Miss Annie, she was layin' there propped up on that big white pillow and . . . you know what she looked like, Miss Jordan? Member them ol' pictures of hers that you used to look at so much? The ones when Miss Annie was a little girl? Well that's just what she looked like. Like that little girl she was in them ol' pictures. She looked so nice and peaceful layin' there. Just like a little girl."

"She looked like a different person all right," J.T. added. "I came in a few minutes later."

Wash laughed out loud. "Hallelujah! Oh, my, my, my! Sweet Jesus!" Wash laughed again, lifting his hands toward the ceiling. "'I will praise thee, O Lord, with my whole heart; I will shew forth all thy marvellous works.'"

J.T. glanced at the door, as if planning a quick getaway, and then muttered nervously. "You got a collection plate, Jordan? I think Wash wants an offering."

"Y'all have to excuse me. Sometimes I gets carried away. You know what she told me then? She said, 'Wash, Jesus is my friend.' That's exactly what she told me. I said I knew that He was, and then she told me what happened.

"Miss Annie said she woke up hurtin' real bad, and she asked Jesus to help her. Then there was a light in the room and she saw Him! I know she did, Miss Jordan 'cause she told me what He looked like, and it was just like He looked in Matthew seventeen: "his face did shine as the sun, and his raiment was white as the light.' She didn't use them same words, but that's what He looked like to her.

"Well, anyhow, Miss Annie said she told Jesus she wanted to be saved and go to heaven. He told her she *was* saved because she already believed in Him in her heart."

Jordan's eyes were bright with joy, tears running down her cheeks.

"I guess that's about all. There she was in that hospital lookin' like a little girl, and she wasn't hurtin' no more." Wash clasped his hands in front of him, closing his eyes. "Oh, sweet, Jesus, thank you! Praise that mighty name!"

Jordan sat at the table, weeping quietly.

J.T. put his arm around her shoulder. "I came in right before she died, baby. She just put her hands under her cheek and curled up like a little girl. She had the sweetest smile on her face. Just like you used to when you were a little girl, and you'd go to sleep in my lap. It was like she just fell asleep."

Jordan put her arms around J.T., hugging him. Then she got up, standing on her tiptoes, and put her arms around Wash and hugged him tightly.

J.T. made a fire in the stove and Jordan made them a pot of coffee. They sat at the table drinking the rich, dark coffee and talking about all the good times they had had together.

Jordan took J.T.'s hand in hers, reaching across the table to take Wash's thick, work-hardened hand. "'The Lord bless thee, and keep thee: The Lord make his face to shine upon thee, and be gracious unto thee: The Lord lift up his countenance upon thee, and give thee peace.'"

"You gettin' to be a real little lady preacher," Wash laughed.

Jordan smiled at J.T. and Wash. "My two dear, dear friends. I thank God for both of you. I'll pray for you every day, no matter where in this old world I am."

* * *

Billy drove his Cord through the streets of Liberty. Passing by Marcell's house, he stared at the red-bordered white banner hanging in the front window. In the center of the white field of the banner, a single gold star blazed in the pale December light. *I'll see you again someday, old friend. "Greater love hath no man than this, that a man lay down his life for his friends." I never think of you without that Scripture coming to mind, Marcell.*

Passing Liberty High, Billy could see the faces of teachers and friends as clearly as when he had been in school with them. He wondered what had happened to various ones of them and determined that he would look some of them up in the next week or two. *Here I am, twenty years old, and strolling down "memory lane" like I'm seventy. War must have aged me more than I thought.*

When Billy turned into Annie's driveway the frost-burned weeds rustled against the bottom of his car. He parked in front, walking around the side of the house to the back porch. Jordan sat on the top step holding a worn and frayed Raggedy Ann doll on her lap as she stared at Annie's wagon down in the yard. She wore a black suit with a white silk blouse.

Standing at the corner of the house, Billy gazed at Jordan with such a rush of emotion that it caught at his breath. Her blonde waves tumbled in a pleasurable disarray along her face and shoulders. Even this far away, her skin seemed to give off a warm glow.

Jordan raised her head slightly, catching sight of Billy as he walked across the side yard toward her. A smile brightened her face as she rushed to greet him. In a silence deeper than words, they embraced next to Annie's wagon in the shadow of her house.

"Oh, Billy, it seems like a year since I left you!" Jordan whispered against his chest. "I didn't expect you for at least two more weeks. When did you get in?"

"Came in on the train about noon. I had to do some fancy talkin' to get out of that hospital this quick, but I just had to see you."

"It feels so good just to hold you." Jordan looked up into his face, pale and worn from his injuries and the long trip.

Billy touched the side of her face with his fingertips, kissing her gently on the lips. "I just found out about Annie. Wash was leaving the church, and he waved me down and told me."

They walked to the back porch, Jordan holding to Billy's waist, and sat together on the top step.

Jordan took Billy's scarred right hand in hers and looked into his dark blue eyes. "I got to see Annie the night before she died. I'm so glad we had that last little while together."

Then Jordan told him Wash's story of what had happened to Annie in the hospital that last morning.

Billy smiled warmly at Jordan, nodding his head slightly. "You know, Jordan, this Christian walk of ours is the most amazing thing in the world. I'm just beginning to learn about the things of God, about how He works in people's lives, and I can't wait to see what's gonna happen next."

"'The unsearchable riches of Christ.'" That's about the best way I've ever heard it described." Jordan traced the scar on Billy's hand with the tip of her little finger.

"Well," Billy announced. "I told the General that we're getting married."

Jordan frowned slightly. "How bad was it?"

Billy smiled broadly. "You're not gonna believe it, Jordan. It all happened, naturally, in that study of his where all I can remember is lectures and grief. Anyway, he sat behind his big desk and looked me straight in the eye. 'Billy,' he said, 'you've become your own man in spite of everything I could do to stop you. I'm proud of you, son?'"

"He actually told you that?" Jordan beamed. "He said he was proud of you."

"First time in my life I ever heard those words from him." Billy's eyes narrowed in thought. "He knew about my getting recommended for the Silver Star—the ol' military grapevine I suppose. Then when I told him I was going to OCS that really topped it off. He's giving us his blessings. It's a miracle!"

"Well, maybe a little one," Jordan laughed. "When do you leave for OCS?"

"Three or four weeks. Soon as I get my strength back. How about you? When do you leave?"

"They're giving me a thirty-day liberty to settle all the affairs. Then it's back to Sydney. I'll have duty at the hospital and on the ship just like before."

"That gives us worlds of time together," Billy smiled. "When do you want to have the wedding?"

"I think we need to have a proper period of engagement first," Jordan teased.

"How about two weeks?"

"Sounds about right to me," Jordan agreed quickly. "Billy, it may sound crazy, but do you know what I'd like to do?"

"Get married tonight?"

"No, not that," Jordan laughed. "I'd like to live here—in Annie's house. It's the only home I've ever known."

Billy looked at the huge old house, drifting into ruin. "I've heard my mother talk about what a beautiful place this used to be. It'll take a lot of hard work, but maybe we could fix it up like it used to be. There'd be room for a bunch of kids, that's for sure."

"I can just see it now," Jordan beamed. "The way it was when Annie was growing up." Jordan stood up, holding Billy by the hand. "You want to walk over to Annie's grave with me?"

"Sure. I didn't get to tell her good-bye yet."

They walked through the dry winter weeds across the field toward the cemetery. "You know, Billy," Jordan mused, "there aren't any good-byes for Christians. It's just a little while apart."

Entering the cemetery just as the sun was setting, Jordan and Billy walked through the shadows among the live oaks and tilting old tombstones. As they stood together before the mound of red earth, a salient of amber light shined through the darkness above the grave of Annie Simms.